The Awakened

Book One
of the Ethereal Series

Julian Cheek

Published by Clink Street Publishing 2018

First edition.

ISBNs: 978-1-912562-19-0 paperback
978-1-912562-20-6 ebook

To the one who saw me and always believes in me, my lovely lady, Mitch. To my grounded and wonderful children, Amelia and Sebastian, and to Becky and Georgia who have always made me feel welcome and loved, and to those who continued to encourage, a little idea can sometimes go a long way. This story started a long time ago in the mist, and I trust you, the reader, will travel with me through this tumultuous experience, and be with me at the end, seeing yourself.

To Sam, David, the Ethereals and all the others who occupy my mind and heart, enjoy the telling and remember the dreaming.

Rain

It was the rain that woke him up. Rain, lashing against his bedroom window as if tapping out a code only he could understand. His bleary eyes looked groggily through the mist as he tried to gather some semblance of where he was. He noticed it was still dark and a low groan escaped his lips, summoned from deep within, as if to curse those who had sent the clouds scudding across the earth to pour their wrath on him that night.

"That night". The night, looking back now, where the first infinitesimal chink in his tightly woven armour had ruptured, and his destiny had begun.

Sam burrowed deeper into his quilt trying to find the last bit of sleep, but it evaded him and despite his tossing and turning and protestation, he eventually gave in, snaking a hand feebly out from beneath the covers to fumble for the light switch. The clock shone its cool amber glow into his mind.

4:30.

4:30! Another 3 hours before I need to get up, but now, wide awake and a prisoner, Sam thought. *Can't get up because that will wake mum up, which will wake dad up, which is just another great start to a typical day. No music, for the same reason. And definitely no sleep!* Frustrated already, he sensed his stress levels start to awaken, so, to counter this, he allowed his eyes to roam around the cluttered room.

There was his wooden window, the culprit for today. A few pictures in dusty frames resting against each other on the cill, looking for comfort. Bedside table. Half-eaten peanut butter sandwich and crumbs marking a trail from bed to table. Bumpy old sofa, bedroom cupboard – open. Bedroom door – very closed! Mirror, "whatever", work table with depressing clutter and unfinished homework. Xbox, bookcase, old, dusty, not used anymore. *Actually, never touched since… No! Don't go there. Not today.* But it held his eyes locked into traversing the room any further, as if beckoning him.

He roamed its shelves. Numerous books lay jostled together, angled like buttresses, supporting each other. Some his, some… David's.

A deep, unbidden shock of emotion sprang up from the pit of his stomach, causing him to gasp, eyes welling up in an instant. At this hour, his now long tried and well tested ability to protect his emotional state was weak, and the impact of that innocent glance caused his world to rock, bringing back emotions forbidden normally to emerge.

David. His glue in this shattered household. His strength and companion in a world gone mad, and his brother, gone forever, cruelly taken away by a *shitty, unseen, unloving, unmerciful, unkind, un-asked-for…* He couldn't go on. What was the point? Ultimately it always came back to one truth. He, Sam, was to blame, obviously. They had made it very clear, from very early days, that he was to blame. For everything! So why stop at death? No doubt, somewhere in that short six week period of hell, he did something to shut David's lights out.

He stretched his hand out slowly and pulled one of the books belonging to David from off the shelf and scanned its cove. *The Power of One* stared back at him. A small smile folded itself onto Sam's face as he remembered this one. One of David's favourites. Science fantasy, lots of explosions, magic… Yes, right up David's street.

Sam aimlessly turned the pages, not looking, not concentrating, just thinking, remembering, as if trying to communicate again with his brother somehow through the pages. And as he delved deeper into the book, each page felt through finger and thumb, Sam started to weep. Tears flowing down his etched face as his mind sent out a message to his brother.

I am sorry, David, Sam thought, *Sorry I couldn't do what I should have done so that you could still be here. Sorry for all the shitty stuff that made your life rubbish. That mum and dad lost you, rather than me…* His fingers rested on a paragraph on a page and he started to aimlessly read.

"… He summoned all his strength and willed his mind and breath to be calm, focussing energy into his fingers. With crackling intensity, bolts of lightning flew from his hands, blasting the rock face into a million shards, leaving the sunlight to once more, filter into the cave."

Wouldn't that be good? he thought, *summoning power and blasting stuff away*. Sleep took him from reading further.

The Ethereals – The first time

Mist.

A deep, clawing, impenetrable mist hung around him. Stillness and isolation, its companions, attacking his senses, and, for a short while, he was at a loss as to where or what he was. Looking down, he could see his feet on a grassed area, trailing away in all directions before disappearing into the still greyness. Despite the loss of most of his senses, he did feel as if he belonged. But the mist. This was strange. He sensed that the ground on which he stood dropped away slightly to his left, so he turned in that direction and started to tentatively walk.

The sound of the damp grass being flattened beneath his feet touched his ears and this encouraged him to explore further. Step by slow step, he walked "down" the field, ears pricking for any sound beyond this ooze, but there was none. It was no use looking around to get his bearings, as the mist effectively shut out all around him.

Well. Not quite. As he did a 360-degree turn, he noticed that a clear path now existed trailing back from where this journey started. As if a hedge trimmer had come along and neatly cut a swathe through this cloaking greyness, enabling him to see. He could see now that his path had taken him down what appeared to be a large field. Damp grass and small vegetation visible, and his wet footsteps disappearing back to his starting point.

On a whim, he turned 90 degrees to the left, walked 20 steps and quickly turned and looked back. Again his path in front of him was lost in the bleakness, but behind, the path was clear, the mist seemingly held back by some invisible power so that his passing was not disturbed.

Cooool, he thought. Concocting a hasty plan, he again turned 90 degrees to the left, feeling now that he was walking "uphill", counted off 20 steps and turned left again.

So, he thought. *If my idea is correct, in a few short steps I should...* And there it was. A clearing in front of him, now disappearing both to the left and the right, but as clear as day. He smiled and did a jig, complimenting himself on his own brilliance. In this place, wherever that was, his route remained open, but his forward exploration remained closed by greyness and silence.

For the first time, it dawned on him that he could see colour and feel the light on his face, and looking up, and up and up, he saw that this "hedge trimmer" had also cleared a path up into the sky so that he could see the blueness above him, some clouds above, now disappearing overhead as they were lost beyond the mist beyond where he stood. It looked like it was in the middle of the day, but what a strange place. What a strange experience. He backtracked now, just testing his theory, and after three right-hand turns on his now well-defined route, he ended up at the foot of his initial track, noticing his newly formed "entrance" into his original path, further up.

For the next thirty minutes, Sam proceeded to run up and down his self-created quadrangle, slowly revealing more of the space, until all the mist within had been burned away and a large-ish square landscape emerged.

Now he could get a better sense of where he was. It looked like he was in a small copse, surrounded by medium height trees, within which this small clearing sat. The clouds drifted lazily across the sky until they, once again, were lost beyond the film of mist, now visible beyond the tree line. Looking up into the skies, he tried to get his bearing as to where north was, but there was too much interference from the mist banks surrounding him to warrant any fixed decision of where "north" was.

And still, the silence surrounded him, now starting to take on a sinister air, as if something or someone lay just beyond his field of vision, waiting for him.

There was no need to explore further really. There was enough around to occupy him, but that background, nagging prickle refused to go away. A prickle, prompting him to step outside this comfort zone and venture, once again, into the unknown. A prickle that got bigger and more uncomfortable until he decided enough was enough and that he needed to explore this new place. Until this time, he still did not question why he was there, or how he got there. It was as if he knew that this place, strange and mysterious though it was, was part of him, in some way. Part of his life. He no more questioned his disposition than he would question why he breathed. *It is as if,* he thought, *the mist represents my life outside of the here and now, and that anything else is still "out there", to be discovered, or not.*

The still woodland beyond held his gaze, calling him, so he decided to continue his exploration, resolving in himself that if the worst came to the worst, he could just carry out a 360 degree "bubble" again, as at the beginning, thus revealing more of the "here and now".

Stepping forward, he moved off into the tree line,

brushing the branches away and disappearing into the gloom until his space lay quiet, empty, yet expectant, awaiting his return.

As before, the mist eased away from him as he ventured further and, reassuring though that was, he did feel a sense of frustration at not being able to see, instantly, what lay beyond. As he traversed carefully through the foliage, brushing around and under the branches, his ears slowly picked up the sound of water running ahead of him, bubbling over rocks and sending out that calming noise, streams are best placed to do. The noise of it increased slowly and he walked towards it, ducking beneath the branch line and stepping over tufts of grasses as he maneuvered himself through the undergrowth sensing that he was indeed getting closer to what he could only imagine, was a small stream working its way through this wooded area.

After a short while, he pushed past the last of the branches and came across the source of the noise. A pond lay in front of him, surrounded by moss-covered, shiny stones and pebbles, haphazardly strewn around and disappearing into the water. A small waterfall bounced over the rocks above him, landing into the pond in front, casting ripples into the mirror of the water, reflecting its surroundings. He felt the soft spray on his face and hands as it glistened in the air around him, slowly painting him in a sheen to match the surrounding area.

He knelt down, reaching his hands out into the water, sensing its coldness as his fingers dipped into the liquid. And cupping his hands, he drew a few eager mouthfuls into his mouth. The silence of the surroundings now eased by the subtle sounds of the falling water and droplets from the surrounding fronds falling into the water's edge.

As he was drinking, he sensed, rather than heard, a subtle disturbance in his immediate environment. For some reason he felt the hairs on the back of his neck start to lift and a feeling of danger began to weave itself into his mind. There were no apparent changes to the noises around him, no shadows casting strange shapes into his field of view, but something was not right. Something was here, he was sure of it. And that "something" was not wanting to announce itself!

He slowly lifted his gaze up from the water's edge, scanning the surroundings, searching for a clue to his sense of danger, but nothing was there. The branches of the trees still bent down to touch the water's edge, the moss and ferns lay quiet opposite him, the water still bubbled down the rock face above him, landing into the water. There was nothing obvious about his surroundings that advertised danger.

I must be imagining things, Sam thought. *The quietness is starting to get to me.* His gaze fell back to the reflections on the water, seeing the tree line, the pebbles just below the surface. But something didn't gel, and his brain made his eyes focus on the surface. Focus on the surface of the water just in front of him. Focus on the reflections on the water just in front of him. And looking back, coming into view, now that his brain, like a radar, had picked up its target, was the shape of an animal. Small, furry, sleek bodied, a long sweeping tail brushing the grasses, talons gripping the rock face. Large eyes, looking straight down at him.

Straight down at me!... With a shock, Sam sprang back defensively as he realised that this creature had crept up behind him and was even now above him on the rock face of the mini waterfall, intent on getting closer without him knowing.

"Aaaaarrggghhhh!!!"

His world exploded as a scream powered out of his mouth,

and instinctively he jumped up, grasping a rock in his hands, and throwing it in the direction of where he thought the animal was, all the while screaming out in shock, hoping to scare this "thing" as far away as possible. Arms flailing and legs kicking out instinctively, Sam shouted and cursed in pure, adrenaline-induced terror.

Nothing!

No noise, no scrabbling, no whimpering. Nothing. Whatever it was, Sam thought, had been scared away by his antics and probably long since disappeared down the hole it had scraped itself out of in the first place. His breathing calmed down a notch and he allowed himself a brief grin, thinking he had scared off whatever terror that "thing" was. He cracked out the tension from his shoulders, which had been building up whilst at the pool, and again turned towards the water, as if to seek some release there.

On the opposite side of the pond, sitting calmly and serenely on its haunches, and not more than two metres from him, the "creature from hell" gazed across as if, for all the world, this screaming banshee, that had been Sam, was a common occurrence here. Its eyes were intelligently gauging Sam's next movements. A thin tongue snaked out, licking its ears, and those big eyes fixed Sam with steely gaze… and then it smiled!

By smiling, its mouth opened, and the most lethal looking row of sharpened, death-dealing fangs shone out from the dark pit of its mouth.

That was it! Sam, casting any sense of brevity to the four corners, sprang up and dived off into the undergrowth from where he had first arrived, screaming in terror, not caring where he went, just wanting to get away from that "thing". Crashing through the undergrowth, any stealth tactics he thought he might have, were tossed into the wind and disappeared in an instance of pure speed and lack of care for where he was going. Branches reached out to swat him soundly across the face. Roots seemed to ease out on purpose to trip him up, and the foliage grew close around him, trying, it seemed, to disorientate him and lose him in the maelstrom in which he suddenly found himself. But Sam was blind to everything. His terror took over, propelling his legs through the woods and downwards to who knows where. At any moment, his imagination was reaching back to see where this creature was, expecting at any second to see this thing appear next to him about to sink its fangs into his neck.

Eventually, his lack of stamina caused his legs to slow and his breath came through in huge drawing gasps and he came to a stop next to a large tree, its base hidden by autumn leaves. He looked back and scanned his route urgently, carefully, but there was nothing there. His mind also did not register at this stage that his route behind him was perfectly clear and he could look back discerning the forms of the trees, the path he had forged, and the slope he had run down. Trying to hold his breath for a few short seconds, he listened out intently to hear if there was any breaking of twigs in the undergrowth, or strange noises that shouldn't have been there, but the woodland had returned to its original serene self and there was nothing other than the sighing of the wind through the trees

"Stuff that!" Sam said, ribs expanding and contracting quickly, trying to catch up with his fears. "No more forests. No more dark places, my friend," he said to no-one in particular. "I want to get out of here..."

For the first time since "arriving", the words he had just uttered by accident sprang out and hit him. Hit him hard! "Where is "here"?" he asked himself. "And how on earth did I get here? Please, please be a dream..." With that final request uttered, he again looked up and out, trying to fathom where next he should go. Backtracking right now was simply not an option, so he resolved to carry on down the slight slope. Gathering his wits to him, he let go of the bark of the tree and stumbled down into the mist, still straining for any sound out of the ordinary.

It wasn't long before he sensed the ground beneath his feet start to level out and looking back, he saw his route still etched out between the planks of mist disappearing on up a hill, and further back, the same forest from which he had burst out in terror what felt a few short moments earlier.

As he looked back, his feet still carried him forward and again, he registered that something had changed. This time, however, this "change" was registered through his legs as he sensed that the ground conditions had changed from grass to sand. Looking down, his second shock of the day hit him as he saw that he had now stumbled onto what he could only describe was a path. A well-worn path and one whose "creators" could be anyone, or anything.

Again, fear crept into his mind like some unbidden squatter and (not for the first time) he had a strong desire to get out of there.

Logic got the better of his fevered imagination, suggesting that if he followed the path (carefully), there would be a chance that he could stumble upon habitation and perhaps, if anyone was there, they could help him get the hell out of here. So Sam, looking in both directions from which the path emerged, chose a route, turned right and started to walk down the pathway, all the while his ears and senses alert for the remotest sound that would enable him to try to find cover if necessary before whatever had made the noise discovered him. And today, he had had enough "discovery" to last a lifetime.

His wanderings took him down a dusty, wide path, well worn over the years. Some stones and small pebbles scattered into the undergrowth to the sides as if tossed there by some vehicle or something that used this stretch. The mist still clung to all the places he had not walked through, and now, looking back, he noticed that the path he was on had slowly been winding down with a long bend, such that the start of his path journey now lay hidden behind the curve of the mist wall on the opposite side.

Suddenly, and again, unbidden, he picked up a disturbance off in front of him. The blanket "grey" of the mist he had been experiencing so far, here, now seemed to hold a slightly darker form and this form was not going away, and, if anything, was getting closer. His "fight or flight" warning light in his mind flashed a lurid red and his first instinct was to dive for cover before whoever was approaching discovered him. But this form was not running or acting furtively. Indeed, if anything "it" was walking quietly, slowly, yet determinedly towards him. Strangely, as he had felt with this place before, this new form approaching seemed to "fit" in his mind's eye and for the strangest reason, he felt drawn to whoever was getting closer. Too late now in any case. The form started to take shape and a young man became more distinct, walking up the path towards him, gazing to either side of the route, as if looking for something. He appeared to be a few years older than Sam, carried what looked to be a bow and a quiver full of arrows, and walked with a sense of "importance" (if that is possible). Eventually, this figure sensed Sam standing ahead of him and looking up, he stopped for a second and stared at Sam, disbelief, if anything, seeming to etch itself into his face.

Then he started running, running towards Sam!

If Sam had not been knocked down through shock yet,

given all the stress levels he had experienced in the few short hours (already??) he had been here, what happened next was way beyond any comfort zone he had ever experienced.

Coming closer, Sam stuck on his spot as if rooted, the man seemed to change his face from shock to pure joy and a smile the size of the sun broke out and his arms reached out in anticipation to greet Sam. Sam of course, saw everything happening as if in slow motion. *Who is this character? What does he want? Why does he seem to recognise me?* All these thoughts rushed into his mind, overloading it and he was aware of a feeling of great dizziness descending on him.

And then…

"Sam! Sam! You have arrived at last! Babu told me you had arrived so I came out looking for you. Welcome, at long last, my dearest friend!" said the man.

Sam's mind was just not able to assimilate all that had happened since arriving and, now with this stranger talking to him as if he was a long lost brother or friend, this was too much.

Sam felt a strong wrench tear through his body, seemingly from nowhere, and a pain greater than he had ever experienced rip through his mind, and the man, the path, the surroundings and the mist disappeared from view entirely.

Mother

Sam sat bolt upright, propelling the open book, which was on the bed, towards the cupboard, where it crashed loudly on the door before slumping to the floor. The quilt somehow managed to equally disappear in his thrashing and he came to, looking around desperately for any sign of this man who had scared the crap out of him!

The early morning stillness was all that greeted him as he gazed around, slowly getting his bearings. Recognition slowly creeping past his fear, he relaxed slightly as his familiar objects came into focus. There was his bedside table, his peanut butter sandwich, book, now on the floor, open but with the spine out of shape.

He breathed a deep sigh of relief, willing his breath to slow down. "It was just a dream," he said thankfully. "A weird, messed-up, but very real, dream." Relief overtook his fear and he smiled to himself thinking that whatever it was he had eaten the night before, was certainly to be avoided in future if that was the outcome!

Looking down, he focussed on the book, now abandoned on the floor. "That was what caused it," he said. "No wonder I went off on a little trip. All that science fantasy is enough to mess up any decent sleep." Thoughts of David, and that this was probably more a reason for his scary dream, had been successfully stowed away into the "Do not enter" part of his mind.

A funny thing, dreams. Even when your brain is convinced that it was all just imagination, you still find yourself looking around just in case a remnant of the dream has found its way into your world and is now resting behind a curtain ready to pounce when you least expect it.

Sam got up, stumbled out of his room, went to the bathroom and started his daily ritual once again. *Light on, Close door (slowly and quietly), wake up on the loo with a quick go on Sudoku, no flushing allowed at this time of course. Careful washing of his hair over the cold bath, deodorant. Done.*

However, today, the dream infiltrated his mind and he replayed parts of it in his mind as if trying to interpret its meaning as something significant. And it was this that really started to reinforce his normal day-to-day feeling of "invisibleness". *Just goes to show*, he thought. *Bloody rain waking me up, David's book catching me unawares…* He stopped himself thinking any further regarding why he was looking at David's book in the first place. That particular stream was never to be crossed again. Never!

"I am lost!" said Sam simply. "Mist is my darkness, weird animal can only be mum and dad. And the boy! Well, what do you expect? Someone reaching out to befriend me? Yeah, as IF! Just a sick joke, really." He scolded himself for thinking this, then turned that anger towards two people in the room next door. *What do you care?* he thought. *I know my place. Know where I should be, and you make it so very clear who you would rather see at the breakfast table…* He recognised his demon and, for the umpteenth time, he told himself to buckle up, close down and just get on with his day.

"Stupid dream anyway," he said, as he left the bathroom and headed back to his bedroom to get changed.

As happened now on most days, since, well, since "they stopped living", Sam shambled downstairs, rucksack hanging limply off one shoulder, jumper ruffled up against his belt, and he made his way to the kitchen to grab a quick bite to eat and try and get out of the house before his parents woke up and started their day by ignoring him.

College today, at least, held some interest as they were running a field exercise later on looking at chemical compounds and their respective reactions when brought together. This was one of his main interest groups, especially after he had demonstrated a particularly nice combination using pool chlorine and household disinfectant. He still laughed at that particular "hum-dinger".

The college bus ride was uneventful as usual. He sat in his normal place, head down, trying to be as inconspicuous as possible. Every now and again, he would look out the window, staring aimlessly at the passing world, getting on with its business. Sometimes they would pass the newspaper delivery man who still insisted on throwing the papers onto the front porches of some of the houses, as if reliving bygone days. It was always nice to see how much his bike wobbled as he threw the newspapers in the general direction of the houses. You could almost sense him cursing under his breath as either a pothole, a puddle or just bad steering caused his legs to shoot out and his face take on a strained look.

But not today. Today it was just grey, cold and still raining. *Hmm*, he thought, *maybe we won't be having any experimentation outside today after all, if this weather continues.*

Later that day, and as predicted, his chemistry lesson did not venture into a field lesson but instead proceeded to look at the molecular structure of glucose, which was about as exciting as watching crown bowls, he thought. Sam doodled out the graphical representation of a glucose molecule, putting "C"s "H"s and "O"s randomly on the page, but something did not "feel" right. Whilst he was happy that he, and practically everyone in the class, knew what blood sugar was, his diagram was wrong and, for some reason, what he had drawn tickled his inner perception.

He looked again at what he had drawn. A straight-ish line wobbled down the page, then turned through 90 degrees, then again and eventually, after a further kick, the line intersected the first, and the overall image looked to be describing a number 6. *Strange!* he thought. *That is not how glucose is represented.*

He continued to study this form he had drawn, something niggling at the back of his mind, until, with a shock, he realised what it was he had drawn. "This is my path I started to take in my dream," he said with surprise. "Why on earth would I be drawing that?" He had surprised himself that something as trivial as a dream had got into his mind such that he was doodling elements of it. He looked up, furtively. The lecturer was otherwise occupied, his feet propped up on his table, eyes glued to a book or something. *No doubt reading something other than the syllabus!* Sam thought.

He looked again at the sketch and, with a shrug, decided to carry on drawing his route as best as he could recall. Why? He could not begin to fathom. *Boredom probably*, he thought.

His pen followed his line away from the original "6" now. He remembered going into the forested area, through a few kinks, exiting eventually at the pond. *Oh yes. The pond!* he remembered. "Silly idiot!" he said, reprimanding himself. Then on he drew, away from the pond now, down and down towards a path, with a bend, and then that stranger. He marked an "X" here. He had no idea why he was doodling.

He had never drawn anything from his dreams before, but, he surmised, he must really be bored today, so he sketched away until the bell went, shocking him out of his musings. The class hurriedly packed away their meagre belongings and trooped out of the classroom, heading in various directions to their next lessons.

Sam forgot all about his doodles and went about the rest of his day, as he did on most. Wishing the day to end so he could just leave, and dreading the day ending as that meant he had to return home.

"Gird yourself, Sam," he said to himself (not for the first time) at the end of the day. His bus arrived and whisked him and his college neighbours back to their respective homes.

"Mum. I am home," Sam called out. Almost as a matter of course.

Dropping his rucksack near the door, he walked into the kitchen to see his mother standing at the sink. A statue, staring vacantly at the pots that lay there. Hands fumbling with a tea towel, her mind, for the moment, lost in whatever nightmare she was putting herself into this time. "Mum," Sam said quietly, trying to get her attention. She looked up, coming back around, turning to him, her eyes trying to focus on this stranger who had come into her world, like almost every day before this, it seemed.

"Oh, hello Sam," she said. "Dinner won't be long. Dad has gone to get the papers so should be home..." Her voiced trailed away, as did her gaze. Sam saw what he hoped would one day be banished for ever; she was lost in a world with no doors and no form and she had forgotten that the "key" hung around her neck like a weighted anchor, right next to the locket she was now playing with. A locket, Sam knew, holding a photo. Just one.

David!

Sam turned away, partly to hide his frustration and

hurt, partly because he just wanted to get away from being reminded of things all the time.

His dad came home soon afterwards. Stamping the rain and mud off his shoes with loud thumps and hanging his overcoat, still damp, onto the clothes rack at the door. He came into the living room, looked briefly at Sam, hesitated for a moment, and then continued into the kitchen where Sam heard him speaking to his mother. *Just as if I wasn't here*, Sam thought. *As usual!*

Slowly dinner was laid out at the table. Sam wasn't sure what it was. He had long given up asking, but tonight's offering defied description. Some vegetables, chicken (?), gravy. Cold. Tired. Lifeless. *Like this bloody house!* he caught himself thinking.

And then....

"Are you going to stop staring at that and at least eat it?" said his dad, accusingly. "Mum spends hours slaving in the kitchen so you can have something nice to eat when you get home. Perhaps you should care a little, and then perhaps you could offer to cook once in a while, but I suppose that is asking too much?"

"I am eating it," Sam said, not responding to the jibe just presented by his dad. It tasted horrible and mum certainly had not spent "hours" slaving away!

"You are not to leave the table until you have finished your meal," said his dad, unhelpfully.

"I am eating it," Sam retorted. "Leave me alone, will you."

"Sam, don't speak to your father that way!" he heard his mother say.

Here we go. Again! Sam thought.

"No that's OK, love. Sam was just expressing himself in his normal "couldn't care less" attitude. Weren't you Sam?"

"Dad! I am here, eating this food, trying to enjoy it and I just want to be left in peace, please."

"Peace!" said his dad. "Peace! Well I suppose it would be frigging wonderful if we could all have a bit of peace round here now, wouldn't it? But unfortunately we are not allowed any peace, are we? No, we have to pretend that everything is just 'tickety-boo', that the day is just filled with wonderful things and we are all so very frigging happy!!"

His dad's voice had slowly risen in volume and he was now starting to get red in the face, spittle and bits of chicken flying out from his mouth.

Sam, with little warning, exploded. "It's not my bloody fault he died!" he shouted, venom in his eyes and anger in his voice. "Everything was just perfect for you two when he was around, wasn't it? But I am so sorry that you are stuck with little sad me!"

"David," shouted his mother, "How dare you?"

"I am not bloody David, MOTHER!" Sam screamed, throwing his chair back in anger. "Never was, never bloody will be!" he said as he disappeared upstairs, diving into his room and slamming the door with all his might.

Sam was too angry now to do anything rational. Looking around at something, anything to hit out at. Instead, he fell onto his sofa, grabbed his iPad, plugged the headphones in, and disappeared into his world of dubstep and heavy metal music, trying to drown out the scream from within. The mess around him scattered to either side.

Sam curled up and looked out at the now darkened skies beyond his bedroom window, still sensing the storm outside shivering his windows as his own personal storm threatened to break through his tinder-dry mind and leave him an empty husk.

WTF! Sam thought. *All the bloody time! Just go on the way you are going, guys. I am so close to just blowing this place and then you can sort out your lonely little worlds by yourself.*

With that, he tried to tune into the thrumming of the music playing through his headphones. Its deep, earthy beat tonight, somehow, lolling him into a place of comfort. Lolling him into another world.

A flickering in Rudhjanda

His sense of perception changed slowly. The thrumming was still there, but now it was as if it came from a far off place, muffled, uncertain, vague even. And, if truth be told, the more he thought about it, the more he came to realise that what he thought was thrumming, seemed now, if anything, to sound like distant drumming. A single, repetitive "call-to-arms" type of noise. Also, where had the music gone to?

He opened his eyes.

A slowly coalescing mass of greyness weaving in and out of focus greeted him. There was no sense of up or down, near or far, just a vast field of "moving greyness". And utter silence all around such that the noise off in the distance slowly drew his mind into the here and now.

He stood in a spot with small rocks and thin grasses around his feet. Something about this type of location tugged at his memory, but, like the moving, sinuous field all around him, nothing fixed itself, other than a vague "awareness" of familiarity. He looked around, trying to gain any bearings of where "here" was, but the only pointer lay in the sound beyond, sometimes clear, as if whatever was making that noise lay within easy reach, sometimes distant, as if leagues lay between him and "it". He sensed, more than felt, that it was very early in the morning, but apart from that, he was effectively senseless. He slowly started to move, heading in, what he thought, was the general direction of the drumming. The greyness draping over him and around him as he moved, like a thin veil, like mist.

Mist! he thought. *This is familiar.*

He continued heading in the general direction of the sound, sensing that the ground he was on was slowly rising upwards. He stumbled over a few clusters of rocks in his way but generally his route led him closer to the sound. As he continued working his slow way over and around the rocks, he was aware of a darkening mass ahead of him that refused to move, and slowly this mass became more distinct until he stood in front of a large cliff face preventing further movement in that direction. He stopped and straightened up, placing his hands on his hips as he caught his breath.

It was here, for the first time, that he turned around to see if another route was available. Behind him, weaving down the small hill (as he now saw) and off into the distance, his track could just be seen through the darkness. He could see some of the outcroppings below casting their shadows from late evening moonlight. This caught his eyes and he gazed up to see a pale dark sky above, clear of clouds, the first inkling of early morning sun sending waves through two banks of incredibly high "mist". The path below him scythed out as if cut by a giant knife, the mist to either side held back as if instructed to stay in place.

"I remember this!" he said. "A place somewhere. Mist and paths." But that was all he remembered, for now.

He turned back to look at the cliff face, gazing as far as he could see in the gloom ahead. He could just make out a few small hand holds above him, and, without really thinking about the implications of going ahead without a recognised route, he reached out and started to climb. Scrabbling higher with each reach, the mist eased around him, as it had done on the path behind, and he progressed higher up the rock face. Now that he was here, exposed to the elements, he was aware that a cold, damp wind was blowing across the face of this cliff. He shivered slightly, gripped the rock face tighter, and continued his upward movement. It did not seem too long before he sensed the rock face start to ease and more grass came into view. The cliff came to an end and he eventually stood on a flat level, clear of rocks but with some grass and flowers around him. Again, he found he could look back, and now down, and see his route to the bottom of the cliff and, cutting away into the near distance, his original path, stopping at a point off at the bottom of the hill. Otherwise, everything else around him lay strangely still. Still, that was, other than the now louder and more insistent drumming behind him and seemingly off to the side but definitely closer than before.

He also noticed that his senses were starting to give this type of drumming more definition, and what had started out as a direction indicator now started to hold some feeling of danger. Also, and this was very hard to pinpoint, another sound. Almost as if some form of interference was cutting into the drumming. Sometimes for a long period, at other times short and sharp, and then it was gone.

Sam started to feel that perhaps he should rather NOT be heading in the direction of the noise, but, he convinced himself, if he was going to discover where "here" was, he had no choice but to travel towards the sound. "Perhaps with a little more care though!" he said to himself.

He set off again towards the noise, noticing that the ground still rose slowly, but this time as if coming to the brow of a grassy hill. As he steadily gained altitude, he started to discern what seemed to be flickering in the distance. It had an unusual effect through the mist, as it seemed to fluctuate between a low ember sort of glow and definite points of light, but not light from a room, more like…

I know! It looks a bit like a camp fire over there, he thought. But it was a camp fire unlike any he had ever seen. The glow seemed to spread out over a fairly wide area, as if multiple sources somehow seemed to merge together into splashes of oranges, reds and purples. Dim through the mist, but nevertheless, a source of calling. *Or warning!* he thought.

And now the drumming took on a more sinister tone. Incessant thumping from multiple sources all around the glow in the near distance, moving around from time to time, and the other noises he had heard earlier, then as interference, now seeming to take form and, if he was not mistaken, sounds of crying, some screaming even. Loud murmurings, deep, as from a male voice; others, keening, coming probably from women, and children.

This does not sound good, he thought. *But where else can I go? Perhaps I can skirt around this place and go on beyond.* A strange power seemed to be coursing through him, urging him, if anything, to venture closer to the slowly emerging event ahead. He was now so intent on what was possibly happening ahead that he failed to notice that he was, and had been for some time, walking on a path, like in his previous dream. A well-worn, dirty, muddy path, rutted with the tracks of many wheels over time, all heading either to or from where he was heading. And then, slowly emerging from the mist, a bent and frail wooden post and sign became apparent.

"**Welcome to Rudhjanda**" was painted in a strange archaic font scrawled across the timber face. The sign was bent down as if, over time, it had given up its ghost and instead was now lying limp, held only in place by a rusty nail, it too looking as if it was about to fall away from the post at any time, to land finally on the ground below. His mind registered all this, but only in part, locked away in his brain for retrieval at a later stage. For now he started to see and feel more of the events unfurling before his slowly horror-stricken view.

The drumming was definitely a call. Not, as he first thought, a call-to-arms, but rather a call to attack, to attack, maim and destroy if possible. The glow was indeed fires, but not happy, comforting camp fires, but, in places, bright sprites of fire burning spars of timber, and elsewhere, glowing stumps of crisp and burnt wreckage of what could only be described as houses.

And, oh my goodness. The "Interference"…

The noise now became clearer. Screams of terror, of destruction. He saw shapes shifting ahead of him. Of people running one way or another. Other shapes held grotesquely in final poses, most definitely not to move of their own free will again. Others standing over dim shapes beneath them, who seemed to be raising their arms in supplication. Thrusting arms powering downwards and then the shapes beneath, flexing for a final moment before slumping to the ground. His mind didn't need to conjure up too many scenarios. He knew what was happening here. A ransack! It appeared as if this village, "Rudhjanda"?, was being invaded by who or whatever lay behind the mists, which was itself weaving through this scene like a sword of Damocles. Despite all this though, his mind was reminding him that this was just a dream. Some sixth sense holding his mental capacity to fear in check, and that other-worldly feeling one gets, that the scene was not really there.

He had just decided that perhaps flight was better than curiosity, when, out of the mist, a young women came screaming towards him, torn cape caught in the wind and trailing back towards the danger beyond as if trying to pull her back into the carnage lying just beyond this grey curtain.

"I don't care if this is a dream or not," he stated to himself, "I am out of here!" And he started to turn to flee from this spectre descending towards him at speed.

"Sam! Sam," he heard. "Help me!"

Now this really got his heart hammering. *What is it with me at the moment?* he thought. *How is it that people know me here?* But by now, the young woman had drawn level with him. Face tear-streaked and dirty with mud and ash, eyes wide in terror and an old, worn blanket tied vainly around her throat, ripped in places and covered in dead leaves and twigs.

"Sam. Stop! Where are you going?" the woman cried. And with that, he reluctantly turned around to confront this apparition. He was about to speak, when, to his horror, he heard a thin "Swack" followed by a meaty "Thunk" and, protruding out of this woman's chest, now stuck out and gleaming, blood and grime attached to its barb, an incredibly large, lethal and death-dealing arrowhead glistened. Someone, or something, had let loose an arrow from within the mist blanket, striking the woman centrally between the shoulder blades, its speed easily sufficient to pierce her through completely, and finally!

Her eyes opened in shock as her body started to shut down and she reached out to Sam, gripping his coat with one hand, ripping the shoulder. Then slowly, almost gracefully, she slid down his side, all the while holding his eyes with hers. Eyes of surprise. Eyes of fear. Eyes that slowly lost their light, but eyes that kept their focus on Sam until, with a long whistling breath escaping her lips, she sank to the ground, falling full-length onto the path. Her hand finally resting outstretched against his leg.

Sam, casting care to the winds, turned and fled, running diagonally away from his already clearly-defined swathe cut through the mist. He ran as if the very demons of hell were nipping at his heels. He ran until he sensed a tree-lined barrier coming into view, and he dived for cover behind the nearest and largest tree, heart hammering and breath tripping in fear.

Looking out from behind his cover, he was relieved after a while that there appeared to be no one pursuing him, and he settled himself against the bark of the tree, hardly daring to move. Pulling his coat tight around him, he tried vainly to burrow deeper into the loam beneath his body, trying to make himself as inconspicuous as possible. His mind was just not able to join all the chaotic pieces together and instead his vision was fully occupied with the sight of that woman, pleading to him, begging him to help.

But how could I? he thought. *And, more importantly, what is going on?* This was definitely a dream he wanted to – no, needed to – wake up from. That thought slowly filtered into his mind and he reminded himself, again, not for the first time, that this was just a dream and that therefore he was not only safe, but also, not actually "here". This seemed to calm him down, and his breathing mellowed and his mind eased at last. In doing so, this allowed him to turn his attention outward, and he noticed that now, the gloom had gone, and instead the early morning light was filtering through the mists around him. The noises and the drumming seemed to have ceased. Indeed, all sounds seemed to have vanished and quietness reigned supreme all around him. He ventured a careful peek from out behind the tree to see what lay waiting for him beyond his sanctuary. Of course, his path was clear to see, arrowing back the way he had come, like an accusing finger pointing straight at him from the desolation beyond. Beyond that, he still had no real perception of space or place, the mist resolutely refusing to move away to enable him to see more of the landscape he now found himself in.

Sam slowly emerged from behind the tree, casting careful looks in all directions. Ears pricking for the nearest sound, and his feet ready and more than willing to take flight as soon as the merest suggestion of danger announced itself. He stepped out from the tree line and walked tentatively back the way he had come, some morbid curiosity perhaps egging him on to go and see what had transpired to this small village.

He eventually came across the first signs of destruction. A mangled cart lay at an angle at the edge of the path, one of its wheels broken in two and its contents strewn over the floor beyond. A form lay on the path a few metres away, and he noticed that it was still. Still, unmoving, and based on the sword sticking out from his chest, very dead! Following rapidly on, he soon came across an arm, whose hand was fixed at an angle, a single index finger pointing up to the heavens. The arm trailed back to the still form of the woman he had had the misfortune to see pierced through earlier that morning, now seemingly a million miles away from where he was presently. Her hair trailed dirtily across her face. A young face and perhaps, in life, one which would have held much beauty, but now, those eyes. Looking nowhere. Fixed in a face doing nothing, attached to a body, rumpled under her cloak of torn blankets and mud. Very, very still.

He swallowed a bitter gulp of bile and looked away, towards the glow which was still evident a little distance away. Moving on past her still form, trying not to look down and study her in any more detail, the village of Rudhjanda slowly came into focus, or what was left of it.

The village lay the other side of a small stream, which appeared to have been starved of water for some time as mud and rocks were more in evidence than the water. It was separated from him by an arching timber bridge, whose spars and balustrading, in part, were either missing, or smoking still from the event that had happened that night. Beyond, and just visible in the early morning mist, broken, bent and ashen-burnt spars speared into the air in all directions. Smoke and small flames still licked around some of the timbers. Straw, fruit, kegs of all different sizes and shapes, lay scattered on the floor, disappearing off into the mists beyond. But all this seemed to merge into each other to allow other details to appear. Details which were all either lying supine or leaning against or over the destruction in front of him. People. All types of people lay scattered in strange poses. All still, yet as if some giant had thrown his toys out of his particular pram and left them as they lay.

Senses on full alert, he carefully and slowly moved onto the bridge, the creaking of the timber in protest at his weight seeming to conflict with the noises of burning timber beyond. He noticed here that a number of people had appeared to have got caught trying to ford the mud covered stream rather than flee over the bridge. Of course, the bridge was covered with broken and burning carts and bodies of people and animals, so no surprise that some unfortunate inhabitants chose the quagmire route, rather than flee past fallen comrades and family. Sam continued forward over the bridge, clinging closely to the edge for some form of support, stepping from time to time over the carnage around him.

And then. A slow, small groan! Sam saw a hand beneath a bale of hay. The fingers were flexing slowly, painfully, but moving nonetheless. Sam hurried to the bale and with some effort, managed to move it off the form of a young boy. The boy was no more than a young teen. Not much younger than himself. Like the others, the boy was unkempt and dirty. His hair was matted with dirt and blood and his blue eyes were lost in pits of dark shadows, but he was aware enough to notice Sam.

"Sam," the boy gasped. "Sam."

The boy swallowed hard, as if trying to extricate some air from his lungs. "If you had been here earlier, this would not have happened!"

Sam was shocked into stillness. "What on earth?" he started, but was interrupted.

"Sam. They came in the night. We tried to wait but they were too many. Too fast. But we waited, as you had asked us to. So we...." The boy rattled a slow breath and then continued. "Why did you go?" he asked with simple boy-curiosity. But any response from Sam was lost on him, for, with a final settling of his lungs, he whistled out one last breath and his eyes lost all light and focus.

If Sam was shocked to start with, hearing his name mentioned, and not for the first time, then the curious comment that he had apparently "asked them to wait" went way past any feeling of being shocked and instead, he just gazed down at the still form, unable to comprehend what was going on in this weird dream.

He heard a single, covert creak of the timber bridge behind him, sensing, more than knowing, that this creak was not settlement. Something about the way that particular noise was made resonated with the deepest darkest recesses of Sam's mind and he was keenly aware of the hairs on his skin standing on end and his temperature spiking. This was definitely not a friendly creak. He slowly straightened up, all senses on full alert, and, summoning what was left of his nerves, he turned around.

At the other end of the bridge, standing centrally as if to stop Sam retreating in that direction, stood what looked at first to be an apparition. At least six feet five tall, draped with a bear skin cloak, fur hat with horns and a massive beard with bits and pieces sewn into it, a huge man glared straight at Sam. His arms, and what was visible of his face, were covered in tattoos of all shapes and sizes, and all of these combined presented a person to whom Sam was quite sure he really did not want to meet on any dark street, or any middle-of-the-day-brightly-shining-thank-you-very-much sort of street either for that matter.

The man exuded evil, anger and malice and Sam was in no two minds that this man and his friends were probably responsible for the carnage that lay all around him.

Sam also noticed, in a slow-motion sort of way, that the man was also armed with a mean looking and very large bow which he held in his outstretched left hand, the biceps in his arm flexing with hidden strength. His right hand was pulled back behind his body holding the twine, now fully extended away from the bow, which was bent and quivering with pent up energy. And between the two lay a wicked looking arrow, pointing straight at Sam.

Fingers relaxing in his right hand, he let the arrow fly.

Sam felt the arrow hit him squarely in the chest. Felt the shaft drive the arrow head through his torso before it punched its way out through his back. And all the while, it was as if he saw this from a third person perspective up in the air, looking back down, as if it was no longer him there on the bridge, but someone else, removed from him. He definitely felt the pain though. Excruciating beyond description. Terrifying in finality. He sensed the wetness of the blood, the sharpness of the arrow shaft grinding against his ruptured lungs. He sensed all manner of things in an instant and yet, through all this, his mind, as if removed from the scene, was calmly speaking to him saying, "Don't worry, Sam. This is all a dream and you will wake up soon!"

He took a few slow steps back, the impact of the arrow alone pushing its energy into his feet and assisting his backward stumble. His final step took him out beyond the edge of the bridge, no longer restrained by the balustrading, and he toppled backwards over the edge, his last sight, of the man disappearing from view, the wind blowing his cape up into a waving banshee.

Again, as if time was snail-paced, he sensed his mind saying, "Relax, Sam. This is how the dream ends. You know that when you hit something, it shocks you back to reality." So Sam relaxed in an odd sort of detached way. The shock he should have felt at effectively being killed there and then oddly removed from his situation.

Sam hit the soggy mud bank with a dull thud, bits of gunk spraying up as he landed.

He did not wake up in his real world. *That's odd!* he thought briefly, as he lay in the mud pool, almost without pain. *Maybe this is what death actually feels like,* he thought in a detached sort of way. *Maybe I am actually dying for real, and this is what it feels like. It's not too bad really, I suppose.*

His strange musings started to get hazy as the light around him started to fade. But nothing, not even being shot by an arrow and dying, compared to what he experienced next when, out of the corner of his eye, he was aware of a slight movement from under the bridge. Some variation in the shadows, which was not a shadow, detached itself from the bridge supports and slowly, ever so slowly, extricated itself from the security and safety of the bridge and started to move towards him.

A small, furry, sleek-bodied animal with a long sweeping

tail moving slowly from side to side came towards him. His legs extended, Sam could see talons gripping into the mud. And once again, those large eyes, looking straight at him.

If Sam was not scared beforehand, despite being impaled or falling off a bridge, then for some reason, this form creeping towards him with menacing, inexorable, slow steps, set his teeth on edge and his deeply rooted and well managed fears exploded from within him and he realised, he was powerless to resist. Powerless to move. Powerless to do anything but just experience what was, for him, quickly becoming his worst nightmare.

The animal drew closer to him, looking in all directions, scanning for any danger but focussing on moving towards Sam. Closer, until his talons touched Sam's feet. And then the creature started to crawl up Sam's legs. Sam was beyond fright now. His lungs were pushing his chest cavity out and in like a trip-hammer against the foreign barb and his eyes were riveted to this creature working its way ever closer to his face. It moved now onto his torso, tongue flicking out to test the air. Sam saw those large, sharp looking fangs, and prayed to all and sundry, begging to wake up. But today, his "help" was otherwise busy and the creature continued its route up along his body until it stood directly in front of his face, looking down into Sam's terror-filled eyes. Sam seemed to sense that this creature was looking at him as if questioning him, which was the last thing he remembered.

Sam's world, at last, gave him some respite and he passed out. But as the light dimmed away to blackness, his last picture was of the creature looking back towards the arrow shaft sticking out of Sam's chest and the animal turning towards it.

Sick

Sam woke up in a fright, sweating profusely and, as a reaction still to his vivid dream, sat bolt upright. A searing, gut-wrenching pain from his stomach almost bent him over double as he felt urgent pangs announcing themselves to him, and he quickly made his way to the bathroom where he promptly threw up. "Aargh!" he groaned. "I thought that meal last night was dodgy. No wonder I had such a horrible dream." After a while, his heaving subsided and he just lay there, holding onto the seat of the toilet, allowing his thumping headache to sort itself out.

He slowly stood up and stumbled over to the sink, eyes bleary and mouth dry. Looking into the mirror, he saw a very tired, puffy youth looking back at him, eyes half-closed in tiredness, a twig stuck into the mess of his hair. *How did that get there?* he thought, and he unconsciously reached up to pull the twig from his matted hair. His fingers were filthy with blackness!

"What on earth!?..." he began. He looked down at his blackened fingers. They definitely seemed to have ash on them, although where that came from he had no idea. The "ash" was wet as if recently applied. Something in his subconsciousness pricked him and he felt a darkness close around him and tie itself around his stomach. He did not want to listen to the one "logical" explanation which presented itself to him. "There is no way that my dream and this can be related," he said with some finality, and he promptly bent over the sink and washed the dirt off of his fingers.

"There. All gone!"

He turned back to his room, stomach still aching, and announced to himself, "I am staying home today. I feel too ill to go to college."

He failed to notice the trail of mud on the floor from the bedroom to the bathroom and now back again. A trail of mud and ash in footprints. His footprints.

He entered his room, closing the door behind him and looked down at his sofa. His iPad lay on the floor, headphone lead trailing away to disappear behind the arm rest. The cushions all squashed with his tossing and turning that night. And then he noticed the dark stain on one of the cushions. A large, dark black stain, still glistening slightly and still attached by some miracle to his pen, and at last, parts of his addled mind connected some dots.

"That explains it! I must have fallen asleep on the pen, which then leaked onto my fingers and it was that that made the stain." He could sense the relief as his mind made this picture fit with his logic and his panic eased as he allowed himself a laugh at his stupidity. He could then look at his dream in a detached otherworldly way. His thoughts turned to the strange creature he had seen, its alien-ness and yet, somehow, it was able to communicate with his spirit in some weird way. He thought about the destruction he had seen. *It was so weird*, he thought. *Seemed so real a second ago. Now laughable and obviously made up*. And with that, it passed out of his mind.

He heard his father clumping down the stairs, heavy breathing and huffing marking his path down to the front door and to his boring "do-the-same-every-day" day. Sam was about to relax when he heard his dad holler up the stairs, "Sam, get yourself out of bed and get to college. You are late and you don't want me to come up there and get you up, do you?"

"No dad," Sam said sarcastically under his breath, "wouldn't want you to bust a hernia or something wasting the effort."

Great, he thought. *Despite my condition, he is forcing me to go to college. Nice one!* Sam rolled back onto his feet, got dressed and eventually left his bedroom, came downstairs, grabbed an apple and went out, shutting the door behind him a little too loudly.

The bus had already left.

"Fantastic!" Sam said. "Now I have a twenty-minute trek and it's bloody raining!" Pulling his hoody up over his head, he did what almost all students do universally. He trudged down the road, rucksack slung over one shoulder, disappearing into his own world of studying the grey footpath in front of him on this grey sodding day.

Cars, buses and trucks all passed by him doing their own thing on their way to who knows what.

And who cares really? he thought, scuffing his feet through yet another grey puddle. *Who gives a stuff about any of this? We just get up, do our stuff, eat things, go to bed, and do the whole thing all over again. I mean, what is the point?* Sam knew this conversation, as he had had it with himself many times, always with the same empty, silent response. His feelings and emotions this morning were already frayed, and pushing his boundaries yet further was pointless.

He entered the town retail parade and passed a number of shops, most still closed till later on, but one ahead of him was open. It seemed always to be open. Its bright warm yellow lighting inside beckoned. It was a lovely quaint café serving all day breakfasts with all the trimmings and steaming coffees and it was always bustling. "The owner never seems to sleep," Sam mused.

Alice, the proprietress, was, for some reason, resting against the door post as he approached, cigarette drooping between her fingers and a lazy trail of smoke escaping from her mouth. She was watching Sam approach.

"Hi Sam," she called. "Not the best of days to be walking to college?" Sam felt like he could think of a great retort to that comment, but something stopped him attacking her with his verbal diarrhoea. Alice always seemed genuinely happy to see him. *One of the few*, he thought. And, if anything, Sam always felt that she "had his back" in some unconnected strange sort of way. There was nothing becoming in her appearance, neither did she ever give him the idea that she was perhaps wanting his company. No. Instead, she seemed to have an inner light that, he felt more than knew, saw him for who he was, and whilst he would never admit it, he did feel comforted when she said hello.

"Hi Alice," Sam replied. "Woke up feeling ill, and got up late so I missed the bus and had no choice but to walk. My silly fault." He tried his best to give her a smile to deflect her asking any more questions.

"Oh, you poor thing," she cooed. "Let me at least send you on your way with an egg and bacon roll." And without waiting for a response, she disappeared into the café, leaving the door ajar.

He entered. Keeping his head down and not looking to either side, in case someone else noticed him or wanted to engage in meaningless banter. He got to the counter and slid up onto one of the available bar stools to wait for his egg and bacon roll. His stomach, despite its earlier efforts to reject all forms of food, now gurgling with anticipation.

Alice returned from the kitchen, saw him and came on over, drying her hands on her apron. "So," she started, "You are not feeling well? Maybe it's the weather," she mused. "This greyness always seems to bring out the worst in our bodies. But, we cannot let it beat us." She said this last statement with conviction, and Sam looked up at her. "I mean," she began, "Look at me. Last week I got so depressed at the constant rain, rain, rain that I had a few days to myself, went down to the coast and had a lovely time in a quiet house overlooking the beach and the waves. So peaceful and tranquil."

The smell of the bacon was wafting over to Sam, who involuntarily licked his lips. Then Alice leant in towards Sam as if to tell him a dark secret. Sam, reflexively leant in also.

"And," she whispered, "you will never guess, but I was befriended by this lovely animal whilst I was there." She looked conspiratorially at him as if to gauge his response. Sensing none, she continued.

"There I was, walking along the beach, as I told you," she continued, "when blow me backwards but out from the bulrushes to one side came this small furry animal, who poked his head out and looked right at me. Now I can tell you, I was shocked to say the least. I mean, creatures are scared of us humans, aren't they? But here was this thing, looking right at me and it knew, Sam, it knew, that I had seen it, and yet it was not afraid."

Sam nodded absently, thinking about the egg and bacon roll, and that he really should be getting on as the college did not take kindly to its students being late. Alice continued.

"So it shimmied out from the rushes and came towards me. Slowly, on all fours. It looked a little like a, well, I don't know what really. A lemur perhaps. But it had these lovely furry small legs but incredibly long talons. I can tell you, they looked sharp!"

Sam, whose mind had already started to depart the café, quickly found that his attention was on her now, as the word "talons" was mentioned.

"Yes, furry, cute, sleek and unafraid," she said. "That was the barmy thing. Unafraid! And those eyes! So large."

Sam felt immediately uncomfortable. His stomach again starting to tie itself in knots. This explanation from Alice of the animal she had befriended now sounded all too similar to that weird creature who had scared the "Bejimini's" out of him in his dream. He slid off the bar stool mumbling, "Sorry, I have to go," and he moved quickly to the door and left.

"But you forgot your egg roll," Alice said to his parting form, but Sam was already out of earshot. He therefore failed also to see Alice squinting out at him from the café window, eyes locked on his departing shape disappearing into the rain once more, a knowing look etched on her face and her fingers teasing an odd looking necklace between fingers and thumb.

Sam decided that he would rather face the wrath of his dad than go to college that day. He really did not feel too well, and, he argued, he could always say he really was not feeling too great. *What could they do?* he thought, *banish me?* Sam retraced his steps, back to his home and, on entering eventually through the front door, he called out, "Mum. It's me."

His mother could be heard scrabbling about upstairs, and it sounded as if she was in or near his room! "Mum!" he called, and proceeded to walk up the stairs. He found his mother kneeling on the floor between his bedroom and the bathroom, a pail of soapy water next to her, and her hands wrapped up in washing gloves.

"Sam Gilbert!" she fumed. "What on earth were you

doing last night? How on earth did you get this place so dirty?"

Sam just stared at her with complete incomprehension. *What on earth?...* he thought. He had no idea what she was on about. "What do you mean?" he started.

"Bloody dirt and, and mud and leaves all over the bloody house and you left the floor in this state. Where were you last night?" Accusingly, Sam's mother turned to him and glared. "As if I don't have enough to do today what with Ken and Marjory coming over later," she railed. "But No. Oh no, you have to leave this place looking like a farmers' market, you slope off to college... Why aren't you at college?" She stopped for a moment, trying to link his appearance with the fact that he shouldn't actually be there at all, but, for the moment, her anger overrode this matter. "Sam, we all have so much to do round the house and I wish you would contribute more rather than leave everything to your father and me to sort out."

That's not fair! he thought, *I am always trying to accommodate their ever-changing mood swings.* "Mum," he began, "I really have no idea what you are on about. I woke up feeling really rough this morning, I was going to stay in bed because I am not feeling well but dad told me to go to college, so I did. I was late, got to town, felt really ill and came back. That's all. I haven't been anywhere else."

"You should be ashamed of yourself," she continued, not really hearing him through her anger. "The floor was a state when I got up here, and I am the one cleaning it up. As usual."

Sam was at a loss as to what on earth she was on about. He really had no clue as to why she was cleaning the floor. Why, for goodness sake? But all ideas drained away. *Why does she think I was out last night?* he thought. *She must really be tripping!* And with that, he unceremoniously mumbled an, "I am sorry!" but not knowing what he should be sorry about, but he always said sorry, so why stop now.

"Sam," his mother responded. "Just show you care about this place. Even for a little minute. It's hard enough as it is at the moment."

Sam sensed where this was heading and did not want to get into yet another argument about a subject none of them wanted to acknowledge, so he went into his room and closed the door behind him.

"Ken and Marjory are over for dinner tonight," she said, moving back downstairs. "I will leave you some food for later if you feel up to it."

And that was it. No, "How are you, sweetheart". No, "Sorry you are feeling ill". Just, "We are having guests downstairs later on. You are not invited, but you can have the leftovers afterwards!"

"Nice," said Sam. Not for the first time. He walked into the room, unbidden frustration bubbling to the surface, and caught his profile in the cupboard mirror. He turned to face himself. A youth of seventeen, trying to be older looked back at him, but with the eyes of nakedness he recognised all too well. His hair wet with the day's rain. Eyes sunken dangerously into their pits. He recognised the look. *You made me this way!* he thought. Rejection, or feelings of the same, reflected back at him from his reflection, passive on the other side of the mirror. He knew he could not escape from this person. He was too honest, too real. Too full of self-loathing and punishment for now. He caught sight of his Xbox in the reflection, and went to turn it on, but today it was just as if the day had handed out all the goodies and he had missed all of them. It refused to start.

Sam breathed in slowly and deeply and his inner self berated him for all the things that had happened today, even those not remotely his fault. And, as often happened, these thoughts then externalised themselves and his anger about the injustice in his world bubbled over into action. He reached for an Xbox game, unfortunately within arms' length, and threw it with all his might at the wall, trying to focus all his anger into that small flat object.

He succeeded. The box bounced soundly off the wall and then went skating over the work table sending pens, papers, and his coffee mug flying, the coffee still in it spewing out over the wall.

"B-LO-O-D-Y TYPICAL!" he cursed. "Mum and dad are going to kill me after all this." He glared down at all the pieces laying scattered on the floor, shrugged his shoulders and climbed under the duvet covers, resigned to doing what he should have done, what he wanted to do all day. He went to sleep. His last thought was, *No one listens. So why should I?*

Tangaroa (God of the sea, rivers and lakes)

Sam rolled over in his sleep, unconsciously moving the duvet up around his neck, sensing the furry smoothness as it gently caressed him. He wanted desperately to disappear into nothingness for a while but the distant sounds of the night nagged at him, pulling him away from oblivion. Something about his surroundings didn't seem to fit and it tugged at his senses, refusing to let go. The noises were not from an outside he was familiar with. The sounds were definitely NOT cars, and since when was his duvet so soft and... well... furry?

He opened his eyes, looking straight up at darkened timber spars, flickering colours dancing around the shadows beyond, reflecting off the canvas of what could only be a tent. He was now fully awake and his hands moved down to feel this strange covering over him, as if to verify that he really was under a fur pelt. He became aware of the noise focussing to a dim throbbing coming from his right and he turned his head to try to seek the source. What he did not expect was to turn and come face to face with what could only be described as the grubbiest, smallest girl looking straight at him, eyes as large as planets studying his every gesture, who, on seeing his eyes open, screamed in a low guttural way, fell off an even smaller stool and stumbled backwards, legs bicycling furiously to get enough grip to turn herself around and out through a flap he now saw open to one side, yelling loudly for someone to come, and come quickly. A fire still glimmered on the sandy floor of his "space", the red embers and glow showing that the fire had been lit some time ago. Lazy smoke curled upwards and out through a slot above, as if undisturbed by the commotion around it.

Sam sat up quickly, which was his first mistake! A pain like nothing he had ever encountered before shot up from his chest, forcing him to cry out in pain and reflexively curl back up into a ball. His chest was heavily bandaged and he could sense a slickness around some of the material. A slickness that felt like blood. Of course, his senses went into overdrive as he tried to assimilate all the various options of where he was, what he was doing there and why he was bleeding, but these were all driven away in an instance when a stranger burst into the tent through the flap, ripping him urgently from his now banished sleep.

"Sam! Thank the heavens. We thought we had lost you. If it wasn't for Babu, I don't want to think what could have happened." A young man stood before him, vaguely familiar, if that were possible, the grubby looking girl hiding behind his legs, peering past to look at him, her eyes impossibly large and flashing a luminous vivid purple from deep within.

Sam, without thinking clearly, could only utter, "Who are you and how on earth do you know my name?"

"Sam, now is not the time for play. Now is the time for you to rise, come on out with me and stop this war. NOW!" The last was uttered with short but raised punchiness before the stranger turned and looked back at the girl, telling her urgently, "Pania. Run quickly and get Ngaire. Run like the wind, child. Tell her. He is awake!" And with that, the girl released her grip on his trousers and with a quick glance back at Sam, turned and ran headlong out through the tent flap shouting at the top of her lungs for Ngaire to come quickly, disappearing off before her voice was swallowed up in the noises from without.

As if the troubles of the night he had already experienced were not enough, now Sam was being accosted by two strangers who he didn't know from Adam, telling him to stop some war he knew nothing about, let alone wanted anything to do with. Sam, despite the pain pounding from his chest, decided that enough was enough regarding this most extreme of events. He stood up and faced this young man, eyes blazing with unsuppressed anger. "Look!" he blasted. "Whoever you are, THIS, is not real! YOU, are not real. Nothing is real. I don't sort things out, I only get abused and told off and sent to bed, so get out of my sight, leave me be and stay AWAY! Nothing good is real, so why should there be any difference here?" And with that, he brushed fiercely past the youth, pushing him back with a shoulder check, before storming out of the tent and into the unknown beyond.

Outside, pandemonium flourished! People stumbled around wherever he looked. Some kneeling over still forms, keening cries renting the air and gazes turned skywards in supplication, as if asking for help from somewhere long since vacated. Others, stepping over shapes and edges, too vivid to digest, looking with stunned faces at a world which had been destroyed in front of their very eyes, never to be healed again. Sam was too pent up to stop; instead he stormed down from the tent and through the crowd, who, as if by magic on seeing him, parted to allow his passing, almost as if reverentially opening the way for him. He was vaguely aware of their chanting as he passed. They seemed to be proclaiming, “He has come. Here is the one who will save us.” This just increased his desire to escape from the nut house he thought he had got lost in, wanting nothing more than to wake up and face his demons in the real world, rather than this self-fabricated one.

Without a backward glance, he steered directly away from the tent and towards the mist bank in the distance, a mist bank he now saw as a saviour rather than an ominous oppressor. Had he bothered to look back, he would have seen those self-same people, who moments before were kneeling around him looking for his help, now looking to each other in confusions and despair, sunken heads falling even deeper as they saw that their Helper was instead fleeing. He would also have noticed the grubby girl trying desperately to chase after him, being held back by the young man who first approached him in the tent. His eyes, grey in the early dawn, staring after Sam’s quickly disappearing form, his ripped cloak flowing behind him, whipped away by the winds that gathered to the top of the enclave.

The mist thinned as he approached, and, like before, it parted allowing him to progress towards a tree-lined darkness ahead of him, the mist staying apart behind him, so, had he looked back, he would have seen an arrow-straight path back to the carnage he had just witnessed.

Sam didn’t look back; instead he staggered into the trees and tried vainly to run into its welcoming darkness. But instead, the tree branches seemed to strike out at him and the roots to trip him up, such that progress was difficult. Eventually, the slow progress had its desired effect, and the fear of the past few minutes eased sufficiently for him to slow down and try to get his bearings. Looking to the sides and up ahead offered little clue of his whereabouts, but looking back, he saw that his path had brought him up through the trees and into thicker, taller trunks that pressed around him, shutting out much of the light that attempted to break through the grey clouds that seemed to hover above him.

It also allowed him to hear what was slowly looming up ahead. Once again, commotion appeared to be occurring in front of him and, for a moment, he thought that his struggles through the forest had instead made him angle back to the place he had just fled from. The unmistakable sound of steel on steel, crashing against one another and yet more sounds of screams bounced through the trees and mist and became clearer as he moved on. He attempted to turn away from the sound, but the trees and lack of visual perception made the sound reverberate all around him such that he lost all sense of direction other than where he knew he had been, by the mist path etched into the cloud banks behind him.

"Why does this dream always have mist?" he asked to no one in particular. "Mind you, at least I know it's a dream, because of it!" he said, helpfully explaining away the location, and thus also the atrocities he had just witnessed. It also allowed him to focus himself back into the "now" and the noises ahead of him, such that he moved on towards them, almost in a trance, as if he had come to accept that he was not actually there, and that, therefore, nothing could affect him.

He sensed, more than saw that the trees were thinning and shortly, he felt the darkness lift and a dappled light start to expand across his field of visions. He stepped out from the tree-line and came across a similar scene to that he had encountered earlier.

Fires were burning in a few locations around him. Huts, once large and proud, were now burning down into ash stumps, their few spars, a lasting testimony of the area, still pointing defiantly up into the sky. He saw many forms, silent on the ground, bent, broken, still. Some with eyes, now sightless, gazing at their last nightmare vision until that was snatched away from them in merciless haste, others, bent down to the muddy ground as if to hide from a fate they wished not to acknowledge let alone view. He saw people moving slowly, aimlessly around him, looking one way or the other, some crying out for people who he felt, rather than knew, would not be responding to the call. He saw a few fights still continuing, but these were sporadic and coming to a logical conclusion. The victor knowing that it was only a matter of time now until their objective had been achieved.

He saw all this, and he felt… nothing!

This is just another dream, he thought. *A dream, which will disappear when I wake up. So I will not let it affect me. It means nothing. Just like life really.* His demeanour, he thought, was impressively kept together. This was not a "normal dream" if any dream could be classed as "normal," but it was just like any other in the sense that he would wake up and go on his way, without a backward glance. Or so he thought.

He was aware of another sound. One just below the threshold of "normalness". A sound of someone or something attempting to move quietly, surreptitiously. A sound of someone or something moving towards him, with intent. He slowly turned towards the source of the sound. It came from the same forest he had just left. It got closer, more urgent, louder. Sam felt the cool trickle of sweat down his face and tickle the small hairs on his neck, which, he noticed, had risen almost imperceptibly, as this new sound invaded his brain. He realised, that despite his outward bravado, this "noise" was getting to him and he started to step back slowly from whatever was coming towards him from beyond the tree line.

Impossibly, the self-same creature, or one just like him, that he had tried in vain to escape from when he had been shot; the same creature, he now realised, had been staring at him at the pond, seemingly so long ago, and yet, actually only one night past; this same creature now burst out from the tree-line beyond and staggered towards him with, in Sam's mind, obvious and not nice intent. Sam felt an almost impossible to control, revulsion towards this creature. Somewhere in his mind, the word "Babu" filtered into his thoughts, but he discarded this against the need to get away from this thing, and get away right NOW! The creature was trailing blood and Sam noticed he had a number of deep cuts on his fur-lined body. But it was those eyes and those razor-sharp teeth that occupied Sam's attention.

He turned and ran headlong, away from this "creature from hell"! But, like often happens in dreams, the creature, rather than disappear into thin air, instead increased its pace and started to run after him, trying to catch up with him, which Sam was not having, in any terms! Sam burst once more into the tree-line, hoping to fool the creature into getting lost in the mist, which surrounded them still. This only heightened the noise level of the creature, who seemed now to be thrashing only a few metres behind him, the mist and trees once more affecting the sound such that Sam quickly despaired of ever getting away from it.

With renewed determination, Sam picked up his pace, diving through thickets and dodging now left, now right, through hedges, small trees, branches now swatting him soundly in the face and chest. All the while running from this "thing" that continued to invade his dreams like a banshee. As he ran down the hill he sensed that the creature was falling behind, and the last sound he heard from it, was almost as if a forlorn cry had left its heaving chest, crying out to him. "Saaaaaaaaammmmmmmmmm. Run no more..." it seemed to say. *But of course, that's not possible,* thought Sam. *Animals don't talk, so yet again, Sam, my man, it is just another demonstration that this is indeed a dream. A very weird and very real dream, but just a dream!* This uttered between ragged breathing as he tried to calm his chest, which now found the opportunity to remind him that it was still bandaged and it really hurt! He looked down at his chest, realising for the first time that he had no shirt on and instead, the bandages around his torso, now mottled and dirty, were flapping in places as the knots came undone. Darker patches were dotted around where the bleeding had started afresh and he resolved to go back to the tent, if for no other reason than to find his shirt.

Sam eventually emerged again from the forest, sensing that he was now a little lower down the tree-line than when he first fled into it. The mist slipped effortlessly around him, but for once, he sensed a slight thinning to his left and he turned in that direction. Moving on, for the first time he saw that the mist in front of him had disappeared partly, with a clear slash running across his vision from right to left. *Hey! That's my original path from the tent,* he thought. He looked to the left and saw this clear route defined, disappearing into the forest, marking where he had entered it earlier. Then looking right, he got his first real glance of the utter carnage he had fled from.

For once, silence lay still over the whole area, like a blanket. There were no bird sounds, no rustle of trees in the wind. It was as if time had taken a deep breath and was holding it before letting it go in one huge exhalation. Beyond, he saw the area, shattered beyond description. Fires licked hungrily at the sides of tents, burning trails from one location to the next. As before, he was aware of the people on the floor. Still. Bent over in exaggerated poses, like statues similar to those found in Pompeii. In his mind, he saw many of them appear to be looking right at him, accusingly. Asking him why he had chosen to abandon them and turn away when he could have done something to stop it, but of course, he had no answer to this. A few people walked around in zombie-like states, searching for their loved ones as he approached. A few looked up as he got closer and on seeing him, slowly hung their heads or turned away from him with shoulders hunched, shaking their heads in dejection. Too tired to speak to him or challenge him on his inaction. It had an effect on him. If nothing else, and as clear as crystal, he walked into this chaos and the message he got from their faces was, "You see, Sam. In dreams, as in life, you can never please anyone!"

For once, he allowed himself to observe what was going on. He noticed the ruts in the muddy tracks. The stones overturned and discarded to either side as vehicles had passed, the puddles forming in the depressions here and there. He saw the blades and arrows too, some lying abandoned to either side of the path, others, broken and notched, either fixed in the sides of timber, hay bales, or floor, other times protruding from people. Men, women, children. There appeared to be no selection process in this strange place. No mercy for the young or infirm. Just some mad group who took it on themselves to maim and destroy, and for what?

Sam was lost in his thoughts and so did not notice at first that his footsteps were being matched in sound by another set, off to his right. Slightly softer, lighter, as if made by a smaller person.

He stopped and looked up and saw her there, peering down at him with dishevelled hair and dirty face and those large, purple-lined eyes. And his walls cracked.

"Pania?" he questioned, not sure if he had recalled her name correctly. "Is that you?" For a moment, he felt an uplifting of his morbid mood as he saw someone he at least recognised, who was not running from him, accusing him, or trying to kill him. "Are you OK?" She glanced fretfully over her shoulder, looking back over a bump in the hill to where he could not see, as if checking for reassurance to continue.

Looking back, she put her full gaze on his. "Why?" was all she could say. With choking voice and fingers clutching the sides of her torn smock, she stood looking down at him, her feet flinching as if ready to bolt should the situation change.

"WHY?" she challenged again. Louder this time. "Why did you go? Why did you leave me?" And it was if these few statements were enough to unlock the floodgates within her, and she started to cry the cry only young children can do. Cries from the deepest natural places of the inner self. Cries of not understanding, of abandonment, of hopeless despair where once there was just total trust in the carer.

And Sam read every sob with complete understanding. Saw all his fears come, unbidden and uninvited, from within the form of an innocent young girl. He recognised them for what they were and he stopped.

"Pania. I cannot explain what I do not know," he began. "I do not know what this is all about and I do not know what message I am meant to receive or give. But I am so very sorry that you are hurting and lost and alone. You are lost and alone, Pania... But I am here, and that's a start at least, isn't it?"

Pania looked through her tangled hair at him, sniffing strongly and shoulders heaving in sadness, eyes blinking back tears that refused to ease. Her fingers now tightly holding her smock across her chest, seeking some comfort in the fabric. Looking at him.

"Pania!" Another voice. "Pania. Come away. Now!" She turned her head in shock, looking back to someone. A male. Beyond the rise of grass she stood on. Slowly a head appeared. A head of a young man. A head of someone he recognised.

"You?" Sam exclaimed in shock. "What are you doing here? You were the one in the tent and the one on the path earlier. You were…" His flow stopped completely as more of the man appeared over the rise. For now, not only could Sam see the man's face, he could also see that the man was carrying something… or someone. A woman lay supine over his arms. Her head hung back wobbling slowly as he stepped into view, long silver hair trailing down towards the ground, arms limp at her side and legs dangling.

Eyes welling up with tears he did not want to show; fierce and proud the man stood. His muscles flexed as he shifted his weight from side to side to balance the dead weight in his arms. "You should leave!" he started. "You should leave now before these people turn on you! You should go, and leave us alone. This appears to be the way you now wish to live. You are not welcome here." The last said with deathly menace as his eyes bored into Sam's, seeking, to the end, to see some form of humanity, some form of feeling. But Sam was unable to feel anything at the moment. As if entering a room of pandemonium and being expected to know exactly what to do, Sam stared helplessly back at this man above him, who seemed to know him, yet, to Sam, was a complete stranger. Sam could only look up at the man in confusion and utter, "I do not know you, or her." Pointing at Pania. "I do not have anything to do with this, and besides, this is not real. So whatever sick dream I am walking in, you are just a part of it and you will soon disappear, just like all other dreams do."

The man looked down at him, then his eyes moved down

to the still form of the woman he held protectively in his arms. His demeanour showed clearly that this woman was greatly loved by him. He looked on her still form, studying its every contour and line, as if seeking a clue to some hope that life still existed in her.

"This is all because of you!" he started softly. "Turi would still be alive if you had acted and stopped this evil before it grew. But now, like all those around you," pointing to the still forms that lay crumbled around Sam's feet, "she must go to that place we cannot enter, though I wish I could alter things so I could go with her. You have taken away my breath. You have taken away my strength. You have killed her."

Sam was slowly, and, to him, surprisingly, getting angry with the man. *What right does he have putting all this down to me? Who does he think he is?*

"Whoever you are," he began, recklessly, "I owe you nothing! You can do nothing to me, and neither can this place. It all means nothing and soon, I will wake and you will all disappear and I will carry on with my existence, for what it's worth." Sam was getting increasingly angry, aware that he was perhaps using this man in front of him as a target for all the confusion his mind was battling to understand and come to terms with. But he didn't care. *Why should I?* he thought, *when everyone around me expects me to be someone else?*

As his anger mounted, he failed to see subtle changes in the man above him, and, had he been more aware, perhaps he would have known to keep quiet, but, it was too late now. The man had beckoned Pania to move behind him while Sam ranted, and turned fully to face him now. Legs widened to take the additional weight, arms locked beneath the still form of the woman he carried. His eyes searching and finding a table nearby, the pieces of crockery that had been sitting on it long since broken in pieces around it. He carefully and protectively lay the woman on the table, arranging her arms across her body, tidying pieces of torn smock and cleaning away bits of mud and dust on her face, the face of his mother. And all the while, his face became as thunder before a storm. Threatening, dark, disturbing. Very serious! Then, at first, very softly, but with increasing tempo, he started to speak.

"Sam. I do not know what demon possesses you at the moment. I do not know why only venom comes out of your mouth, but I sense that whatever it is, you believe it! Completely! All I do know, is that we were friends as children and friends for life, until today. Today, you took away the one who set me on my path, the one who cleaned me up when I fell, who comforted me when I was lost. Today, you took my mother away from me. From us! And today, Sam, you died to me also!" And with that, he released his arm from under the form of his mother, and started down the grassy mound towards Sam, slowly gathering pace as his loss translated into pure, love-fuelled anger.

Shouting out loudly as he hurtled now towards Sam, his last words to him were, "… and as for me and who I am. I am Ma-aka, head of the Watamka Clan. And you. You! "Sam-of-the-Shades", you are Enemy and you belong where we cannot enter." And with that, he pulled out a club, which had been concealed in his cloak, and swung it out at Sam with all his strength, hitting him squarely in the chest. Sam felt his ribs crack and, not for the first time, had a sensation that, *surely if this was another scene where I was falling, am I not going to just wake up back in bed?*

He did.

Sweat

He awoke sharply, his legs kicking out at some unseen character, and in so doing, fluffing his duvet up into a mess over his knees. *Bloody hell*, he thought, *that was not a nice dream!*

Sam was in a cold sweat, breathing heavily, but eventually he calmed himself down on recognising his familiar surroundings. His hands subconsciously moved down to his chest and, on feeling no bandages, moved on down to rearrange the duvet around him. He breathed in the silence, enjoying its peace for a well needed moment. As often happens with dreams, the detail of what had just transpired evaded his thoughts and he did not think to question why not only the characters, but the location and "feel" were the same for his recent dreams. Even the recurrent mist fields failed to make an impression on his mind.

His chest throbbed, but again, he put that down to his stomach slowly recovering from food poisoning the night before. *Seems so long ago*, he thought.

The events of the last night had faded somewhat but the broken mug and dark stains of the spilled coffee on the carpet stared accusingly at him. Outside, the day was grey and miserable. Yet again, the weather had stepped in and a cold front coming across from the ocean had ensured that rain was the major state of play. Sam got up, grimacing slightly at the pain in his stomach, and proceeded to the bathroom for his morning ritual of trying to wake up whilst not looking at himself in the mirror.

David's door was open, which in itself was unusual as normally his parents kept his room firmly shut as a testament to his absence. He walked down the corridor towards the door, hearing slight noises coming from within. His mother was inside, standing at the mantelpiece over the fire place, her hands moving slowly over the marble, tracing the contours of the edges. Her eyes studying the nuances of the changes in colour from one place to the next, deep in lost thought. She was humming something or other as if to a child, but softly, almost under her breath. No rhythm or order, just noises, random and lost. She moved towards the window, easing a picture frame on the wall slightly to be straighter than it already was and then stopped in front of his old bedside table, now empty of his stuff other than a lamp and a picture. The picture was of the two boys when they were much younger. It was one of the few pictures he was aware of where his mum was smiling. Smiling out of the picture and holding both boys, one on either side, protectively. She reached out and picked it up, studying the image for a while, before her finger snaked out and rested on the glass in front of David, rubbing the surface. Then she drew the picture to her chest, folding her arms over it and sank down onto his bed looking down at the pillow, clean and soft, and unused.

Sam softly retreated from the room, letting his mother deal with whatever demons were currently ripping through her mind but also allowing her that private time, to hopefully allow mourning and healing to occur. He knew that if he were to invade her space, especially in that sanctity she sat in, his dad would hear about it and retribution, unfair and unsought, would be swiftly dealt. For his part, Sam argued that it was no use sharing his hurt with his parents about his feeling of loss, as had been clearly demonstrated many times since that horrible day. When he tried to express how he was feeling, he was shut down immediately by his dad for disturbing and upsetting his mother, or his mother glazed over and lost herself in a world he felt partly guilty of creating.

His dad's approach to mourning was to deny himself any form of emotion as, in his world, David's death was solely his responsibility, mad though that was. His dad could no more have stopped things happening, than King Canute could have stopped the tide rising. But to him, he saw his wife, a shell of what was once a vibrant and lovely lady, go through her day lost and alone and unreachable. It made him feel, if anything, impotent. He was supposed to be the carer, the defender. What type of defender allowed their child to suffer needlessly and all the while, stood silently by seeing death take him? What type of carer allowed his wife to be destroyed? What type of father allowed his feeling to push his surviving son away such that, for all intents and purposes, he too was lost to him? And so, his own internal battles had only one form of release, and that was to strike out at anyone who even dared to question his position and lack of feeling. Sam got it fully. With both barrels!

Sam got his college bag from under the mess of clothes in his bedroom and trudged down the staircase and out the house, getting to the bus stop just in time. Moving to the back of the bus, he slumped down, the greyness of the new day reflecting his mood and he stared morosely out into the world. A world he felt detached from. A world with greyness and rain and death and sadness. A world full of aliens who neither saw him nor heard him. "Come on, Sam," he said to himself. "Where is this darkness coming from today? Snap out of it. No one else will give a rat's arse about things, so just man up and get through today." With that rebuke posted, Sam breathed in deeply, looked up and out into the greyness, and tried to think about other things.

The little girl, Pania, came to mind suddenly. *Where on earth did that image come from?* he thought. *Why a grubby little girl who seemed to look up to me? And that guy. Warrior, or something... What was that all about?* Sam allowed the train of thoughts to progress and, with a shock, he realised that indeed, the last few dreams he had had, that he could remember, all seemed to have the "Warrior" bloke and similar geography. *And that creature, Babu! That was it, Babu. I remember. What a weird one that was.*

Sam could not, at first, answer the unbidden question in his head, *Why is it that I am dreaming that I am important in that place?* Importance led on to people who were seen to be "important" in the media, and this led to thoughts of David, who was obviously more important in the household than him. And then it clicked. *Of course! The dreams are a reflectance of my feeling inadequate. No wonder I am seen as some hero there, for whatever reason.* That decided, he promptly forgot about the dreams and, as the bus was now pulling up in front of his college, got his bag together and followed the crowd of grey people clambering off the bus and walking in cold dreary steps towards the uninviting entrance to Greyshott Sixth Form College.

"Boring day. Boring lessons. Boring teacher. Boring life. Just a bore, really..." *Stop it!* he reprimanded himself, not for the first time, and proceeded into the college doors, disappearing into another world he wanted nothing to do with.

That afternoon, after college was finished, Sam decided to walk home rather than "hurry back to mommy" by catching the bus. The weather had cleared slightly, and darkness was a few hours away at least, so a walk, after the trials of geometry and trig, would be much appreciated. His route, as normal, wounds its way up a slight hill, passing through a fairly built-up housing area, a few trees lining the sidewalk and the odd dog lover taking "Fido" for its afternoon constitution and, more often than not, failing to pick up the crap it had left behind. For some reason, those little "parcels" really got his temper up. *Why can't they bloody pick up their mess rather than let someone else do it?* he thought.

At the top of the rise, the housing stock segued into the start of the town where the college got its name from.

Greyshott, or "Greyskull" as he was often tempted to call it, was a small, non-descript rural hamlet, with a high street, as was standard in just about every small town in Christendom it seemed, housing a number of small shops together with a larger department store. The village church (and adjoining pub – yet another necessary attachment that made England's rural life what it is known for... *boring!*) nestled into a small corner behind some huge oak trees, their branches, like witches' claws, hanging out over the street, ready to swat the unwary foreign visitor back to whatever country they had escaped from in the first place.

"By the power of Greyskull," he proclaimed, on arriving at the start of the official town. But today, as every day, whatever Master of the Universe was in residence, was certainly not parked out in this particular place. It remained small, and cold and, to him, unwelcoming. Unwelcoming that is, other than the one place he did feel welcomed. Timber's Tea House always seemed to have that special something about it. The warm yellow glow spilling out from within always seemed to be there, regardless of whether it was a bright sunny day, or the coldest, dampest day in history. The condensation on the windows seemed to give a sense of weariness to the place, but this didn't stop people entering its quaintness. Once inside, the smells that escaped from the kitchen were something to enjoy. It had fast become one of the town's "must-visit" destinations and it was often the case that the Sunday church community meandered down to Timber's for a well-earned "full English" after the morning service, rather than go to the pub next to the church, much to the landlord's annoyance.

Its proprietress, Alice, never seemed to get flustered and indeed, seemed to spend inordinate periods of time chatting to its customers and never seemed to spend any time in the kitchen, and yet, with just a skeleton staff, and a dog, she produced the nicest, tastiest, stomach pleasing English breakfasts he had ever had the fortune of tasting. Originally, Alice was also known for always having a half finished cigarette dangling from her mouth as she served, and whilst this unusual "attachment" took a while to get used to, her cooking skills quickly overcame the hardiest of opponents against smoking. Now, however, as the laws had changed, she was often parked outside having a quick puff, rather than risk having her establishment closed down by the authorities.

She was there as he approached, standing outside, leaning against the door jamb, one leg cocked up behind her, resting against the timber frame, cigarette dangling from her mouth and the smoke gently curling up into the air. She had already seen him and was looking at him through squinted eyes against the smoke, looking at him intently.

Sam, over the years, was aware that she seemed to do that a lot with him and, at times, this "attention" was unwelcoming and a bit creepy. She gave him the impression that she knew him at a deeper level than most others, although how she could and why she would want to, escaped him. But she seemed to be able to look inside him and communicate with him in ways that did not have words. Of course, in his boyish moments, he would joke that she obviously fancied him, as if to ignore those feelings that someone seemed to "care". Alice was in her mid-forties. Not married. No other relations that he was aware of. One dog, Bumper. She always seemed to live in her kitchen frock and her long silver hair was tied loosely with a green ribbon. She rarely wore any make-up but her eyes, a piercing and honest deep bronze, did not seem to need any enhancements, as they cut through and seemed to see what one was really about, rather than the façade so many people built around themselves. There was something different about her, Sam sensed. Something other-worldly. He could not put his finger on it, but he was sure she knew more about him, and potentially others, than she gave away, and this lent her a certain "strangeness". A strangeness, however, that Sam took comfort from.

"Good afternoon, Master Gilbert," she intoned. "And how is the intrepid traveller today?"

That is the other thing, he thought. *It was a little odd that she seemed to say things as if she knew where I had been, or what I had just experienced. She must be a witch underneath all that appearance*, he thought, jokingly.

"Fine, thanks," he replied. "Just off home." That in itself, he realised, was a stupid response. Of course he was on his way home. Where else would he be going to in this direction and at this time?

She smiled at him, sensing this internal argument going on. Pushing herself expertly off the door jamb, she threw the cigarette butt into the bin and, turning once more into the open door, said, "Well in that case, you must take something with you," and disappeared inside. Sam felt he could never actually argue with her. What she said always seemed to be logical and right. He followed her in, distracted and curious at the same time. Alice disappeared behind the counter and re-emerged with a small plate, on which sat a perfectly formed and utterly eatable cinnamon whirl. "For you, sir?" she questioned, holding the plate out towards him, her eyes sparkling in jest.

"I, I … er, I don't have any money with me," Sam exclaimed embarrassingly, looking both at this delicious pastry and Alice at the same time.

"That's perfectly OK, Sam, "she said. "It is going spare in any case. Bumper doesn't eat pastries, and you seemed to need a little pick-me-up, so, here," offering it once more to him, "take it and enjoy. Who knows when you may next have a chance to rest and eat?"

What a strange thing to say, Sam thought. *She must be pulling my leg*. But, looking at her now, her eyes had lost that sparkle and instead, were looking straight at him with understanding and, if possible, instruction. As if to say, "I see YOU, Sam-of the Shades. I see you and I am next to you."

Sam grabbed the presented pastry and turned quickly away from her and towards the door, throwing a brief, "Thank you," back into the depths of the tea house before exiting and walking as fast as possible away from his fears, which had sprung up and bit him when he was least expecting it, and from a place he considered to be safe.

Alice's form filled the door threshold shortly thereafter, gazing after Sam's rapidly disappearing body whilst, once again, clutching the necklace around her neck and teasing its shapes as she muttered something under her breath, almost imperceptible to those around her. Her eyes flashing a purple glint for a second before she turned back into the warmth of the store and the other customers.

"Sam," said Sam. "You're such a dweeb! Who would want to hang around you anyway?" His rapid departure from the tea house, and away from Alice, now settled down into anger at himself for running away for no reason, other than from his own fears and loathings. The cinnamon whirl, at first a delight to behold, now cold and lifeless in his hand. The stickiness assaulting his short-lived happy moment. He threw it away in disgust, unable to accept the gift. Unwilling to allow himself a respite or to accept that someone seemed to care.

He got to the house and walked rapidly up the pathway to the front door, sensing that for some unknown reason, anger was bubbling around inside him suddenly and that he did not like where it was going yet was almost powerless to resist its outcome. He went straight upstairs and went into the bathroom, slamming the door behind him, which rattled the implements on the wash hand basin in protest. The mirror caught his full attention. A red-faced youth looked angrily back at him, goading him almost. Without controlled thought, he heard, more than directed what happened next.

"Why did you have to die?" he said to David, represented as the image looking out at him from the emotionless mirror. "Why did you have to die and leave me here with THEM? We were mates. Best mates. Brothers. And now I get all the anger. I get all the hurt. But it's not my fault!" The last spat out in anger and frustration.

The mirror image looking back at him, and in his mind's eye, looking back at him with derision and pity, made his fingers unlock themselves from the edge of the wash hand basin and, almost as an automatic gesture, turn themselves against him.

SLAP
"Sam."
SLAP
"is."

SLAP
"such."
SLAP
"a."
SLAP
"baby."
SLAP
"and must."
SLAP
"grow UPPPPPP!"
SLAP

Steel eyes and determination mixed with self-loathing and anger combined to create a cold, calculating monster in front of him in the mirror as he watched. He was powerless to stop him and his red, ruddy cheeks throbbed in protest at the recent assault, but he was beyond caring right now. *I deserve it*, he thought. *I deserve everything coming to me.*

Sam breathed deeply, gasping for air in huge, half-sobbing lunges, but he had control of his "weaker self" and he did not allow himself to cry, to be human. Oh no, that was for other folk. Not Sam. Not Sam who let his own brother die.

He sank down slowly against the side of the bath. Feeling the bathroom mat under him, the reassuring warmth of the radiator pulsing against his body. He brought his legs back under him and gazed up at the ceiling light. For once, letting the fight ease out of him. Sensing, once more, that what had happened was a process he needed to work through. Necessary, but painful, nonetheless. He just sat still, feeling his chest move up and down with the exertion and his eyes never leaving the burning light from the ceiling...

The Gathering

For one brief moment, he was sure that the light had got noticeably brighter and bigger and he focussed his attention on looking at what had caused the fluctuation. Instead of a ceiling light, he was now gazing directly at a large and very real looking sun, dappled as its rays filtered through a mist bank which appeared to cover the whole visible area in front of him. Sam was also aware now of the smell. A heady sappy smell of wood surrounded him and invaded his senses. "What on earth..." he began. Looking around, his face almost immediately came into contact with incredibly large and very wet fronds of forest fern and scrabbling back in panic, his hands groped for purchase on beds of damp leaves and mud. *Where am I?* was all that escaped his befuddled mind. Panic, which had been slowly bubbling under the surface, erupted out into his consciousness and the only thought he had was to flee. Anywhere! Somewhere!

Pushing blindly through the lush foliage, Sam started to shout out for help, hoping that someone was within earshot who could come and rescue him from this bizarre place. Only deep and impenetrable silence returned his pleas and he soon gave up, concentrating instead on trying to gather his wits about him and work out where the hell he was!

That's weird! he thought, pushing yet another large fern

branch out from is path. *This mist is everywhere, and yet behind me, it is as clear as day.* This announcement opened a padlock in his mind and he smiled to himself in relief. *I know where I am. Dreaming. Again.* He allowed himself to relax now that he started to get his bearings, but this lasted only for a brief moment as he remembered the other elements of the last dream he had had regarding this place. Death and destruction, strange people and animals rushed through his mind's eye and he resolved to take things very carefully for the next few minutes so as not to stumble on any more strangeness.

Sam continued on his way, slowly forging a path through the branches and fern banks until he started to be aware of the sound of running water ahead of him. Slowly he drew nearer to the source and, after a final push through the last tangle of branches, he emerged next to a pond into which a small waterfall tumbled, the source of the noise. It took some time until he noticed that the pond and the surroundings, the rocks and trees around him were now all visible. The mist, prevalent up till now, had disappeared and he saw the whole area as one. It was majestic! Majestic, and also very very dangerous, he realised with a start, as he recognised exactly where he was. As if for confirmation, he looked past the pond and the waterfall and looked intently at the edge of the forest beyond. Sure enough, Sam saw a clear carved line off across the other side of the pond. A line carved through the mist beyond. A line made by someone. Him!

"This is THAT pond!" he exclaimed with fright. He quickly ducked down and scanned the area in case the creature he had first encountered was lying again in wait to scare the shingles off of him. Today, however, all was quiet and peace settled in the area like a warming blanket. Sam relaxed and breathed out his angst.

Still, Sam was resolved to move away from the setting, just in case, but also knew that if he followed the route he had originally made, he would eventually find the path. And the path, he remembered, introduced him to a man he had met later. A man he had no interest in meeting any time soon. *Warrior, or something like that*, he remembered.

Sam stood up from his hiding place and, gazing out for inspiration, decided to head in the opposite direction to the route he had first made. Cutting through the tree line, he now headed uphill to see what other as yet unencountered parts of this world awaited him.

His route took him up through the tree line and occasionally he intersected a river which, he assumed, fed the pond below him. As he travelled further, he started to think about the mist that always seemed to be present and yet, never closed up behind him. *Why is it*, he thought, *that this mist is always here and yet refuses to act as mist should act?* Curious, he decided to cut in a different direction and sure enough, the mist path now forged the same route as he was travelling. Almost as if it were following him. "This is a bit creepy," he commented to no one in particular. He soon came out into a clearing where the trees were less dense and the grasses more prevalent. The sunshine filtered through the mist banks and formed many strange patterns as it was refracted by the mist above. Sam was noticing this when his eyes fell on a change of texture beyond. Another path cut across his field of vision. As before, this dust path was well worn and tracks were evident criss-crossing the surface. *A route well travelled*, he thought. He moved towards it until he was centrally positioned on the path and stopped. Hands on hips, he looked in both directions deciding which direction to go but there were few clues to go by. He turned left. Despite his encounters so far in this dream space, he still recognised that it was best to try to find some form of civilisation and a path must eventually lead to someone or somewhere.

Sam continued walking along the dirt track, senses heightened and alert for the merest sound of things beyond. Today, however, peace seemed to reign in this particular neck of the land. The track undulated over fields and through more fern banks dotted here and there. *Things are so silent here. In fact, since coming here, I don't think I have heard or seen a single bird!* This made him look up from his wanderings to scan the skies beyond, but there was nothing. Only a long, meandering track to who knew where, fields, and nothing else. Not that he could see anyway. Slowly the track started to go downhill and, after a bend in the road, Sam stopped. Quickly. Beyond, and just visible through the shifting folds of the mist banks, he thought he could see a largish body of water. The sunlight, he saw, seemed to glint off the water and send welcoming shafts of light up towards him. There were no waves evident so he assumed it was perhaps a lake. Closer towards him was the source of his focus, causing him to stop in the first place. A small hamlet of huts and shanty houses nestled along the bank of the lake, smoke wisping lazily upwards from a few fires within. The houses were all made of timber spars, he noticed. Felt and peat roofs were standard here and occasionally, he noticed a few of the houses were built of stouter rock. The path he was on wound its way down an incline and through the centre of this scattering of huts, pausing at a larger square within the community. A square which had a number of people sitting together, or standing to one side or another chatting to each other. He felt a sense of peace pervaded the area. Here there were no rebels, no death or destruction. Just a community going about its business. Sam carefully moved down towards the village, ready to bolt if the need arose.

The first person to spot him was a young boy of about 10 who bounced out of a hollow in the rocks just off the path in front of him, intent on a game he was playing. Sam gasped involuntarily, which in turn attracted the attention of the youth who stopped his "game" immediately and just stared at Sam with wide eyes, mouth open in shock and hands still grasping the bent stick he had been playing with earlier. The boy's face was streaked with sweat and dirt but his eyes shone through this self-made mask with clear intensity as he appraised Sam from his vantage point. He was clothed in rags and wore a short pair of trousers. His shirt still possessed a few buttons and a pocket, out of which, Sam noticed, a small snout poked, sniffing the air carefully to appraise this new potential danger. The boy's eyes roamed over Sam like a watch dog, and, curiously then, also around the space that Sam occupied. He appeared to be puzzled at something, scratching his head in some confusion as if weighing up what he saw with what he thought he should have seen.

"Where is your Padme?" the boy asked with the innocence of youth, rubbing a grubby arm across the face of his nose and sniffing at the same time... "Is he hiding in your cloak, mister?"

Sam had no idea who or what a Padme was and was at a loss how to respond. Instead, Sam asked the youth, "Where exactly am I and what village is that over there?" pointing down into the hamlet below, shrouded slightly in the mist.

The boy appeared unfazed that his question had been ignored and, squinting down towards the village, replied, "That's Baradin. I live there. Do you want to come and visit?" Sam was not expecting that invitation and at first was at a loss what to say, but he was rescued from further speech when the boy jumped off the rocks and without waiting for an answer, bounced off down the path, beckoning Sam to come and at the same time, looking back over his shoulder to make sure Sam was following.

Sam followed! With some trepidation he argued that it was better to enter a village with someone the inhabitants recognised than alone and as a potential stranger.

The boy waited for Sam to catch up, but his boyish curiosity meant that the waiting was more like bouncing back to Sam and then circling him like a predator looking at prey he did not yet realise was going to be his dinner. All the while, the boy was looking Sam up and down, and more than once, his gaze roamed over Sam's clothing looking for something, and scrunching up his face in confusion when what he was expecting to find wasn't where it should be. Occasionally, as if to seek some reassurance, his gaze slipped off of Sam and roamed the surrounding fields and the skies above, looking in vain for something that Sam had not the slightest idea was supposed to be there. "Where do you hide him then?" he said. "Is he invisible?"

Now Sam was the one to scrunch up his face as he wondered what on earth this boy was asking him. "Sorry, ummmmm." Sam thought it was wiser to change the subject so he asked the youth what his name was and waited for an answer.

"Pit!" said Pit, jumping between puddles on the path, almost distracted by new found things to occupy his world. "I am Pit. Who are you?"

"Sam," said Sam. *Better,* he thought, *to keep where I am from and what I have experienced to myself for the time being. I can't afford for Pit to go screaming off down to his folks in fear before I have had a chance to introduce myself.*

By now, they had reached the outskirts of the small village. Typical noises of someone cutting wood, or hitting things to make implements, or babies crying and mothers cooing to them filtered through the normal sounds attributed to any rural village he was familiar with. He was able to see more of the activities now that he was close enough for the mist to play little part in cloaking things. The village looked beautiful. Peaceful. Something settled softly into his comfort zone locked deep within him. "Baradin. I like this place," he declared to himself.

Ahead of him, some people were sitting around a log fire which was burning grandly in the centre of a clearing. Odd groups of people sat or stood together, discussing or chatting about life, he assumed. Elsewhere either mothers or fathers were jostling with various children who were either running around them, or dancing between them with laughter. Further beyond the clearing, he noticed the water's edge of the lake which now appeared to have a deep sky blue hue rather than the normal greeny-blue of cold water lakes he was used to. In fact, the more he looked, the more he was sure that the lake itself seemed to have some sort of glow emanating from within. *Something to enquire about at a later time*, he reminded himself. The houses all had that well worn appearance as if they had been built a great while ago. Lichen and moss grew from out of timber spars and roof shingles and the buildings spoke of strength and community. Of welcome and of security. Sam felt at peace in this place.

Sam's sixth sense managed to awake a strange curiosity in him as he slowly became aware that everywhere he looked, animals of all shapes and sizes were either running with the people here, or were being carried, or slept comfortably next to the folk. In fact, he was sure he had not seen this anywhere else, ever!

Pit by now had disappeared, looking for his parents, Sam assumed, and it was not long before a small crowd formed off to one side of the village square, jostling around an excited small form, Pit. Pit was gesticulating, and his body tried to reinforce what his fingers were describing. Many times he looked up and pointed towards Sam and slowly, the crowd started to move towards him as he hovered at the edge of the village fire. As the villagers got nearer, some started to raise their hands to their faces, others pointed at Sam, turned to their neighbours and spoke in hushed tones, seeking an answer to their questions. Sam sensed that he was being inspected and dissected like an insect, and instinctively took a few steps backward in defence. By now their voices had reached babbling proportions as they all started to appear to discuss and argue amongst themselves, almost ignoring Sam in their debates. Almost!

Snippets of sentences came floating over to him. "How can you say that, Marika? It surely cannot be..."

"It is He. I swear it!"

"...Tread warily..."

All this and more jostled for attention as the crowd gazed at Sam in shock, disbelief or horror, it seemed. Pit, whose initial excitement was of being the one to introduce Sam to his village, now was fighting with conflicting emotions as he sensed and heard things that scared him. His parents didn't normally act this way when other people came to their village.

One of the older men, after looking at a few of the elders for agreement, stepped out from the crowd and the people fell silent. "I am Niko, leader of the Baradin," he proclaimed. "We welcome you here in peace, stranger, although we have some who feel it is their right to make pronouncements before you can introduce yourself!" This said, pointedly as he looked at some of the crowd, who shrunk back for a moment. "Our son," he continued, resting his hand on Pit's head, who beamed from underneath it, "often brings curious things back to the village and it would appear that today he has outdone himself for indeed, what we see before us is both curious and a portent. We must ask who you are and what brings you to our humble village."

Sam heard all this but the way the man asked him these questions, seemed odd. *Why am I a portent?* he asked himself. *Why the strange greeting?*

"My name is Sam," he began. "My name is Sam and to tell you the truth…" He got no further as voices took over for a second as a clamour from within the knot of people gathered around Pit and Niko.

"You see? I told you…"

"It cannot be I tell you. He was lost to us…"

"Has he returned to save us?…"

"Where is his Padme?"

"That word again," Sam said, amongst the other feelings shooting through his mind.

"Still!" ordered Niko. "Be quiet, all of you. All will be made clear when Sam is allowed to speak…" Looking directly at Sam, he then asked, "I have lived many years and seen things I wish never to see or experience again. I have heard of things both impossible and amazing to consider. Of news from the distant corners of our empire. Of death and destruction as the Ethereals were decimated by the hand and direction of 'The Nameless One'. I have heard, as well, of one who came and stood and brought to an end, the power of him. I have heard and seen all this, and yet today, of all days, one stands before us who is recognised and seen. But this cannot be. For he was lost to us and lost forever. You cannot be! And you travel without your Padme. All this is too much to understand, so we must ask, are you indeed, 'Sam of the Shades' and have you come to stop that which must be stopped? Or are you a spirit?"

Sam sprang back in shock. *There is that name again!* he

thought. *Where have I heard "Sam of the Shades" before?* And then he remembered a previous encounter where someone had called him that also, shortly before knocking him out with a massive club!

Sam, who, a few moments before, thought that Baradin was perhaps the most beautiful and peaceful village he had ever visited, was now thinking that these people were affected by some mental blight and he resolved, yet again, to leave this place as soon as possible.

He looked first at Pit, who was now looking at him from under deep and dirty eyebrows, then at Niko as he stood fierce and determined in front of his people, then at the people themselves. Many of them, despite Niko's instruction to be quiet, were talking angrily behind him, pulling shirts and dresses for attention and casting furtive glances over to Sam to check he was still really there.

Sam straightened up and looked at Niko, saying, "I am afraid I have absolutely no idea what you are on about! I do not know what a Padme is and I am definitely not from any Shades. Furthermore, it does not matter. You will all soon disappear anyway!" Sam said this last as an attempt to make light of what he thought was quickly becoming a bit of a farce. It had the wrong effect!

The people suddenly all stopped talking and looked at him in fear. Some started to move back into the safety of the village and others made glances back to their huts and houses for possible weapons that might be necessary. They started to speak amongst themselves asking whether this person was actually here to destroy them. As panic increased within the throng, a movement started towards the back of the crowd and slowly but surely, a "bubble" moved its way forward, people parting as it moved inexorably onward, despite all the frightened and, at times, angry comment coming from these people. An old lady emerged from within the protection of the people, and they, on recognising her, started to quieten down until there was absolute silence.

Everyone looked at this wizened old lady, who appeared to have no fear of this person who had come unannounced into their village, and waited on what she had to say. Her face was lined with age and bronzed through many years of being out in the sunlight. Her hair, like many of the women, was worn loose and it cascaded down over her shoulders, tied at the ends with small bones and twigs. She wore a fur pelt and she held a long, thin pipe in her hands, still smoking from the substance within it. Her eyes, however, were crystal clear and full of deep and hard fought intelligence.

"My name is Ngaire," she began, holding the attention of everyone with her poise and inner strength. "I have walked these roads for countless years and speak to both man and beast. I have seen events which made the earth shake and I have witnessed The One who came from the Shades to destroy 'The Nameless One'. While it was still dark this morning, I sensed a calling and I have travelled in haste to get here. I have headed and I have now seen… But not for the first time! For you," looking now directly at Sam, "you have been here recently. And death and destruction is at your door. If you were indeed He of whom we speak, you would have stopped the Bjarke from ransacking and killing the peoples of Watamka and you would have fulfilled your destiny. But this person I see before me is cloaked and I cannot fathom his aura. You cannot be him, for HE was bright and brave and true. But you, you have had placed on you a burden that is unfair and unjust, and we must therefore wait for The One to arrive again and pray that his coming would not be delayed."

As if a potential prophecy had been awaited and then not been fulfilled, the people listened to Ngaire and began to relax as they understood that Sam was perhaps not who they thought he was, and that he was just a stranger. An innocent stranger that they should make welcome after all.

But Ngaire was not finished.

"And yet," she continued, "you come here from without and the mists listen to you." At this she pointed back behind Sam, where his passing could still be seen through the mist bank moving off into the distance. "You walk and the mists part, yet you walk without companion." Summoning her breath in slow resolution she continued, "How is this possible? Where is your Padme, Sam?"

The people again stopped their discussions as this point re-emerged, having been lost in the last few minutes of surprise and all turned to look at him with renewed fear.

"I have no idea what a Padme is," began Sam, "and I have no idea why I would need one. I have seen my fair share of crap, thank you very much and I do not need anything else to 'accompany' me in this world." Sam was getting a little annoyed with these people who appeared to be imposing their ideas onto him. *Just like at home, again*, he thought.

"Without a Padme," Ngaire began, "you cannot exist! And yet here you stand. Breathing, aware, of apparent sound mind..." Sam did not like that comment. "I must consult with the Ethereals," she said, causing yet more gasps from within the throng. "I must ask how this is possible. How you can be here unaccompanied. This is indeed a mystery, Sam, and I can see that you are truly unaware of what this means about you and your existence here."

Sam was rapidly getting tired of this discussion and wanted nothing more than to move on and wait to wake up. "Well maybe you would be so kind as to enlighten me what a Padme is, then," he said. "And then perhaps I can tell you where mine is!"

Ngaire, unaffected, continued. "A Padme melds with

you on your birthing. When a Turangai, a person, in your words, first enters the world, they form a bond with a creature. This bond starts a life-long relationship and it is the creature's role to protect them and assist them in their walk. To train them in their belief and to fend off all who would try to attack them, for they are chosen by the Ethereals for us when we are still being formed. No one can exist without their Padme and no one has, till now!"

Sam, smiled inwardly as he recognised that once again, dream worlds played funny tricks on one's mind and that this was therefore yet another proof that pretty soon (but not soon enough) he would wake up and carry on with his life.

Sam knew what he needed to do and, without much thought to the consequences, said, "I am afraid I have to upset you there then. You say everyone must have this 'Padme' thing and without it they cannot exist? Well I have no Padme and yet I exist here before you. I am breathing. I have sight. I have movement. What I don't have, is a Padme and neither do I have any desire to have one, whatever it is. So," he said with mounting determination, "if I have no Padme, and to have one is essential, then either that fact is untrue, or I am not real, or you are not real! Which means that this place is not real and in fact," pushing now to the edge of the fire which had been glowing merrily up till now, "I bet that if I pick up a red hot coal from that fire…" gesturing to the coals within, "nothing would happen to me."

And before anyone could move to stop him, Sam bent forward and reached out to the closest glowing coal he could find, and picked it up.

A coalescing electric blue energy field shot out from his fingertips as he came into contact with the burning coal. The field blasted out in a circumference around him, knocking those closest to him away in a blur of scattering bodies and objects and his hands flared into white hot orbs, glowing and pulsing with an intensity that shocked him to his core.

"What the f…" he began, looking at his glowing hands for a brief second, before he passed out with the pain.

The radiator

Almost instantly, the shock of what had just happened jolted his body into an automatic reflex movement, jumping away from the perceived danger and moving his hands protectively against his chest. His hand burned and he could feel the pain screaming out from it as a warning. He opened his eyes.

The bathroom was just as it should be. The light still glowed above his head. The mat still lay, now dishevelled, under him. The radiator, however, did not look the same. The towels that normally rested over the unit were now scattered over the floor and he sensed his hand throb acutely in awareness of this situation. "You stupid, stupid idiot!" he began. "No wonder your hand is in agony. Fancy falling asleep here of all places, and leaving your hand to rest on top of this very hot and very efficient radiator! No wonder you are in agony." Sam realised that the source of his pain was NOT as a result of him picking up the red hot coal from the village, but instead was as a result of his utter stupidity of leaving his hand on a hot radiator and then falling asleep with it there, waiting for nature to take its course and burn the stuffing out of his extended digits!

"Muppet!" he scolded himself.

He clambered up to his feet and went to the wash hand

basin, holding his hands under the cool cold water from the tap, thinking about what had just transpired. *You know, Sam,* he thought, *when you are dreaming, you think that place is real, but it isn't, and this is shown to you time and time again, when you wake up and a logical explanation always stares you in the face. Well, my son, today you have outdone yourself and I jolly well hope your hand stays throbbing for a long time to hopefully teach you not to be so bloody stupid! Why would you want to live in a fantasy world like that anyway? One is forced to walk about with a weird creature hanging round your neck all the time. What happens if that creature dies of natural causes? Do you die then? Nice!*

Sam sensed that his anger was bubbling up again and he forced himself to calm down. Turning the tap off, he moved his hands to the towel draped over the towel rail to dry them. The throbbing was still there and a distant pain still reminded him of what a dangerous position he had put himself in. He admonished himself roughly, looking down for any scars as a result of the close burning he had just encountered. Luckily there did not appear to be any lasting damage to his hand and he flexed his fingers to test the joints. *Strange!* Sam thought. *My hand seems to be glowing!* And indeed, his right hand not only throbbed with the blood pressure coursing through it, it seemed to also emanate a subtle glow that he was sure was not there before he dropped off for a quick power nap. He studied his hand carefully, but all seemed to be in order now and he turned his attention to other things.

Exiting the bathroom, he noticed that all was quiet around him. *Mum and dad are not yet at home,* he thought to himself. *Dad is out at work and who knows where, or when he is due to arrive? Mother? Well I have absolutely no idea where she is or what time she is back to start to prepare dinner. Surely they must have come on by to see how I was. They would not have left me there all day without either waking me up, or moving my hand off the radiator, would they?* The last, he sensed, not said with much conviction. Sam trudged down the staircase, looking under the gap in the staircase out into the living room ascertaining if indeed anyone was home. There was no one. "Nothing prepared," he started. "No dinner laid out. Nothing started in the cooking department. No table laid. Same ol', same ol'."

But today, something was different. Today, Sam looked up across the living room furniture and spied "it". A recent addition to the mantelpiece looked back at him. A picture of David smiling out at the room. Hands on hips and bending forward. His torso bare and dripping with water. A big smile shining out from the prison of the frame, mocking him! Sam remembered the day that picture was taken. David had just competed in a swim-a-thon and, naturally, as he always seemed to do, David had won. Mum had taken the picture of her lovely son and was "oh so proud, wasn't she?" Of course, other than a few other knick knacks, the mantelpiece was bare of adornment. No picture of Sam shared this "hallowed" surface with their beloved older and better son… In fact, looking round now, he noticed that there were absolutely no pictures of him, anywhere! Without intending to, Sam was overcome by a deep and uninvited jealousy.

Without thought he launched himself at the mantelpiece, grabbing the picture frame and staring at the image within.

"It's not my fault you died!" He glared, accusingly at the image smiling back at him. "It's not my fault you were and remain their favourite. What did you do that I couldn't? Why were you planned when I was obviously just an accident?" All his pent up anger and frustration and hurt coalesced into these pointed questions and he was aware of tears pressing out from his eyelids. Tears he really did not want to acknowledge or, for that matter, did not want to be expressed, given his anger. But there was no one around that evening. No one to admonish him or tell him to be quiet. No one to tell him that he was not to blame.

"Why couldn't I have died, rather than you?" he said, more quietly, as if, for a moment, communicating with the one he had always felt closest to, now cruelly ripped away. "Then everyone would be happy!" he continued. "Their Wunderkind would be alive and their bloody abortion would be dead. Dead! Dead! Dead! I HATE YOU!"

He hurled the picture from its place on the mantelpiece, smashing it and the pieces around it onto the floor and the coffee table. The frame exploded in a cascade of glass and wood against the table and fell in pieces onto the floor.

He often looked back at this moment with a particular jolt, as he distinctly remembered the feeling that his spirit had somehow slipped out of his body and was looking down at his form carrying out the action, and yet he was powerless to stop it. His mind was saying *stop, Sam. Stop!* But his emotions were yelling *do it, do it, DO IT!*

His emotions won. With anger exploding from his demeanour, he turned to find something else, anything, to vent his frustration on. The coffee table was nearest. Picking up one of its legs, he tossed the object off to one direction, its frame spinning around as if lost in space, the glass inlay failing to keep a grip to the wooden frame and flying off to shatter against the wall. The reclining chair, "dad's beloved sanctuary from life!" followed suit. Sam's hefty kick lifted the frame backwards to fall against the glass doored book case, which spewed its contents and shards of glass onto the carpet. Books, tables, chairs, fire surround. All succumbed to Sam's uncontrollable anger and frustration.

In short order, he brought havoc to the room, hurling

abuse at the top of his lungs to whoever cared to listen. To his friends for never seeing him. To his parents who lost him years ago. To David, who should have been there to help him, but wasn't.

"Why did you die?" he sobbed, slipping down the wall to lay on the carpet. "Why did you die, and leave me here all alone?"

His slump down the wall caused the last object on the mantelpiece to finally lose its grip and the heavy candelabra, toppled end over end, striking his forehead a hefty blow and sending him reeling off into the stars.

Ōmakere, the place of abandonment

"Oh my head!" he moaned softly, reaching up to rub his forehead and searching in the dark for the candelabra. ".... The dark? Why is it dark all of a sudden?" Sam slowly opened his eyes and looked around, scanning the room as he started to notice that things were not quite as they should have been. He noticed at first that rather than a well worn and comfortable living room (albeit it should have been in utter chaos), now, a dusty, hard worn dirt floor greeted him, and a field of many fires burned all around him, fires that were moving slightly, agitatedly. These small fires focussed themselves into torches held by many hands illuminating a crowd of deeply lined and worried looking people.

From calamity to this! he thought. *I must be going mad. But this feels so weirdly real!*

One of the torches detached from the rest and came towards him. "Master. Master! You must rouse yourself and help us. Our time is at hand and we look to you, as before, to save us. Get up and get ready. Our enemy is at the door!"

Sam looked up at the man who had addressed him. His look was returned by cloudy eyes in a well worn, tempered face. The man was rugged in complexion with long white hair loosely tied behind his back and the grizzled look of someone who had been around for a long time. The man was looking intently and somehow reverently at Sam and his arm was outstretched towards him, reaching and beckoning Sam to take it and regain some semblance of order in this chaotic world he had landed in. Sam just stared at the outstretched hand as if in a trance, noticing the veins, aged and destroyed in places, the dirty nails, broken through poor diet and the thin arms disappearing into the folds of a torn tunic. For a brief moment, the man's arm fascinated him.

Gathering his wits, Sam tried to stand up but the floor quickly started to ebb and flow beneath him as a dizzy spell ruptured this moment.The man quickly and expertly reached out to gather Sam up and as Sam straightened, he was amazed that he was almost a full head taller than the gathering around him. The people, on seeing him stand, all reached out their hands towards him in supplication. Yearning, looking, hoping. Men, women, children. Some looking around in abject fear, others holding hands protectively. Children gripped the apron tails of their mothers, gazing either shyly or with uncertainty at this strange person in their midst. A few were crying with either tiredness or sadness.

Sam saw all this in a blink of an eye, but it would take some time before he was able to assimilate what on earth was going on. This was definitely not the living room but for the time being he allowed the flow to carry him onward.

"Come," said the man again, trying to manoeuvre Sam forward and away from where he had been lying. "Come, Sam. You must carry on your work. We need to protect the young."

All Sam was aware of was that his mind was quite detached from the goings on around him, almost as if he was moving through treacle. *Almost*, he thought, *as if I am walking through a dream!*

"What work?" said Sam. "What am I supposed to be doing and why am I here in this strange, other worldly place?"

Sam felt it first through his feet rather than through hearing. A slight vibration coming through the floor, sending tremors pulsing up his legs and throbbing through his nervous system... A distant, low toned buzzing sat at the periphery of his senses. He noticed a few people towards the extremities of the group around him, start to turn around looking for the source of this "irritation". Slowly, the buzzing increased in volume and intensity and took on more definition. A strange cackling noise wafted between the drone that gathered outside and now Sam was aware that this noise seemed to be coming from all around, and it oozed something. Something sinister.

Louder and louder it became, growing in depth and anger, seeming to descend into the surroundings like a storm of bees until the buzzing in his head had become so intense that he had to reach up to cover his ears, crouching down to escape this audible attack.

And suddenly, the noise stopped!

The crowd froze in place. Eyes now locked on Sam; in expectation of what, he had no idea.

Beyond the crowd, gashes started to appear in the darkness allowing light to filter through, illuminating the once darkened place, which, Sam now realised, was a very large and very big tent. These gashes, Sam realised, were the flaps of the tent being lifted up, taking on a circular route as each one lifted away until the "circle" was complete. A large group of men were slowly revealed surrounding the tent, their demeanour leaving little to the imagination and their sharp evil looking blades, held with intent in their hands, made sure that their message to the crowd was very clear indeed. These men were not here for a chat! Slowly they entered the tent, first in one place, then through more and more openings until at least 20 men, well built and of varying heights, surrounded the people, who in turn, surrounded Sam.

Then they stopped. Silent. Waiting.

Their hair was adorned with bits of feather and bone and some were wearing head dresses from some wild fantasy, but none were as terrifying as the individual standing in Sam's direct line of vision.

The largest and most evil of them all stood proud of the group of men, his eyes staring intently around the quivering community as if seeking out his first victim of the day. This "leader" was covered in tattoos of intense patterns and Sam saw a fretwork of cuts and gashes over his torso and legs as if his position as head of this clan of dogs had been a hard fought occurrence. Long, dirty hair hung loosely down his back in contrast with the others. Black, soulless eyes stared out over the crowd until they settled… on Sam. A scar running from forehead to chin flexed as he chewed on a piece of grass sticking out of his mouth. He was grinning wickedly from ear to ear and then spat the green squib out!

"What is this?" he asked, expecting the crowd to be running in fear but instead they were standing still, their backs turned outward and away from his men, looking, he noticed, at a solitary figure, Sam. "Are you their chief?" he queried. "If so, you will be the last to die. Do you not know who I am?"

"We know who you are, Half tooth," said the old man who had first addressed Sam. "But do you know who stands before you?" gesturing towards Sam, who, for all the world, wished he could just disappear. "If you did," he continued calmly, "perhaps it is you who would be afraid!"

As for Sam, he found himself frozen to the spot, not believing this nightmare he had stumbled into. His fear clutching at his throat prevented any sound escaping from him.

The leader's eyes grew enormously large in his face as he battled to understand what had just been said, and that from a frail, old, bent runt of a man who, even now, was insulting not only his name, handed down from his forebears, but also his position and rank as leader in front of all his men.

He pushed out his already extended barrel chest and cried out, his voice carrying over those around him. "I am Napayshni, the Strong, leader of the clan of P'rui of the people of Bjarke. Run, little chickens, run, and try to escape that which lies in wait here to cut you down. Let's have a little sport with you while you still have breath." And with that, he drew his crescent shaped sword from within his tunics and held it aloft.

No one moved! Not the men, not the women. Even the children stood still, all looking inward. All looking at a small, insignificant young whelp who, for some reason, held their eyes, and their faith.

Napayshni had never been insulted or made to feel worthless like this, and his anger bubbled out of his mouth as he spat and dribbled out his next command. "So. You stand as men? You die as dogs!" And he slid his blade up to the hilt into the back of a man nearest to him, who, without a sound, looking pleadingly at Sam, slipped slowly off the dripping blade and sank to the floor. Napayshni became enraged that his planned "sport" for the day was not going well. "What?" he cried. "Is this some sort of holy man that you feel no pain? No fear? Men… Kill or be killed and tomorrow we will pray over their bones."

Needing no further excuse, his men sprang to the attack,

their war cries renting the air in sick jubilation. The outer row of people fell quickly. There was no order to things. No decision to spare those nearest. All started to be hacked down where they stood, the knot of people remaining, slowly becoming tighter and tighter, still focussed on Sam. No cries of fear tore through the space, though an electric air of emotion was tangible to all. To Sam, this was like a silent slasher movie gone wrong and he, the sole spectator.

"Stop it! Stop it! Stoppppppppp itttttttt," he screamed, as, one after the other, the people around him fell where they stood. All keeping their eyes on Sam. All hoping. All believing. All dying. He didn't know these people and yet, for some reason, they "saw" him. Believed in him. "For what?" he questioned. "What possible purpose could this all serve?"

All around him was utter carnage. The living now being pushed forward by the dying falling into them. The dying seeing their life force drain away and their outstretched bodies, concentrically arranged like petals of a flower, with Sam, the centre. He willed himself to awake from this nightmare but it evaded him and slowly but surely he witnessed what no person should. Wanton death and destruction was occurring all around him, and, for some inexplicable reason, he was supposed to be partly responsible for this mess!

The torch bearers lost their grip on the torches, which fizzled out on the sand, merging flame and smoke with the blood of the innocents.

Only one man remained. The tribe of blood-thirsty men seemed to pause for a moment and in the eerie silence, Sam was dealt the worst blow.

The old, wizened, half-blind man who had first greeted Sam spoke. "I am Arana, the Rock, of the beloved clan of the she bear, Ia-pea. I refused to listen to the others, Sam. They said, at Tangaroa, that you stood there and did nothing. That you allowed their deaths to occur, but I did not believe it, until now. You stand here before me, and refuse to help. How long, Sam? How long will you exist without being? Do you despise us that much?"

And then he gasped as the end of a dirty blade blasted out from his chest, pushed with huge force by Napayshni. A soft, almost whispering breath escaped Arana's mouth and he too, like his kin, slid off the blade and slumped to the floor.

There was no noise to cover the screaming silence Sam now experienced. He was lost in emotion never before felt. His eyes scorched with the smell of death and the smoke curling up as insence mocked him. Before him stood this so-called "leader", but all Sam saw was a coward. And his anger focussed itself solely on him.

"What?" Napayshni spat. "You still do nothing? Are you, nothing? You will die just like these around you and then we will feast on your flesh, just like we did to those at Tangaroa, and P'nui and Rudhjanda." And with that, a low cackle escaped his lips as he raised his sword high, ready to chop down yet another life.

In the periphery of Sam's vision, a blur of lightning seemed to shoot through the open tent flap behind Napayshni, lancing through a few unfortunate men, who for the briefest of moments, were not aware of the gaping holes in their chests, revealing darkened cavities, ribs and lungs. Shock took them shortly thereafter and they fell hard, landing amongst those they had just killed. The "lightning" headed straight for Napayshni, who sensed this new disturbance before he registered it on his face. His body froze as he recognised that this energy was indeed, even now, at his door, and looking to break it down with force.

His chest burst outward with a loud "clap" spewing sinew, bone fragments and bloody gore onto Sam, who now saw that, rather than a bolt of energy, this "thing" was indeed something animalistic. All fur and teeth and claws. Eyes of steel and teeth as sharp as knives. Napayshni was dead long before his body felt the weight of gravity and succumbed to it, falling before Sam in bloody finality.

Sam stepped back instinctively from this new "enemy", finally shocked into movement after what seemed an eternity of terror. He was aware of a questioning thought escaping his mind. "Babu? Is that you?" But before he got any further, his backward steps took his feet into contact with an inert body and he started to fall. As at the bridge, seemingly eons before, he felt himself looking at this scene almost in a detached sort of way. He sensed his body falling backwards, his arms rising up into the air. He was also aware of this animal now turning its attention to the remaining attackers, who slowly started to flee and scatter, but it was too late for them. Way too late, and the furry blur disappeared into the throng, ripping, slashing, repaying the damage caused.

Sam hit his head hard on the dusty ground, one last thought firmly etched on his mind.

I did nothing!

Rain on the windows

Sam became aware once more of his surroundings. His eyes remained tightly shut as he fully expected that "thing" to turn on him at any second and end his miserable existence, as it had seemed to do for the other invaders. His hair on the back of his neck crackled in expectation and he felt his skin go from clammy and hot to shivering and cold in rapid succession. There was no noise, however, from outside the comfort envelope he had created for himself through the closing of his eyes, so he carefully opened them to see what dangers waited in store for him, out there.

Silence! Emptiness. No animal, no people on the floor writhing in agony, no dead enemies around him. No! Instead of this, he saw another form of destruction all around him with the coffee table, mats, glasses, chairs and destroyed picture frame dotted around like so much broken kindling. He was home. Lying on the living room floor, blood trickling down and into his eyes, stinging them into an involuntary blinking movement. It looked for all the world as if a giant had trampled through the room and left chaos in its wake.

"Oh my goodness," he moaned. "What on earth has just happened to me?" His mind flitted back to what he had just experienced, convinced that the enemy would, at any moment, come bolting out from behind the curtains and stab him through the chest. But the only thing that launched to stab him was the sunlight of the late afternoon sun filtering through the living room window, which, miraculously, had remained intact. His mind went back over the things he could vaguely remember from his dream a few seconds ago. At the time so vivid, now, apparently so unreal. Arana, the old man, who appeared to have thought that Sam was some sort of hero, Napayshni, that weird Indian, now most definitely dead, but where? He thought of these and the people who had died all around him, worshipping him, and he felt embarrassed. *Why on earth would I dream such a load of old codswallop?* he thought.

Looking around the decimated room he recalled why it had become like this. "David!" he began, "You were the reason for all this." He saw now that his fit of frustration and anger a few minutes ago almost definitely was the cause for his blacking out, and the toppled candelabra besides him with a few dried blood stains evident on the stand proved that this was no freak occurrence. "And it bloody hurt!" he said to himself, rubbing his temple gingerly. He linked the sight that greeted him here with the articles in the dream, and peace settled onto his shoulders lightly and gently, as if massaging them for him. The loss of his brother and the resultant grief and frustration that he could have, or should have, done something to save him from that cruel death, even though he knew in his heart of hearts that he really would not have been able to do anything to save David, merged with the dream world he had just been "swimming" in as if hand-in-glove. Merging. Becoming one. And the only message that stayed true when everything else faded into silence was a simple fact weaving through both situations.

"I did nothing!"

He stood up slowly, the blood pounding in his temples as the pain ebbed and flowed through his head like a whirling Banshee. A groan escaped his lips and he moved falteringly out of the living room, pushing the weird dream away from his mind, putting it down to the emotional turmoil he had just unlocked by stumbling unexpectedly on the photo frame. If he was being brutally honest, he thought afterwards, it was more to do with not being able to cope with yet more guilt at doing nothing, and this time, for a world that didn't even exist, rather than as a result of it being a dream in the real sense. Sam walked slowly out of the destroyed room, not bothering to clean up the mess he had made. He knew, and yet was seemingly unfazed about it, that he would have a lot more to deal with when his parents returned back from wherever they were, if they were at all bothered.

At around 6pm, Sam heard the car doors close below from the driveway and the sound of feet heading towards the front door, crunching through the "river-washed" pebbles dad had bought from the DIY shop last year. He heard the keys rattle the front door and the voices of his mum and dad as they entered the hallway, talking about one thing or another. They seemed to be quite animated, for once, which in itself was a miracle. But that would soon stop… It did. The voices were cut off as if by a knife as Sam imagined them entering the living room and seeing the damage that had been caused. He heard the sharp intake of breath by his mum as she saw her "sanctuary" destroyed by some evil hand. A loud, "What the…?" from his dad.

Sam waited!

Downstairs, Paul, Sam's dad, was at once at a loss as to what on earth had transpired here, as when he had left earlier this morning, the room certainly hadn't looked like this; and also was acutely aware, at some subliminal level, that "whoever, or whatever" had caused this mayhem may yet still be in the house. He quickly scanned the room for any sign of a break-in. The windows were intact, the door appeared to be secure and there did not appear to be any forced sign of entry. In his "male-ness" he did not look at the actual damage around him. This task fell, naturally, to Margot, Sam's mum. It was she who looked with increasing horror at the smashed table, the broken chair. Saw, with some increasing confusion, the candelabra sitting amongst the jumbled articles which should have been on the mantelpiece. Noticing, without registering at first, that the stand had blood dashed on it. Her eyes swept now over the rest of the floor as some sixth sense started to warn her that something prized was missing from where it should be in her mind's eye. *What is it?* her panicked mind was shouting. *David!* It came at her like a thunderbolt. *Where is the picture of David?* Now real fear overtook her addled brain and she scanned in terror, trying to find him amongst the wreckage, any similarity to her thoughts that he had been "trapped" once before, and was now no longer with them as a result, too true and painful to accept.

There, under the plant pot. A glint of brass and shards of glass. She leaped forward, crying out as it dawned on her. The picture frame was bent and distorted and the glass cover was long since shattered. His picture, at one time smiling and innocent and "her's", now torn and crumpled and wet from being trapped under the plant and the now cracked pot.

"Noooooooo," she keened. "Nooooooooooooo." Margot was lost in utter despair and blackness as she was forced to face this physical manifestation of her loss and emptiness at losing her son. She was not aware of anything else at that moment other than a total emptiness and blackness upon blackness as David was, once again, lost to her under the unmoving fronds of the plant. She sunk slowly to the floor cradling the crumpled image of David to her chest, deep, cutting sobs rattling through her body.

Paul looked down at his wife of 25 years. From where he stood, the sunlight filtering through the window landed on Margot's face, illuminating her deep sorrow in high definition. He looked down at her and, as always, yet never expressed, felt utterly helpless to help her and bring her out from her deep pond of depression she kept swimming in. Hers was the externalisation of a deep motherly despair at the loss of their son, so cruelly taken. Hers was the need that had to be fed, to be noticed by their friends and consoled. *But what about my needs?* he felt. *Where is my helper to resolve my loss? My despair? My guilt! I am the one that keeps quiet so she doesn't hurt any more. I am the one who has to sort things out...*

Paul didn't like the way his thoughts were going and he turned away in anger. Anger at himself, and anger at whoever had caused this chaos and opened up the wounds again within Margot, that he thought should be healing. Paul looked out through the living room window, lost for a moment in his own battle and then, like a switch had been turned on by some unwanted and evil hand, he saw his thoughts coalesce into a strange, yet to him now logical, answer to all this destruction, and he was powerless to stop it avalanching off his mountain of pent up frustration.

Sam! Where the bloody hell is Sam? he thought. Now, as if a strong ray of light had cut through his mist bank, which had prevented him from seeing an obvious answer, he saw a clear cause to all this chaos, and, unfortunately for Sam, also saw a scapegoat to unleash all his anger and guilt at not being strong enough to reach his wife.

"Sam!" he shouted, startling Margot out of her darkness.

"Sam. Are you here?" Looking up through the ceiling into where Sam, had he been here, should now be sitting. There was a slight movement upstairs, but sufficient for Paul to launch himself off towards the living room door and out through the hallway to the foot off the stairs. "Sam!" he shouted with his face already turning red, "get yourself down here and get down, NOW!"

Margot's head appeared at the living room door entrance, peering down towards Paul with confusion etched in the lines of her tear-streaked face. "Paul, dear," she began, but he was in no mood to listen to anyone right now.

"Darling," he said with some tightness, "let me handle this, OK?" And he turned back to look up the stairs to see the slow shuffling form of his son appear at the head of the stairs and gaze down at him in evident guilty mode.

Sam came down the stairs, all the while acutely aware of the arrows of wrath being shot at him from his father. He didn't care! *What could he do to me which I haven't already had done to myself previously?* he thought.

Paul could sense that his anger was just washing off the shoulders of his son, which just added to his anger and guilt. *Not only am I incapable of reaching Margot, even my son despises me!* This from a mind long since prepared for a battle against one, he thought, who would give up easily and allow his anger to be placed on his young shoulders but instead, saw his wrath and batted it away like an annoying fly.

For the first time in many years, Paul was aware of a part of him leaving his body and looking down at the unfolding events as if dissecting it for future analysis. He saw his arm snake out towards Sam before he had reached the foot of the stairs, grabbing at his shirt and yanking him off the last two treads and hauling him back down the hallway and into the living room, Sam's feet furiously backpedalling trying to maintain his balance. Margot was in the way and Paul pushed past her, Sam bouncing into the door frame and Margot at the same time. "Paul, please!" she cried.

"Margot. Be quiet. It's about time he answered for his bloody ineptitude." And Paul propelled Sam into the middle of the room amongst his "creation" and glared at him with uncontrollable malice.

"What on earth did you think you were doing?" Paul began, not even allowing Sam to defend himself, or even to check whether he indeed was to blame for this in the first place. "Your mum and I are not even allowed to go out for a minute without you coming in here and, for some cracked and spiteful reason, feel you have the right to trash our things as if they belong to you. Do you think it is bloody funny to smash our things? Do you think it is funny to leave the house in a state of total turmoil, lacking even the smallest modicum of respect to be careful and have a bit of care for this house?" Paul had to stop for breath, casting a quick glance at Margot, his eyes demanding her silence. "Look at what you have done to mum," he continued. "It's not enough that she has to suffer every day. No. So far as you seem to be concerned, every attempt she makes to try to move on, you feel the need to disrupt and destroy her peace." Paul pointed down to the destroyed pot plant and the remains of the picture frame. "So, can you please explain why you felt the need, this time, to break that which wasn't yours and why you insist on stuffing up mum's life?"

Sam felt the venom pour into him from this person who was supposed to be his dad. He was still reeling from his own throbbing from the fallen candelabra. He didn't need yet more pain.

"Paul," began his mother, "I am sure Sam didn't…"

"I am not finished!" Paul said with definite finality. "You know what?" he continued, glaring at his unemotional son, "it would be a whole bloody lot better if you weren't here.

Why don't you just go away and leave us in bloody peace for once in your little sheltered life?"

Paul knew before the words had stopped echoing off the walls and fallen objects around them that he had gone too far. He wished that the few seconds just past had never existed. Hell, he wished a lot of things had never existed. What a bloody better life they might have been enjoying… But it was too late.

"Paul!" exclaimed his wife in shock. "How can you say that? Is it not enough I have lost one son without you tearing my world up with yet more cantankerous bullish and, basically, crappy attacks at Sam who probably didn't intend to do any of this in any case?" She turned to Sam, for once, her eyes clear and her emotion focussing purity to their last remaining son. Sam was already turning to walk out. Too much pain and demands on his young shoulders. He mumbled something saying he was going upstairs. He did not want any of them to see him in the state he was in. He just wanted to escape this place. Escape the pain, escape everything to feel alive and happy again. For him, at this moment, his only sanctuary was a room upstairs and a door firmly and forever closed.

Through the walls and carpeted floor of his room, he was aware that his parents were still refusing to climb down from their positions. "… But dear," he heard his mother say, "you know he didn't mean this! Why on earth did you lay into him like that?"

"Marg," replied his dad, somewhat gruffly, " it's about time he bloody woke up and got his head out of his cloud, sorted his life out and started to help out around the house once in a while. All he does is…"

"Paul, stop! Please," she cried out.

And then…

Sam heard his dad's footsteps move towards the front door, his voice rising in untameable anger. "Why can't you of all people stop for once and see that I too bloody miss him!" he screamed. "It was not my fucking fault he died!" And with that, the door opened and then slammed shut, rocking the frame and Sam's world into a shattered place he felt would never be fixed.

Sam couldn't cope with any more emotion. For him, he had reached the tipping point and he just stared mutely around his room, not able to assimilate what had just happened. In the silence, he saw his room, for once, for what it was. His poster clinging to the wall was more than ready to be replaced. His bed was all scruffed up from the morning and his desk held an assortment of things that were just that, things. This was his world, he realised. A world of stuff, a world of misery. He even needed "crutches", looking down at his Xbox, to get him to escape.

It was this which caused a "click" to occur in his head, and he saw a simple, yet until that moment, never brought to the surface, idea. An idea which was now so obvious, he felt, if it were possible, he should have acted this out eons ago. He glanced up at his window, thinking. The rain was again beating against the pane, which he thought was quite apt. The rain was cleaning the window, and he was about to clean his own space as well.

Without another thought, he rummaged in the back of his cupboard, found his old backpack and proceeded to throw in a few clothes, a torch and passport. His wallet and phone went into the back pocket of his trousers and his jacket was taken off the hook of his bedroom door and placed over his shoulders. Without a backward look, he opened the window, threw his backpack down onto the garage roof below, clambered out himself, jumped off the garage into the rear garden, and walked off into the darkness.

Breaking out onto the street, he was, for a while, undecided which way to go. The street lights seemed brighter heading into town, so he headed off towards it, pulling his hood up over his head to keep the rain off. A wonderful, uplifting sense of elation permeated through him, and he allowed a smile to grow as he walked away from the turmoil and pain, and hopefully, at long last, was going to be allowed to walk into a better place with no demands and where the sun shone just that bit brighter.

The glow of the town slowly drew him closer. The houses slowly got larger and more grand as he entered the outskirts of the main shopping precinct. At this hour the streets were deserted. One lone fox in the distance spied him, had a last sniff at something on the floor, then disappeared under a fence and away. Otherwise, things were blissfully quiet. Sam was happy just to walk. There was no agenda, no place to be, no time by which he was expected anywhere. He just walked, looked at the passing architectural landscape and enjoyed, for once, the serenity that wrapped around him, healing and soothing his raw emotions.

At this hour, everything was shut. Even the welcoming ambience of Timber's was absent, with only the slow glow of the letters above the shop front filtering onto the light patterns thrown onto the street by the other units. Unconsciously, he glanced up at the windows above Timber's but the curtains were drawn and darkness was the only shadow in those windows. *Why did I think about Alice then?* Sam mused. *She "got" me at least*, he thought.

Opposite the main entrance doors, a bus shelter stood. For years just a drop-in to wait for a bus, but tonight, a refuge from the weather. Sam walked towards it and sat down on the bus bench and started to plan his next move. The lights of the shelter were faulty, it appeared, as the fluorescent tubes behind the advertising banners were flickering, almost hypnotic. He certainly was not interested in the wonderful "smells of the forest pines" advert on the wall, but his gaze unfocused itself and became mesmerised with the flickering, warming light behind. The flickering of the lights and the gentle wash of the rain against the sides were enough. Before he knew it, his head fell slowly onto the side panel of the bus shelter and he fell into a peaceful sleep.

Had he been more aware, he would have sensed the movement behind him. The soft padding of someone coming up behind him. Someone who did not want him to know they were there. But sleep had taken a firm hold of him so he didn't see Alice slowly come up behind him, then slip beyond the side panels until she stood in front of him. Silent. Studying him. Then, as if prompted, she glanced down, undid the necklace around her neck, and placed it carefully around Sam's, then left.

Ngaire, "Silver Fern"

The flickering lights continued to pulse into Sam's awareness and the sounds of noisy trucks passing close by assaulted his peace bubble. He tried to turn in his half sleep to shield his eyes and ears from this invasion of his senses. His movement was enough to tip him off his perch and to land in one unceremonious heap on the sodden grass! "Grass?" He was so shocked that he immediately woke up. "But there is no grass here," he continued, confusion racing through his mind as he tried to assimilate this impossibility with the fact that he was indeed, lying in a large and very wet patch of nature's finest grass. "Where on earth……?" he began, looking all around him in fright.

The cause of the flickering he had sensed earlier now became apparent. Lightning was flashing through the air off in the distance, followed by loud thunder claps and deep reverberating rumbling. *Trucks!* he registered. But this lightning storm was like nothing he had ever seen before and it certainly wasn't lighting up any familiar townscape he knew, and definitely no bus shelter either!

At that moment, the heavens decided to open up and rain lashed down on him with unmerciful fury. Sam had no choice. He stood up quickly, looking in vain for his backpack, and for the safety of the shelter, but both objects eluded him. Still in some shock, he proceeded to move off and down what he felt was a slight fall in the topography. The lightning, he now noticed, illuminating a very real and very dense mist bank all around him, robbing him of any sensory powers in terms of sight. He instinctively stretched out his hands to try to feel his way out of wherever he had "landed" and was surprised when even his arms disappeared into the impenetrable bank of mist. Slowly he stumbled down range, and felt, more than saw, that his feet had got him onto a rutted path, which he slowly followed. Small rocks and muddy water covered his feet from time to time as he lost his footing in various places. Still, when he did volunteer to look back, he was shocked to see that, rather than the emotionless banks of mist enveloping him, a swathe of "mist-less-ness" preceded behind him, familiar in an "other-worldly" way.

Sam continued stumbling slowly down the semi-illuminated path, trying to filter the sound of the lightning whilst trying to engage his befuddled mind to tell him where on earth he had "landed". Darkness was his only companion and all sense of three-dimensionality had long since been scattered to the four corners. There were no sounds to assist him, and the lightning continued to flash strong patterns into his retinas, after each bolt.

"There!" he cried. Just off to one side and noticed through his peripheral vision, a small light, constant and fairly fixed in place glowed out through the mist. Sam headed in its general direction with haste, careful to watch around him for debris and puddles. Gradually the light took on more definition and started to illuminate the structure to which it was attached. A small, wooden house set on rickety posts emerged from the mist. The light, (he could see now that it was a flame from a wick, protected by some miracle from the wind and weather, by a dirty, broken glass surround) gave out a mysterious, silent glow seeming to make the whole structure float above and through the mist. Surrounding the timber building, a dangerous looking porch reached out, cracked and missing boards dotting the surface. He stopped at the last tree, looking intently through the lashing rain for any sign of life from within, but nothing moved.

The light continued to beckon warmly and, with some trepidation, Sam crept closer, slowly climbing the steps up to the porch and moved towards the door. Breathing deeply and casting one last glance around and behind him, he turned to the door and knocked.

The dull thuds of his knocking seemed to him to be incredibly loud and he realised that the lightning had stopped just as he knocked. Beyond, he heard the unmistakeable sound of a chair being scraped back and footsteps heading towards him, slowly, loudly, scarily. Sam was just about to turn and flee when the door opened.

An old, incredibly bent and stooped lady peered out at him from within. A fur pelt over her shoulders was tangled with a cascade of silver hair, and twigs and bones appeared to be tied randomly in amongst the braids. She was also smoking! A long, thin pipe was gripped between her lips and she was puffing its rich mixture, smoke trailing up and around her, and Sam. Beyond, Sam was aware of a healthy warm glow coming from a fire which was crackling madly, a rocking chair, a large mirror and odd ornaments were arranged around this source of heat. It felt homely and Sam, without questioning, sensed he was safe here.

He looked down at the lady and was somewhat surprised to see her lined face going through a series of weird expressions as if trying to fathom whether this bedraggled creature in front of her was friend, foe, or a nightmare from her deepest recesses.

"Sam?" she said, tentatively, "is that you?" If Sam had been fazed leading up to this, given his confusion as to where he was, hearing a strange old lady address him as if she knew him was certainly enough to stop him in his tracks. *How on earth does this woman know me?* he thought, and he started to step back away from her and think that perhaps the mist, rain and gloom beyond were now more inviting and "safe" than this woman's house of welcome.

The woman unbent herself slightly and said, "Sam, I am Ngaire, the healer. But you used to call me Silver Fern." And with that, she opened the door fully, turned and shuffled back towards her rocking chair, somehow knowing that Sam would follow.

Sam followed. Entering the house and closing the noise of the weather behind him, he moved into the heart of the house and went to the bench that the lady (Ngaire?) was pointing to, and sat down.

Ngaire busied herself pouring some water into a pot before setting it on a stand over the fire. She grunted slightly as she then sat back into the rocking chair, which sprang back under her weight. She reached to her side and pulled out an old box from which she got a match and proceeded to relight her pipe. A contented smile etched her face as she started to feel the draw of the smoke in her lungs and the wisps permeate her space. She remained silent, not looking at Sam, which he found intimidating, until the pot was whistling. She pushed herself slowly off the chair and offered Sam an outstretched cup. "Tea?" she offered.

"Yes please," was the only thing he could utter at that moment.

As she got the tea leaves and hot water working together, she looked sidelong at Sam, almost in a quizzical, questioning way, trying to gather her thoughts and her confusions at seeing him outside her door and on a night like this. Eventually, she offered him the steaming cup, turned around and sat herself back in her rocking chair. Plucking up her courage, she began.

"Sam, what is going on?" *What a strange question*, he thought. To this he had no answer, wondering why she had chosen that particular question to start a conversation and he looked blankly back at her. She was looking intently at him. Focussed. Aware. Perceptive and, somehow, compelling. Compelling something in him. The glowing, homely embers radiating warmth into his bones and the "safe" surroundings almost won him over. Almost! He caught himself and laughed inwardly. *Another dream*, he thought. *Oh well, best just get on with it and wait to wake up again.*

"Silver Fern," he began, "I am afraid I don't know who you are, or this place, but…" (And this with some smugness), "as this is a dream it doesn't really matter, as soon I will wake up and none of this will exist!"

Ngaire responded with a strangely mellow voice. "I cannot speak for your dreams, Sam, but I do know that I am very real, as is this place." She paused as he raised his cup to his lips. "As is that steaming cup of tea you are about to drink." (That said with a downward look away from him, a small smile hidden beneath her hair which had fallen across her face.) Sam was already in mid sip when this was uttered and it was hot. Too hot! The brew burnt both his lips and his mouth as it flowed down his throat and he coughed and spluttered loudly as a result, quickly putting the steaming cup down on the table and trying to regain some dignity as Ngaire-Silver Fern looked on, chuckling.

Sam regained some feeling to his mouth and looked up at the old lady. "Somehow you know my name, but that is OK in this weird place. I am wet and cold, but that can be explained away. This is just a reflection of the inner me, so let's just have some fun with this and see where it goes. Besides, I cannot die in a dream, so it should all be fine ultimately. A bit of a mind trip but otherwise, fine! So tell me, Silver Fern, why do you know me and why do you give a damn?"

Ngaire did not respond at first. Instead, she reached down and found her pipe and busied herself with filling it once more with her rich smelling tobacco before the heady smell of oak wafted towards him as the pipe was lit and she drew her first puff. Then she settled back in her rocking chair, and began.

"Sam. The story you are about to hear is heavy in its telling. The questions, many. The answers, I suspect, very few. But the reasons for this will only be discovered when we start to travel down the route we are about to embark on. But, you have been brought here this night, once more. And I cannot stand in the way of the Ethereals and question their motives or reasons. All I can be is a servant to them." She paused. "And a friend to you, Sam." With that, Ngaire started to explain to him all that she had witnessed and seen relating to Sam, and Sam's world started to reform again after so very long.

Ngaire, the healer, started to heal him.

"Our works are governed by beings from a higher plain," she began. "Their rulers are the Ethereals and few there are here who have seen them, let alone been able to communicate with them. Their presence is felt more than seen, if that makes sense?" Sam found himself nodding. Ngaire continued. "The Ethereals created all that you see and can feel in this world. They have sometimes been known to walk in the world to touch that which is in need of them, but I have never seen this. (This said, it seemed to Sam, with some sadness, and possibly regret?) They are the ones to whom we owe our lives, our joys and our faith. For my part, they have blessed me with the art of 'seeing' and being a vessel for them, such that healing can occur to those who are ready and willing to receive. Sometimes, though, I feel this can be more of a weight around me than a gift!" Ngaire said the last with wise humour.

"For millennia, order and peace reigned in our world and there was a time..." Ngaire choked back a sob. "Oh Sam, once, the trees were vibrant and proud. Tall and powerful, they stood. And the fields and the plants sang with energy. Now," Ngaire hung her head down, "now darkness weaves through their spirit, through their essence like a deadly disease, and I fear that that which once was proud and alive is lost for ever." Ngaire drew another large puff of her pipe, trying to regain some strength before continuing. "The Ethereals are supposed to be above petty squabbles and discord. It is their role to maintain and nurture this world. To them, this was and is their gift to themselves and a joy to share with us, their people. But discord and evil lay at their door, and slowly, inexorably its presence was felt both in the kingdom of the Ethereals and here in our home. The Nephilim were created by the Ethereals to act as servants for them and to carry out their orders here on our world. The leader of the Nephilim is Lord Elim." She said his name as if it was poison! "Lord Elim revolted against the rulers of the Ethereals and a huge battle ensued. The very fabric of the heavens was rent and terror more than has ever been experienced reigned here whilst the battles continued. There appeared to be no let up in the battles, which lasted eons, as both friend and foe knew each other's strengths and weaknesses intimately, and whilst the Ethereals were more powerful, the Nephilim had larger numbers. An end to the 'Age of the Snake' seemed a mere dream.

"And then, in a master stroke that none could foresee, the Ethereals did something that, to this day and forever more, will stay in our heads and lives as a sign that the force for good will emerge victorious."

The embers of the fire had dimmed and the tea, long since cooled, lay untouched besides them. Ngaire got up and placed more logs on the fire and offered Sam another tea, but he was captivated with the story and quickly shook his head. Ngaire turned back after inspecting the flames beginning to lick around the new kindling and sat back down.

"Where was I?" she asked of herself. "Oh yes, I was about to tell you where you come into the picture!" Sam, entranced though he was with the story, was awake enough to hear that suddenly he was now front and centre stage to this very strange but very captivating story and his hairs on his forearms began to lift. Ngaire continued. "The Ethereals knew that to battle with the Nephilim using just those elements around them that they had created, was not working, so they assembled the mighty Anahim together, the ultimate leaders amongst the Ethereals, to discuss a plan so extraordinary, so brazen, that were it to be ushered anywhere else, all hope of an end to the battles, and victory over the Nephilim would have been an impossibility. The Anahim saw that the only way to beat Lord Elim and his troops was to go *outside* of the ordinary!" She looked now directly at Sam. He should have seen it coming, but he was, to this point, blissfully unaware of the clues she had been dropping into the explanation.

"We mortals know not how, but somehow, the Anahim knew of another place in another time and another dimension. They knew that only there could they find an answer to defeat Lord Elim. How else could they hope to end the battles unless something from another dimension could be used as a weapon, which neither the Nephilim nor the Ethereals could have any power or influence over. There was great debate and discussion about this. On the one hand they saw this as a possible end to the Nephilim, and on the other, saw a potential calamity should that weapon decide to turn itself on them. After much soul searching and wise thought they decided to send one out to find that which no man, nor being could be in this world." She paused. "Sam. They sent one to come and get you!"

Sam did not know where to look. He could not, would not accept the words he was hearing. It just could not be. This crazy woman was mistaken and lost in her myths and the amazing story he had been listening to with joy and amazement a few short moments before, now started to sound discordant and cruel. Sam felt his anger build. He knew it for what it was and even here in his dreams, he sensed when those around should rather go whilst they still had a chance. Ngaire, or whatever the hell she was, was about to fall into his line of fire, and he had both barrels loaded, waiting.

But Ngaire was not finished and before Sam had an opportunity to scream, she dropped one small time bomb which blew his anger to smithereens as so much mist. "Sam," she started, "the Anahim who went across space and time to seek that weapon, went knowing that all the powers they had in this world, and all the strength they imparted, would have to be lost when entering your world. That on starting down this journey, they could never return. They could never enjoy immortality. They were to be stripped of all just to find The One to rescue all. The fairest and bravest of the Anahim hesitated not one second but, taking up her cloak, she stepped forward and entered the chaos and was lost to us forever. Her name is sung and her sacrifice held in all folklore and myth. She was the one who left to find that which needed to be found. Her name, Sam, was Aronui and she will never come back to her world again! Instead, she now lives, we presume, in your world, and who knows what she experiences as a mortal where once she was a leader of all you behold, and more."

A small piece of an, as yet, incomplete jigsaw, fell from the skies and landed slap bang into the middle of Sam's rapidly confusing world as he recognised something that his soul *knew* was true. "Alice!" He choked in incredulity. "Alice? The lady from the chippy who serves full English breakfasts to me when I go there! That Alice? You are saying that she is, was, a mighty leader here, like an angel, and had powers no mortal would ever have, and instead of all that, she chose to give it all up and come and find me?" Sam had to stand up! He paced rapidly up and down like a caged lion, unable to assimilate his emotions and thoughts. "You are having a BLOODY laugh, woman!" he shouted. This was sooo way off beam that his mind simply could not hold the import of what had just been stated. But Ngaire sat there. Still. Arms folded, her pipe still clenched between her aged lips, smoke still oozing out from the end. Waiting. Silent. Unbroken.

"Sam," she continued. "Search your heart and hear. You did come back to this world and you did have powers none here had ever witnessed and you battled the Nephilim who fled in terror from your anger and your wrath, and for a time, we started to believe that perhaps an end to the evil would happen in our lifetime." Ngaire once more dropped her head and continued in a whisper. "But then one day you went to confront the Lord Elim, perchance to end the One who had caused all this misery, and you never came back; until this week, with no memory, no recollection of anything that transpired before, and no knowledge of the powers you had, and should still have. And now, as you have witnessed yourself, it appears all that Aronui, your Alice, set out to achieve, has been cruelly destroyed by the destroyer himself!"

Ngaire hung her head at last and stared down into her dishevelled shawl, which lay ruffled on her lap, and she toyed with a loose thread or two as dejection hovered around her like the darkest of mists. "I know not what happened in your encounter, Sam," she breathed, "but you went in with victory on your arm and faith as a shield and now you are a ghost, a shadow. I cannot bear it!"

Ngaire's shoulders started to shake as a deep well of sorrow bubbled over at last from within and tears of grief coursed down her weathered cheeks.

From somewhere deep within Sam's psyche he heard, *Typical! Here I am in a dream world and even here I am useless!* He did not like what he was hearing so he turned to Ngaire, moved over to her bent body and held her tight, trying to protect her from the demons who toyed with her frailty without remorse. He could feel anger build again, but this time in defence of someone rather than as a mechanism to protect himself.

The candles flickered dimly in the late night gloom and small sounds of crackling from the last vestiges of the fire interrupted this moment. Sam was about to get up when they heard a knock at the door. Ngaire shook herself into the now as she heard the knocking and turned her face up to Sam's, reaching her thin, bony hand out from within her shawl to touch his face. "That should be Ma-aka," she said. Standing up heavily and walking to the door, she half turned, saying to Sam, "Be careful, Sam. He carries great conflict in him at this time." Ngaire got to the darkened door and opened it.

Sam couldn't see the person beyond in the darkness of the night, but he was aware that firstly, it was very late, and who therefore would be out at this time of night? Secondly, he had a feeling that whoever was out there had come for him and that set his fears racing. He heard Ngaire speak to the form which stood just outside. "Be ready, Ma-aka.

He is here as I had hoped and prayed. He is here and much confusion hangs over him, like this mist hangs over us." She said this as she peered out into the shifting gloom. The mists that lay over their world, never seeming to move or alter. Then she stood to one side to allow the person to enter.

There, in the dim lamp light of the porch, wet from head to toe, stood the same young man he had encountered right at the *start* of this strangest of dreams, the same man who had run up to him in greeting on that path. *And was he not the same man who was there when I woke in the tent?* Sam mused. *And, now that I come to think of it, the same man who had also come at me with a club and tried to kill me a few short days later!* Parts of his dream came back to him, flittering in and out of his consciousness.

"You?!" Sam said in shock. That, for now was all he could manage. There were too many emotions cascading through his field of vision right now for him to be able to tackle yet another potential encounter. Sam recalled that this man, Ma-aka, had lost his mother the last time he saw him. He also remembered the girl.

"Pania?" he mumbled. "Was she OK? Was everything alright with her? Where did those thoughts come from?" All rushed through his mind in a second. Both Sam and Ma-aka looked across the chasm of the room at each other; Sam with incomprehension and surprise, Ma-aka, with fear, loathing and anger all mixed in together.

For once, Sam was able to study the man who stood in front of him. He stood slightly taller than Sam but appeared to be around the same age. Like many others in this world, his eyes also glinted a purple hue and it was as if this colour became more intense as emotions flared. For now, his eyes were of deepest purple and were almost iridescent. His tunic was soaked through and his hair hung down over his face in wet, long streaks. Almost as an after-thought, a large eagle perched on his shoulder and looked sideways down to the floor, perhaps looking for a mouse or other tasty rodent. Ma-aka seemed not to notice this proud bird of prey perching on his shoulders, but with a quiet "snick" aimed at the bird, it lifted off his shoulders and flew back off out into the darkness, its cawing echoing through the air as it slowly faded into stillness... Ma-aka stood facing Sam squarely and Sam noticed that he was very much more muscular than he had remembered. The tattoos, which appeared to be normal "adornment" here, were carved up his forearms and resembled sinuous dragons and other objects too confusing to decipher. Sam remembered that Ma-aka had proclaimed that he was a head of some clan before he had decided to try to kill him. His mind was at a loss with many jumbled emotions and he could sense that this man opposite him was similarly tackling a myriad of feelings within his stiff pose.

Ngaire broke the stand-off. "Ma-aka," she called softly. "We all need to re-learn that which we felt we knew intimately. We need to allow The One to be who he is and to listen, even though the hearing of it may pain us beyond despair. For this is our task. This is our duty. And, Ma-aka, this is our friend!" And with that, she turned to Sam and looked at him with deep feeling and love and moved to him, to embrace him where he stood.

Sam was taken somewhat aback with this show of emotion, and clumsily lifted his arm to embrace Ngaire, all the while trying to see what Ma-aka would do. Ma-aka stayed silent and immovable, blocking the front door, his eyes looking first at Sam, then at Ngaire's bent back, his face a blank canvas that Sam could not read.

"We first met when we were both quite young." Ma-aka mumbled down to the floor. "I was helping my father catch some fish for our tribe in the mighty Manganui-a-te-Ao. She it is who has fed our people for generations, and our clan, like many others, settled on its banks many generations ago. My father was head of the Watamka clan. Wise, strong and brave he was. His name was Ari, the Eagle, and he led our people with strength of character and wisdom." Sam heard the regret in Ma-aka's voice and wondered what had become of his father, Ari.

"As the eldest son, it was my duty to take over as clan leader once my father died, but I did not expect his leaving to be so early in my life, nor so unexpected. Where we often fished, the water is funnelled through a series of large boulders and the fish fly upstream and launch themselves into the air there to escape the cascades. We were thigh deep in the cold waters, balancing on the wet rocks under the strong flow trying to catch the flying fish when suddenly a bright and dazzling light appeared hovering over the waters right before our eyes. The other men, believing a spirit was awakened by our fishing, ran in terror and disappeared into the forests, but my father and I held our ground. My father was not afraid and he looked at me and said just one thing. 'My son, the Eagle, protects us and the waters feed us. Be not afraid for this is less than they.' Then the dazzling light exploded and I lost all senses. My ears and my sight failed to function for a while and I fell back into the waters, tumbling end over end as the current threw me downstream. I feared then for my life, as I have never done since. The boulders could have taken my life and I would have been powerless to resist the current, but I was spared and it was not long before my feet touched the river bed and I managed to stand. Of my father, there was no sign and I scanned all around for him."

Ma-aka was lost in the telling and he did not stop the tears which pressed out from within him. "My father had disappeared, and finding him was paramount in my mind. I looked all around for him until my eyes alighted once more on the boulders where we had been fishing and there I saw the strangest sight. Where once there was no one, now lay one unconscious on the boulders in amongst the raging current. Dressed in the strangest apparel. That person was you, Sam. My amazement at seeing someone appear from out of thin air was only matched by my determination to hunt for my father. I needed to find him, yet I needed to save you at the same time." Ma-aka looked up at Sam, "I chose you over my father, Sam. I came to save you and, to this day I do not know why I did this. I beat myself every day for failing my father, but he was gone, and you were found. What choice did I have?" Ma-aka continued. "They found my father later that day! His body was torn and his bones crushed. The torrent must have swept him over the falls to plunge into the rocks at the base and just like that, without a goodbye, he was gone, Sam. Ari, the Eagle, my father, was gone."

Ma-aka stopped then, his loss palpable in the air. Sam without knowing how or knowing anything of this person who stood before him, knew then why it was that this man who stood before him, had become his friend. Why, according to Ma-aka, they had become inseparable. Sam connected with Ma-aka in an instant as they stood separated by a few dirty wooden planks and the air of despair and loss. "David!" Sam gasped. "I lost my brother, like you lost your father, and nothing I did could bring him back, Ma-aka. I too blame myself for something, I realise, I had no power over and no control of its passing. He was here, then he was gone and I never had a chance to say goodbye either. I failed him, but I didn't, Ma-aka. And neither did you fail Ari."

Ma-aka was silent. His head hung low for a moment as he digested what had just transpired, then he looked up slowly and gazed at Ngaire. "Perhaps there is a way back, Ngaire," he said. "I do not pretend to understand what happened when Sam went to confront Lord Elim, but, as you say, here he stands and despite hurt and loss, I see that he is not to blame." And with the first of a slow grin he continued, "So put him down, Ngaire. Put him down so I too can crush the life out of him!" Ma-aka, at last, entered fully into the shack, closed the door and crossed the gap between him and Sam. Ngaire stepped back respectfully and Ma-aka faced Sam, close enough to strike, close enough to embrace. Ma-aka stretched out his arm and placed it on Sam's shoulder. "Sam? I am a simple man and I am not worthy to replace Ari, but the spirits chose otherwise and so I must obey. They also sent you. Sent you to change the events that are unfolding around us. That too I do not understand but..." And now looking up at Ngaire, he continued, "One here at least, believed enough to defend you, and who was I to second guess our great healer, Ngaire? She who is mother to me where Turi no longer stands." Sam sensed a sadness flicker across Ma-aka's face as he gazed directly at Sam and he tensed, expecting Ma-aka to take his anger out on him, but instead, Ma-aka, with some humour, said. "As a human, you should not be here. You appeared out of the light and battled the powers who sought to unbalance that which was perfect. The fact that both Ari and Turi are now lost to me has nothing to do with your arrival, and departure, and arrival again." Ma-aka had a twinkle in his eyes as he said this and the purple glow had eased. "You came from the light and who am I to continue to promote you as 'Sam of the Shades'? No! Instead you are who you always have been. You are 'The One'. Chosen by those who we worship for reasons beyond me. But, if you will permit, I would like to stand again by your side one more time, Sam, and face our enemy together, as we did in the past, and, I hope, can do again in the future."

Sam looked over at this man who stood in front of him. His eyes on Sam and his hand on Sam's shoulder, and for once, Sam saw honesty, and more importantly saw a kindred spirit. He did not know what was going on but for now that didn't matter. For now he felt welcome and loved. By two weird looking strangers, who, for some reason believed he was worth a damn, and that was fine by Sam. He reached up and put his arm on Ma-aka's shoulder, mirroring Ma-aka. "Ma-aka, I will try to find that which I lost and try to be worthy once more of your and Silver Fern's trust. Who knows, maybe we can stand side to side again and kick this Lord Elim's arse into the depths of darkness once and for all, and if we do, then I know you and Silver Fern will have my back and protect me with your lives, as I would for you!"

The moment was broken by Ma-aka. "Ngaire?" he asked with confusion, "what is "arse"?"

She just laughed and said, "Oh, my heart feels the healing. My spirit soars to the eagle and to the Helpers this night. But my body hears the bed and so I leave you two. It is late and I, for one, need to be up early tomorrow morning." And with that, she put her hands lightly on both their heads, in blessing, then left them and shuffled off into the darkness and to bed.

The night disappeared as Sam and Ma-aka talked long into the early morning hours. They spoke of bringing Sam back to the clan and how Ngaire cared for him through the fever, of the hunts they went on and of their lives as they bonded as brothers. Ma-aka also told Sam about Pania, the orphan girl who they had found abandoned in the forest one bleak winter's morning. "If we had turned back a few minutes earlier," Ma-aka proclaimed, "Pania would not have been found and, I fear, the wolves would have taken her that night. When you arrived, Sam," he continued, " Pania took a direct interest in you and could often be found by your side, helping Ngaire bring you to health. You became a father figure to her, Sam. More than any other, she looked to you for guidance and protection, and you, in turn, loved her deeply." Sam felt the truth in his word even though he could not recollect any of what had happened in the past, which annoyed him no end. However, he did remember enough to recall seeing Pania and how, for some reason his heart went out to her. The first person he had met "here" who he did seem to bond with. *Perhaps*, he thought, *memory has a habit of retaining key pieces that we hold on to in our unconsciousness. Who knows?*

"Is Pania well?" he heard himself ask.

"She is well, thank you." Ma-aka responded. "She asks after you often and, like me, is in some confusion as to why you are different from the person she grew to know and love. But that bridge you will have to cross yourself one day."

For a while now, Sam had been aware that Ma-aka seemed to find it hard not to slide his glance off Sam and appear to search for something, almost apologising in his demeanour when he sensed that his actions were being observed by Sam. *Almost*, thought Sam, *like that boy in another dream, who was looking for something I should have had with me, though I cannot recall now what that was.*

Eventually, Ma-aka could contain his inquisitiveness no further. "Where is Babu?" he asked.

"Babu!" recalled Sam. "That was it. Babu." Sam responded after some time in thought, trying to assemble a reasonable answer. "Ma-aka, I know you may find this difficult, but, like this place," (he didn't mention, "and you"), "I am afraid I have no idea what Babu is or what relationship I am supposed to have with it. I have encountered a creature from hell from time to time who scares that crap out of me, who seems to be called Babu, but personally, I would rather be on the other side of the planet than have to meet up with him again!"

Sam remembered with some revulsion that evil looking creature crawling up his body when he had been shot with that arrow, now seemingly so long ago in dream world. He also remembered seeing it come out of the forests once, bloody and scratched as if in battle. He recalled fleeing from it as fast as was possible, fear taking all logic and casting him down the valley in head long flight. "I am sure I heard something," Sam thought out loud, "when I tried to run from him when he came at me out of the forest, but of course, my confusion at the time as believing that creature was calling me quickly dissipated as my logic took over. Of course the call could not have come from it, but I was sure…" Sam stopped as he noticed that Ma-aka, instead of looking concerned, as he should have done if he was a friend, instead, had a smile on his face as if enjoying a joke, lost on Sam. "What?" Sam asked. "What is so funny?"

"Sam. It would appear that Lord Elim took not only your memory, but also your awareness. He has a lot to answer for when we meet him. And meet him we will, Sam. And when we do, this time, he will answer!" Ma-aka said the last with cold determination, then continued after tending the fire. "Babu is your Padme, your 'protector' if you will," he started. Sam's eyes shot up into his skull in total surprise, not ready to accept this stupendous and actually quite ridiculous assertion by Ma-aka. Ma-aka continued. "Every person born, when he or she reaches youth phase, receives a Padme. No one actually knows where they come from but, without exception, on the 9th birthday, every person awakes to find a creature of some form waiting for them and that creature stays with them for life. Every person, Sam," Ma-aka reiterated, "on this whole world!" Ma-aka could see that this concept was as alien to Sam as Sam appearing out of thin air was beyond the understanding of Ma-aka. "Sam. These creatures, we think, are a gift from the Ethereals when we reach youth phase. Most seem to exist just to play with the individuals but, and this is important to understand, no one can survive past their youth phase without a Padme and no one can exchange a Padme with one belonging to another. Never!" He paused. "EVER! Not until you appeared, that is, for you are the only person who appears to be able to exist without one, and indeed, Babu, as your Padme, appears to be able to exist without you as well! This is not supposed to be possible and yet we must accept that the Ethereals have other plans for you and Babu, that are beyond the comprehension of us mere land folk."

Sam's mind battled with the idea that the creature from hell he had encountered on more than one occasion appeared to belong to him. "But that thing. When ever I met it, seemed to want nothing more than to eat me!" he said with some defence. Sam recalled the occasions he could remember when Babu had been a part of his dreaming, and something did not seem to back up what he had just stated as being truth. He remembered of course, lying totally surprised in the mud, an arrow sticking wickedly out of his chest. *That was a bloody hum dinger!* he thought. He remembered Babu as he lost consciousness, crawling up his chest and whilst the thought of it still revulsed him, he had to admit that the creature did not actually attack him. He also remembered the first time he met Babu at the pond, and yes, it had scared the crap out of him, but again, it had not seemed to want to attack him.

Then of course, there was the time when it stumbled out of the forest in some distress and all Sam did was run away.

"Good move there, Sam, my boy!" he reprimanded himself. That was when he was sure it had called after him.

And then there was the time that he wanted to forget. "When those people all stood around me like idiots, dying, for what? And as the leader came up to me to stab me, Babu came hurtling out from nowhere and killed those scary people. Again, it did not try to attack me!" Sam mused over these "facts" as he tried to assemble what he was hearing, despite it not settling easily in his idea of what made for a nice family pet!

"So you are saying that every person on this entire world MUST have a Padme, and that if they don't, they are effectively toast...?" Ma-aka scrunched up his face, not understanding how toast could have a place in a sentence about Padme. "However," Sam continued, "for some weird reason, I, who should be dead according to your theory because I don't have a Padme with me, apparently, break the rules because actually I do have one, but it is neither with me nor needs to be and instead, my Padme turns out to resemble my worst nightmare and scares the willies out of me every time I encounter it!? Well all I can say is that your Ethereals were having a massive laugh when they chose that one to be my pet!"

"You and Babu," Ma-aka noted, "like all other people here, connect together as naturally as breathing! However, I must correct you on one matter. The Padme are not pets and you are not their master, Sam. They fuse with your spirit at some deep level connecting both within and without."

Now Sam was confused so Ma-aka continued. "Why don't you give it a try." Ma-aka looked straight at Sam as he said this, and he might as well have said that Sam could float and fly through the air in this world at the same time, so weird was this explanation sounding to Sam. However, Sam did pick up on Ma-aka's last comment.

"What do you mean exactly, give it a try?" he asked, the air around him feeling cold and clammy once more. "Sam!" Ma-aka said with some frustration. "Have you really forgotten everything? You must call him. Call him, and he will come." Now Sam felt at a loss.

"How?"

"By using your charm!" Ma-aka answered. And before Sam again thought that Ma-aka was trying to play him for a fool, he continued. "And, NO, I do not mean your *natural charm*, which at the moment is seriously in question…" (*Oh, funny one Ma-aka*, thought Sam.) "…I mean, call him with your Charm, the one around your neck, Sam!" And Ma-aka now looked directly at Sam's neck.

Sam fumbled up to feel what could be on his neck to make Ma-aka stare like that, as he knew that he certainly was not wearing anything. His skin went icy as, instead of the feel of skin on his neck, his fingers found what appeared to be a necklace! "What on earth?…" he cried in confusion. "Where did that come from?" He tried to look down to see what was around his neck, but of course, nature had designed things such that he was unable to, so instead, he sprung up and moved quickly to the mirror which stood over the fireplace and gazed at himself with yet more shock.

There, lying naturally around his neck, hung an unassuming necklace. It had a few beads and shiny objects together with what appeared to be leather strips hanging down off a thin string tie. Right in the middle, and now resting lightly against his Adam's apple, hung a thin, wooden tube, almost resembling a flute, but much smaller. Holes were to be seen down its length and at the bottom, the tube ended in the shape of an unmistakable whistle. For some reason, in the deepest recesses of his mind, he thought he had seen this thing before, but for now, the where, how and why of it escaped him.

"Blow!" he heard from behind him. "Blow your pipe and see what happens." Ma-aka now stood behind him, looking at his reflection as Sam wrestled with finding something around his neck that he sure as heck hadn't placed there, whilst at the same time trying to not think about that creature. Sam, after long deliberation, slowly, carefully lifted the wooden pipe to his mouth... and blew.

If he was expecting any sound to come out from the end of the pipe, Sam was not expecting the noises emanating now. Instead of a flat note, the pipe seemed to have created a three dimensional warming tonal hum. It resonated and grew rather than dispersed, and filled his senses with electric expectation. The pipe dropped out of his open mouth yet the sound continued. A thrumming, soft and palpable resonance was the best Sam could describe it. Warm and somehow safe as well. It hovered around him and then seemed to move out into the surroundings. Looking. Hunting. Seeking.

"It won't be long now!" Ma-aka said, prophetically.

In the silence that followed, Sam's senses were on full alert. His ears were waiting to hear any difference in the blanket of sound he had grown accustomed to since coming to this place. He was waiting for something, anything, to change that. He did not have to wait long.

A thin, tentative scraping was heard outside and Sam felt beads of sweat trail down his face as his fears played a dance with his emotions. Ma-aka was looking at him though, encouraging him to trust, so Sam relaxed slightly. *After all,* he mused. *This is just a dream anyway and if the worse come to the worst, at least I know I am going to wake up and IT will be nowhere around.*

The door opened, almost by magic, creaking slowly as if whatever had pushed it, was trying to do things quietly. For a brief second, time stood still. The door was open, the darkness undisturbed outside the door, the lamp still glowing over the door frame. And then, a head appeared at the door. A head Sam had seen before and one he had no desire to see again!

Babu peered slowly from around the door frame looking furtively into the space. His eyes roamed the room carefully, searching for potential danger finally resting on Sam, looking fully at him now. Keeping his eyes firmly on Sam, he stepped into the room. *There are those claws again*, thought Sam.

He had an opportunity to study Babu properly now. He remembered that thin, scrawny looking furry body, but one which held immense pent up energy, which, he recalled, was able to spring at an enemy and carry out swift punishment. The muscles under the skin flexed as Babu paced around the room and the sinews moved like water under a sheet. Babu walked on all fours and of course, at the end of each foot, those long, deadly looking claws sat. Sharp as knives and equally deadly, they glinted as if metallic. Babu had fox-like ears which stood proud of his head, twitching every now and again as its senses reached out beyond itself, testing the air for danger.

Over everything though, Sam was struck by the eyes. The eyes, in proportion to its face, were huge. Deep set and feral in quality, they held Sam's gaze like pools of dark water. They spoke of intelligence, hidden beneath the surface, and something more. Knowledge perhaps. Deep, "larger than this place" knowledge and wisdom. Babu's tongue snaked out now and again, sensing and tasting the air for changes in tension. It resembled that of a snake's, forked slightly at the ends and now it was tasting the air as it paced slowly around Sam. *Like a predator would pace around prey!* Sam thought, absent-mindedly. Babu continued pacing, drawing closer to Sam, not quite sure if it was safe. At the last moment, Babu moved right up to Sam, as if finally deciding that he had passed a test, and settled down at his feet as if nothing was any different to the way things were.

Sam looked down at the form, curled up beneath him, then looked up at Ma-aka with some amazement. "What now?" said Sam.

"Now?" returned Ma-aka. " Now the rest is up to you."

Sam slowly moved back to the chairs they had recently occupied and sat down. He felt amazingly tired and looking up he sensed through the open door, that morning was not far away. He could scarcely keep his eyes open any longer and sleep started to take him into its welcoming embrace. But not before he sensed Babu get up from the fireplace where he had stood, and move back to Sam, jumping lightly up to Sam's chest, crawling up to his face as before, and settling himself down to sleep.

"Hot Dog and Chips with Plenty of Tommy Sauce"

Sam woke slowly, as if pulling out of a vat of glue. He wasn't ready to open his eyes as yet, instead enjoying the tranquility of the house and the sanctuary of it all. Life, for once, was good and… "Hey mate, you can't sleep there! Some of us need to get to work you know?" A coarse, loud voice invaded his sleep and he awoke instantly. There, staring down at him with unmistakable disgust, stood an elderly man, wrapped up against the wind, a scarf tight around his neck and a hat rammed hard down around his grey wispy hair. Behind him, a younger lady tried not to stare, but she found that difficult. Sam got up quickly, the events in front of him, catching him unawares.

Three or four commuters stood around him and one more sat on the bench, as far away from Sam as was possible. They were all staring at him, as if dissecting a vagabond. His hair was dishevelled, having been pressed up against the side billboard for most of the night. His jacket was hitched up around his chest and his shirt had similarly become unhitched from his trousers such that he did indeed look like someone from the great unwashed. He stood up. Quickly. Mumbling his apologies, he retrieved his back pack, almost absent mindedly, and walked away, straightening his clothing as he did.

Well that was bloody embarrassing! he cajoled himself. At once trying to get as much space between him and the bus shelter, the people still staring after him and then turning to each other to continue to "dissect" him with their fellow travellers. "Wankers!" he muttered beneath his breath.

He made his way to the children's park and hid behind the trees near the swings to get a breather and to bring some semblance back into his world. Straightening his clothing and patting down his hair in semi-respectable fashion, his mind naturally replayed what, for him, was the most amazing experience he had had for a long time. With some regret he acknowledged that he had indeed been dreaming, again, and this was his world and those, looking out to the commuters sat now in the bus shelter, waiting for a bus that definitely wouldn't come on time, unfortunately, were his people. He looked out from behind the trees and considered his position, now that reality had kicked back in, the dream was consigned to that place where most dreams resided after waking and he was still getting wet from the rain which still fell from the skies! *When can we bloody well have some decent weather?* he heard himself think. "Well," he said sagely, "at last we don't have as much mist as that other place! I wonder what Babu would think of this place?" That caught him by surprise and he unconsciously moved his fingers up to grip the necklace off which the pipe to call Babu hung. His fingers found only flesh. No necklace adorned his neck. No Padme prowled around the area protecting him. "You are bloody ridiculous, Sam Gilbert," he rebuked himself. The opportunity he had had, albeit in a dream state, to feel some sort of freedom and happiness, was snatched away by his state of mind and, pushing those "childish" thoughts away, he wondered what to do next.

He scanned the street in front of him. The commuters were still moving around, some looking down at their watches. *Probably tutting under their breath because the bus is just not coming, Sonny Jim!* thought Sam with some humour. Behind the shelter, and already flickering its neon sign to the world, Timber's seemed to be open for business. A few people could be glimpsed behind the shopfront glass. "Sitting having a coffee or something, and eating fantastic food no doubt," he mused. His hunger pangs chose at that moment to make their presence felt and he was compelled to at least get fed up before deciding what to do for the rest of the day. *Besides*, he thought, now that his reality was etched firmly in his head, *mum and dad probably don't even know I have left!*

Sam peered once more from out behind the trees and was rewarded to see the No 57 bus pull up to the shelter. "So those horrible people can bloody well sod off to wherever they have to be today!" he said to himself. The bus pulled away from the shelter and, luckily today, it appeared to be the right one such that all his fellow travellers who had stood around him earlier, had now departed. He walked out from behind the trees and made a beeline for Timber's and walked inside.

Inside, the normal chaos of a typical "caff" could be heard. Cups chinked, knives and forks scratched at the chinaware and the buzz of various voices deep in discussion or laughing at a particular joke could be heard wafting through the atmosphere. Over it all, from time to time, he heard the waitress shout an order to someone behind the wall that separated the kitchen from the dining area. He found a table, thankfully near the window, and stared out into the gloom, waiting patiently for someone to come and take his order. The rain had taken a turn for the worst, if that were possible, and it now lashed down in torrents outside, forcing those hardy enough to venture out, to seek shelter under any overhang possible. *Why is it always raining here? Over* there *it's always misty,* he thought, for no apparent reason, other than he was bored of waiting. He was very hungry. *…and if someone didn't bloody hurry up…*

"Master Gilbert. What a pleasant surprise this dreary, bleak day. What can I get you?" Alice stood slightly behind and to his left, pen and pad in one hand the other reaching out to Sam with a menu. She had a look of guile on her face as if knowing she had managed to creep up without him sensing her.

"Hello, Alice," Sam started. "I didn't hear you come up as I was deep in thought…" Sam stopped in mid-sentence as a link jumped out at him and bit down hard. "Alice! The Alice. The one who had come over here to find him… that Alice." But, looking at her, straightening her smock and keeping her head down for now, the thought of her being some super "alien" with immense powers, now lost, seemed not only absurd, but frankly, a bit creepy to him. "Erm, I mean, um, well, um…" His vocal dexterity abandoned him as he found himself lost for words.

Alice looked up. "I am sorry, Sam," she said, "I didn't get that. What is it you would like?" She was looking straight at him, her deep eyes seeming to bore into his. Purple flecks visible within her irises… *An electric aura seeming to hover around her … Bloody hell, Sam! Get a grip, mate. She will think you are starting to perv over her soon if you are not careful!*

Trying hard not to stare back in turn, Sam forced his eyes to turn back to the menu, proffered by Alice, still sitting in her outstretched hand. "Full English please, Alice," he blurted out. "And some toast as well if possible?"

Alice wrote down the order saying, "Toast comes with the full English, Master Gilbert," another smile playing over her face.

"Of course it does, you bloody idiot!" Sam ranted at

himself under his breath. "I am acting like a bloody love-struck teenager!" He could sense that his face was starting to redden and he quickly turned around to look out the window, knowing that his actions could be perceived to be rude, but all sense of politeness were rapidly running out the door, calling him to come with it. Sam stayed put.

"And?" he heard Alice ask.

"Huh. What? I mean, sorry?" Sam asked, tripping over his words, his face surely now resembling a red sunburnt idiot!

"What would you like to drink with that? Tea, or coffee?" Alice asked, innocence dripping from her mouth like honey from a bees' nest.

"Tea. No, coffee please," he bumbled, trying desperately to regain the "customer is always right" demeanour, failing miserably though. Looking up, he concluded. "Milk, no sugar please Alice." *That showed her*, he thought as she started to turn back to the kitchen, but not before she stopped, hesitated for a second and then bent in low towards Sam. Wondering what she was about to say, he too leant in towards her, not knowing why exactly other than he felt somehow compelled. She waited.

"Sam," she half whispered, "the sugar is already on the table. You don't need to tell me whether you want some or not. That is up to you to sort out yourself!" And then she stood up and walked off. A slight swagger visible in her walk.

Sam fumed inside for the better part of a minute, furiously trying to straighten the knives and forks which were already expertly placed and straight as arrows and sorting out his serviette into odd shapes, the same finally giving up the ghost and tearing down the middle to lay in pieces on the table. *Damn! Get another one from the basket before she comes back.* He ordered himself to calm down and chill.

This was definitely not how he envisaged his morning turning in to.

He slowed his breathing, allowing himself to work out fact from fiction. *Sam. You know that what you had was just a dream. You know that Alice is no more than the owner of this place and you have known here since you moved here. You have never seen her fly around the place on a broom stick and you probably never will. So bloody well calm down and be real, before she comes back and finds you still gibbering on like some loony!*

He was pleased with himself. He knew that, at times, he needed to be hard on himself otherwise he would be lost in a world of…

"Sam. Can you move back a bit please? I have brought you your coffee. No sugar!" Again Alice had crept up behind him to deliver his coffee and again Sam was shocked into movement.

"Of course," he said, trying to regain order. He looked up, to force himself to face his demons. Alice had a smile on her face and her hair fell forward slightly. Sam, unwittingly, followed the line of it as it cascaded down her neck and then he noticed something. Where was her necklace? *She always had that weird thing around her neck and now it was gone. And, more importantly, from memory, it did look a lot like the one I had on in my dream!* Sam did not like the way his thinking was going, and he definitely did not like the outcome should his thinking follow some logical conclusion. Before he could pose a question however, she turned back to the kitchens and was gone.

Alice returned a short while later, but this time, Sam was prepared. The plate was presented and he had to just enjoy the picture for a second. Strips of bacon with the edges crispy, just the way he liked it, fried egg (two of those, if you please!) some heavenly smelling sausages, baked beans and at least three slices of brown toast, adorned his plate. A Full English in every sense of the word. He licked his lips enjoying the anticipation of diving in to this beautifully normal past time.

"Will that be all, Sam?" Alice asked, again her eyes looking into him as if to speak to his inner self.

"This looks lovely Alice, thank you. All good here for now." Just before she started to leave he blurted out, "I, um, I notice you are not wearing your necklace today. Have you lost it?" Even as he heard himself utter the question, he was kicking himself at how stupid it sounded. *So what if she isn't wearing her necklace. It's not as if she gave it to me when I wasn't looking and breathed some spell on it to make it enchanted, you idiot!* All this flitting through his mind in an instant of rebuke to himself.

"Thank you for noticing, Sam," Alice responded. "It's nice when people take an interest in others. Don't you think?" She started to move away but not before she uttered one more sentence which hung in the air in front of him. " I gave my necklace to a friend. He needed it for a while. It's what friends do, don't you think?" And with that, she disappeared into the kitchen leaving Sam open mouthed in mid bite, wondering whether he had heard what he was sure she had said between the lines.

As he ate, his mind played over the events of the last few hours and, as often happens when one has a chance to dissect things in peace, a logical sense of order eventually settled in his mind. *Of course Alice has nothing to do with my dreams and I am certainly not going to tell her that I dreamt of her! I am sure her friend needed it for some reason and of course she is free to do with it what she will. Dreams are dreams and life goes on. Hey?* With that, he turned his attention on what to do with himself that day, as well as consider the situation back at home. *Am I being a bit melodramatic?* he thought. *No! Mum and dad deserve every bad thing going for them. Stuff 'em! They couldn't care a monkey's whether I am there or not. Let them suffer a bit so they can see what it was like to feel rejected. But where to go and where to eat?* He continued. *And, where to wash, dress, earn money? What about school, fees, living…?* All the details of a mundane life flowed into his head threatening to upset his feeling of happiness pervading him at that moment. Instead, he decided to see if he could turn things into an adventure. *Hey. Maybe I could just hop onto a bus down to Sandhaven and hang out there for now. I could walk along the beach, chill and spend the day there.* Sandhaven was a village on the sea side about 30 minutes away and the thought of going there lifted the clouds that were threatening his day.

That decided, he looked around for Alice to pay the bill, but she was nowhere to be seen. Instead the other waitress approached him. "Can I help you?" she asked.

A young girl, probably doing this for pocket money and an opportunity to pay for some make up so she could go and spend it all at a night club, getting drunk and throwing it all up a few short hours later, shot through his head. *Weirdo!* he said to himself quickly. "Just the bill please."

She returned soon afterwards and he paid and got himself ready to leave. Looking at his watch, he saw he had a few minutes to wait, assuming the bus bothered to pitch up! "Say goodbye to Alice for me?" he heard himself say to the waitress, who just looked at him with some consternation. "Just leave now, Sam!" he said.

Outside, he got himself to the shelter, his backpack firmly on his shoulders, and waited for the bus to appear. It trundled down the road a few short minutes later and disgorged a few passengers before Sam climbed on board and clambered up the stairs to the upper deck. As he settled and the bus started to pull away, for some reason he looked out the window towards Timber's. Alice stood at the door, a cigarette dangling from her mouth, and she was unmistakeably looking right at him. She reached her hand up to her mouth, kissed it, and blew it towards him then turned and walked back into the darkness of the café, and was gone.

Sam tried to focus on the journey but her actions had thrown him. He knew that there was no love motive in her actions, that would be a bit weird. Her actions were more of a mother kissing her son off to school for the first time. To say not to be afraid and that she was right there with him. It was a send off of comfort, of belonging, of being protected. Somehow…

The journey took slightly longer than he was used to. Traffic coming out of Greyshott seemed to be against them and the traffic lights seemed to be red whenever they approached, but eventually they left the outskirts of the town and settled into the windy lanes of the countryside, slowly dropping down towards the coast ahead. Seeing the openness of the countryside and the thin blue line of the sea in the distance was a breath of fresh air to Sam. Sheep were scattered everywhere today and a few lambs could be seen clinging protectively to their mothers in the fields on either side of the road. "Lambing season," he thought. The whole event was an adventure in itself and he enjoyed seeing the various areas open up to him from this lofty vantage point. Slowly the blue of the sea got closer and it did not take much longer before the bus dropped into the village of Sandhaven and stopped at the Town Hall and the last stop. Sam got out, slung his backpack expertly over one shoulder, and considered his options.

He moved down towards the beach, seeing it slowly open up and get larger and more expansive as he approached. The beach was predominantly made up of small pebbles, washed clean by the repetitive nature of the waves. Sandhaven was not actually much of a tourist destination in this neck of the woods, but for him, for today, it was paradise on earth. He laughed freely as he walked up and down the beach kicking pebbles into the water and hearing the reassuring crunch of them beneath his feet. As was normal at these places, he could not resist trying to skim a few into the waves.

Lunch was a hot dog and chips with plenty of tommy sauce.

The day slowly moved into the late afternoon. A short spell at the beach gaming hut, laughing to himself as he saw his money disappear into the slot machines knowing full well that they would NOT be paying him a cent. Time then to think about where to stay that night. As he walked along the Esplanade he saw that a few people were out walking their dogs. Some of the owners having the unenviable task of stooping down to clean up after "Mr. Bubbles has done a poo poo then?" A few couples walking hand in hand enjoyed the slowly dimming twilight as the sea continued to crash its greeting to anyone interested in hearing. One old man had an easel ahead of him and he was painting a fairly good seascape of the sea and the surroundings; otherwise, things were fairly quiet.

Up ahead, and flashing a cheap neon light, a YMCA waited. *That will do*, he thought, making a beeline towards the gaudy colours flashing in the skies. A spotty youth stood behind the check-in counter, chewing bubble gum and gazing down at a small monitor, boredom etched on his face as if he was born with it. "Checking in just for one night?" he managed to say to Sam, already clicking on various tabs on his keyboard in automatic expectation. "That will be £35 for the room. Breakfast is extra. Room with or without a bathroom?" Sam wanted to punch him there and then. "Bubble gum chomping youth meets early painful death in YMCA brawl!" The headlines of some imaginary tabloid newspaper rushing into his mind.

"Yes please," he said, over politely. "Yes, that is, for staying one night only. No, to breakfast and yes to a bathroom." There was no way he was going to stumble down a darkened corridor in his smalls looking for a bathroom in the dead of night, thank you very much, and the thought of a cardboard breakfast at this place, given the delicious one he had had earlier, did not inspire him.

A few clicks later and "zit kid" handed over a piece of paper to sign. Sam forged his signature. The keys quickly followed along with a, "So go along the corridor there," pointing to the only corridor present, "call the lift and go up to the third floor. You are in room 322. Have a pleasant stay." Sam walked off towards said lift thinking that "pleasant" would not be his first choice word for this place. *Still, it is a bed for the night and no parents to get moaned at, so not bad really.*

The room was small and barren. A tiny window was at the end of the room, looking into a rear service yard, and the bathroom was off to one corner. No bath, just a plastic shower cubicle, cracked frames and a toilet and wash hand basin. Also, no towels! "I don't care!" said Sam to no one in particular. He sat down on the bed, which was surprisingly comfortable, to decide what to do that evening. He knew that Sandhaven had a cinema further down the Esplanade and he had to admit, it had been a long time since he had seen a film. That, together with the idea of a Chinese from one of the numerous take away shops, was sufficient for him to feel his evening was well and truly sorted.

Looking at his watch, he saw it was still too early for the films to start and he was not hungry enough yet to warrant going out just to eat something. "Perhaps I will just take a

30 minute power nap," he thought, lying back to put his head on the pillow and staring up at the ceiling. Within a few short minutes, his body lay still, and the deep, regular breathing of someone who had fallen fast asleep could be heard from the bed. Sam's last conscious thought was that of sensing the waves crashing onto the beach just beyond the Esplanade, then this too disappeared into the darkening ooze of sleep.

The grinding of the rocks

Morning broke through into his consciousness assaulting his sleep. Bright rays filtered through his eyes and he tried to roll over to at least try to get a few more minutes' shut eye. Strangely, the waves sounded incredibly loud and very close. He became aware of an echo which reverberated around him as each wave crashed against the rocks, almost as if the water was trapped in a cave, the "swooshing" sucking noise following afterwards as the water receded again, louder than normal. Cracking noises above him, unmistakably that of rocks dislodging from a rock face and pitching down, down, bouncing onto the rock face to eventually crash into the sea below him. "This doesn't sound right?" he started to question, becoming more aware of the un-rightness of the situation. It was the steady breeze on his face that eventually snapped him out of his semi-sleep state. "Where is this wind coming from?" he started, thinking he was certain he hadn't left the window open overnight, and even if he had, the breeze would not be that directed on him.

He opened his eyes and stared out at a scene from an alien planet.

The room had disappeared and instead, in its place, he found himself on a sandy floor of what appeared to be a cave, set back into the rock face, the opening about five metres in front of him, through which the early morning sun was streaming. Totally disorientated, he staggered up and stumbled towards the opening and gasped as the scene opened up to him. The cave in which he found himself was carved out of a near vertical rock face. A few hardy scrub trees dotted around tried desperately to cling to the fragile surface, which itself was cracked and eroded by wind and age. A few rocks from above bounced down the face crashing into projections before disappearing into an impenetrable mist bank below him, from which came the sound of those rocks slamming into the seething water of a sea and of a place definitely not in Sandhaven. Strangely enough, his first thought on seeing this rather inhibiting view was to wonder why the mist was so thick if the sun was out and shining. Sam had already grabbed the edge of the cliff face, fearful that gravity would somehow pitch him out of his precarious position and hurl him into the mist bank below him. Salt spray wafted up the rock face and made the area damp. He could feel the spray on his face and, looking down, he sensed the waves he had heard earlier as they crashed against the rocks of the cliff on which he found himself crashing loudly before sucking back into the embrace of the sea to be replaced by yet another thumping wave. This definitely was not a place he was familiar with.

"Where the..." he began, totally confused. The fact that all his surroundings of the night before were nowhere to be seen did not register; instead he found himself seeing this place as a fact, and one that he was trying to figure out how to escape from. Sam peered again out of the hole in the cliff face and started to look around to get his bearings. Somehow he had to get out from this perch he found himself on, and try to find help somewhere. The "how" or "why" of the situation, for now, evaded him.

Looking down, he saw only a deep, dank mist bank, and

below that he heard the crashing of the waves on many boulders. "No. Going down was not an option!" he concluded. Looking up and to the side, he noticed that the fissures in the rock face were large enough to use as hand and foot holds, and besides, the mist was less dense above him, partly due to the sunlight filtering through it. "Up it is then," he stated, looking out to consider his first plan of attack. The fact that he couldn't see his route clearly or that he may get into difficulties on the bare rock face, and who knows what would happen then, did not play a part in his thinking. These thoughts of self preservation were reserved for a future time, assuming, of course, he survived the next few minutes. Sam reached up and out, slowly, testing the soundness of the vantage points he found, and sensing that they would hold him, he stepped off his safety platform and started to climb.

As is normal in a dream, the disappearance of his familiar surroundings, his bed and bathroom, and indeed, the lack of any backpack, which had been next to his bed when he went to sleep, failed to make any impact on him. It was if where he was now was where he "should be" and he did not have the wherewithal to challenge it.

Sam crept up the face slowly and carefully, at first being very aware of searching out his next grip point, the adrenalin coursing through his body, preventing any other emotion or thought to hold fort. The wind had picked up slightly and it was now whipping around his face and lifting his coat up to be buffeted around him, threatening to dislodge him from his precarious position. Occasionally, as he climbed higher, a few clippings and larger sections of rock came free beneath his fingers and fell to the sea below, but each time, his balance was such that this did little to disrupt him. What did disrupt him was when he lifted himself up so that his face was level with a small recess in the rock face, and the largest seagull he had ever seen chose that moment to fly off the same recess, flapping his wings and screeching into the air in disgust. Sam reflexively ducked his head beneath his shoulder and in the process, lost his grip and started to slip and fall off the mountain. His fall lasted a few seconds only as his feet were stopped on a small outcropping, but the shock of it brought him crashing to the reality of the situation he had put himself in. Halfway up a near vertical cliff face with the sound of deadly waves below him and who knows what awaiting him above, he rebuked himself for the utter stupidity of his actions. "Sam, without doubt the most hare-brained, stupid position you have ever put yourself in. If you fall, you die, if you climb, you probably die also. Nice one… again!" Nevertheless, he gritted his teeth, rubbed the dirt and blood off his hands on the rock face, and proceeded to climb up again, wary this time for birds.

As he continued, he passed a few other roosting ledges, thankfully clear of birds but with feathers and guano spread about indicating that the nesting places were being used. The odd sound of a seagull cry broke through the air, warning Sam off, but otherwise they left him alone. Sam continued to climb, slowly but surely working his way up the cliff face, looking out for his next hand or foot grip until he started to notice a subtle change in the incline. More grasses started to appear and his passage increased in speed until at last, he found himself able to stand on a grassy patch, then, reaching the top, he was able to stop and pause for breath and allow his heart to stop trip-hammering in his chest.

As he slowly gazed at his surroundings, he was surprised that some things appeared to be familiar to him. To his left and off in the middle distance, he saw a few hills disappearing into a tree line. Something in his mind was trying to register that the view itself was strange, but at first he couldn't put his finger on it. To his right, and looking down the valley, he saw what had tickled his mind as being familiar. There, nestled in the lap of the landscape, a lake glistened and shimmered. It was the same lake he had seen when he was introduced to.... *Now what was his name?* he thought. "Pit! That's it. Pit," he said. "He introduced me to the village folk who lived there. Now I am on the opposite side." And peering intently, he could see the village across the lake, shimmering slightly in the heat haze. Again, no mist blocked his view, but as his gaze moved further past the village and on to the tree line beyond, the mist was cloaked again, silent and brooding. The same as he had seen below him. *Below him!* Something clicked in his mind and he peered back down the rock face from where he had just climbed. Strangely enough, he could see his route clearly, going all the way down to the cave entrance, but beyond that, the mist was impenetrable. *What is it about this mist?* he thought. *Why can I see clearly in some directions, but elsewhere, it is thick as a pea-souper?* Sam could sense that there was some link about this, but it evaded his mind for now as if swirling just out of arm's reach, just like the mist.

Sam stared down into the mist bank below him, the sounds of the waves and gulls bouncing off the rock faces and his thoughts floating in and out of his consciousness. Snapping back into reality, he decided to turn and head to the village on the other side of the lake. He was still musing over why the mist was not acting at all like mist should as he walked down to the lake edge and started to follow its banks towards the village. The day was bright and the air was calmer compared to when he was trying to climb earlier. The waves of the lake were lapping gently against the shore, giving off a calming zen-like noise. Off in the distance, near the middle of the waters, a few fishing boats were seen, the men throwing their nets into the water and the sound of shouted commands and chatter carried over the water to him in snatches. Normality appeared to rest in this place, but something was tickling his sixth sense. The scenery looked perfectly normal, for a dream, but it was almost as if the picture was fake. *Something's not right!* he thought. *I feel like someone has thrown a large sheet over a building and then painted another scene on the sheet. One is aware of a shape behind the picture, but the picture takes over. It's almost as if someone was deliberately trying to conceal reality from the viewer.*

Sam was aware of something else. Energy fields, if that were possible, that coalesced just beyond his perception, but enough for him to look around carefully, senses on full alert.

As he continued around the lake he started to hear the sound of falling water. It gradually became louder and more intense. Deeper, booming tones and light high-note tinkles linked in together creating the sound of a waterfall. The trees and foliage blocked his view off to the right but the sound was unmistakeable. Sam eventually came out into a clearing and noticed the water of the lake bubbling and spitting and crashing across a few boulders. As he approached, he saw what was causing the commotion. The lake did indeed funnel itself into a tighter flow, which, after a short journey, hurled itself over the edge of the cliff and fell down and down to smash itself into the rocks below, hidden from view. But what a sight it was. Clear water, powerful and determined, pouring itself in one final leap out from the confines of the lake to join finally with the ultimate power of the crashing sea below. Sam had to stop to take in the scene. Hands on hips, he revelled at the taste of the spray on his lips and the feeling of the droplets on his face.

In an unconscious gesture, he reached up to his neck to

undo the buttons of his shirt to allow the spray to cool him down even further. It was then that his fingers felt an object resting on his neck that was not there in the hotel. "That charm necklace!" he exclaimed, feeling the strips of leather between his fingers. "How on earth has that reappeared?" His fingers came to rest on the smooth length of what he recognised as the pipe by which he had called Babu the last time he was there. *I wonder...* he thought. And, lifting the thin pipe to his lips, he drew a deep breath, and blew.

As before, a deep, melodic, thrumming noise emanated from the end of the pipe and he could sense the air around him fold and play with the shape of the sound, forming it, building upon it and increasing its intensity. It did not become louder so much as "deeper" somehow. More expansive, more powerful until the very air around him seemed to crackle with the resonance.

Off to his left and back where he had first come from earlier, he heard the sound of the undergrowth parting, as if a large animal was pounding towards him. He looked back from where he had come from in some shock to see the grasses bend and break as a line cut a swathe through the landscape heading for him. Arrow straight and just as fast! He stepped back defensively and through natural self-preservational instinct as this *line* seemed to gather pace, his fear growing as all manner of dreadful nuances as to what was causing this disruption shot through his mind in a second. All he remembered about this afterwards, was how very fast the *line* was approaching him.

Suddenly, the line stopped dead a few metres from where he stood. There was no sound coming from the spot, no smoke, no evidence of anything that had caused this bullet to be sent his way. Just a slight sighing as the grasses eased around whatever hid beneath his line of sight within the grasses. And then, Babu peeked out of the undergrowth, looking straight at him with those same, deeply intelligent, and now questioning eyes. Its tongue was hanging out between those now familiar yet still scary fangs as the body strained to get more oxygen and Sam could see its rib cage flexing quickly with exertion. Babu's tail, scaled and shiny, swishing strongly from side to side like that of a snake moving this way and that as it focuses on its prey.

"Babu!" Sam exclaimed. "It's you!" Needing no further excuse, Babu ran the last few metres and sprang up at Sam, who promptly fell back onto the soft ground, gripping the creature around the midriff both in fright and welcome. "Hello, Babu," he said. "How are you then?" Had he owned a dog, he would have said the same thing. His greeting coming naturally to him. Babu's response was anything but!

The words, "Hello, Sam," came booming into his mind. Without thinking, Sam quickly scuttled up and looked around, wondering who had snuck up behind him, for he knew he had heard something. There was absolutely no one in sight! Sam stared intently into the tree line from where he had just emerged, assuming that perhaps the person was there hidden behind a tree or branch. The place was empty. "Strange," began Sam.

"We welcome you back." Now he knew he had heard *that*! "Come out, whoever you are!" he shouted into the undergrowth. "Show yourself and stop all this malarkey and hiding. Is that you, Ma-aka?" Still nothing moved. After a while of silence he surmised, "Must be another dream anomaly." His eyes fell down to Babu as if to ask it if it knew who was calling him and, if anything, it appeared as if Babu was looking at him with a very strange and eerie, almost human intelligence. Almost as if it was saying, "Yes? Can I help you?" Which would have been ridiculous of course…

"Can we help, Sam?" This seemed to come from his mind.

He didn't actually hear it. He sensed it this time. Sam saw that Babu had tilted its head as this thought entered his mind, and blink.

"Ha!" he said to himself, "as if...!"

"As if what?" came jumping back.

Sam's face turned an ashen shade of grey as a thought snapped to attention within him, shouting to be heard. "Babu?" he began, not daring to believe an impossibility, although, in hindsight, accepting that this whole world was an impossibility and so one more into the pot made no difference! "Is that YOU?"

"Who else did you expect it to be?" came the witty response.

"You can talk?"

"No! But we can communicate!"

"Bloody hell!"

"You say that a lot!"

"How cool is this?" Sam proclaimed to the ether. "A mind-melding, super freaky creature, who talks! This dream is awesome!"

"And you can communicate with us in the same way, Sam." Babu replied, its eyes blinking as if to reinforce what it had said. Sam was awestruck at this new discovery, following his mind through a myriad of permutations as to opportunities and possibilities too numerous to mention. "Hey," he thought, "I wonder if I can get it to..." He stopped. "Can you hear *everything* I am thinking?" he asked Babu with some consternation. Babu just gazed into his eyes and replied, "Do you know what we are thinking?" That seemed to settle that particular worry, which, for some reason, had sprung up in his mind. Babu continued. "Communication is one thing, Sam. Thoughts and hopes and ideas are completely another. Ma-aka warned us that you had disappeared into a sea of forgetfulness, so it would appear we need to start again and start quickly. Time is short and we have little time to waste."

Sam didn't like the way that last bit sounded and so tried to ignore it by asking a rather surreal series of questions. "Do you mind me asking, Babu, are you a girl or a boy?" As he asked it, he was kicking himself at the same time, wondering why on earth that should be relevant.

"We are neither male nor female, singular or multiple," Babu replied. "We are what we are and made as we are made. We are melded to you and so, as you are *male,* we adapt to your maleness. Had we been melded to a female, we would have been similarly adapted."

That seemed to make some sense to Sam, who continued. "So how far away can you be before you can't hear me anymore?" Assuming that, like talking, there was a limit to how far away each could be before sound was inefficient. Again, had he thought about it, he would have realised, yet again, what a stupid question it was!

"Whether we are next to you or on the other side of this world, we can hear you when you call. For when we melded we became one, Sam. One! What you say, we hear, and what we say, you hear, when we speak to each other. We are, in effect one and the same, like brothers, if you will. Brothers together and linked forever, regardless of circumstances or events." The last said by Babu as he reminded Sam of the past few *days* and how Sam had acted in Babu's presence.

"But this is just *so* ridiculous," Sam said. "How do you expect me to believe all this when I know full well that a dream is just something momentary and, when you wake, everything you have experienced disappears into the mist and all the wonderful things are as nothing, leaving you empty. Empty and alone, just like life." Sam hung his head as his real life imposed itself on his dreaming and, he found himself bending down to place Babu on the floor. "Brothers?" Sam said quietly, "I have no brothers." And he walked off towards the waterfall, sadness upon sadness heavy on his shoulders.

His mood didn't last long! It was his feet that first started to announce that things were not as they should be. A slight vibration under his toes pulsed and permeated under the soil and shot out in waves around him. He noticed that the waves closest to the shore were now quite agitated and the water in the lake was getting choppy. Babu was circling around Sam now, all focus on the surroundings, protecting his charge, his fur bristling and his eyes wide, searching. "We need to move, Sam," Babu said. "We need to move now!" Sam looked down at Babu and then at the ground around him, which was shaking and moving like a live thing. Stones and pebbles jostled together and some of the larger boulders by the waterfall were dislodged, tumbling end over end down into the churning seas below, crashing heavily as they hit the rock face. The lake was now broiling with anger and the fishing boats were being tossed around like toys in a storm. Strangely though, there were no clouds in the skies above him and the mist banks beyond remained still and impassive. It was the earth itself around him that was active.

"Earthquake!" was the one word that entered his mind. In an instant his attention switched from his predicament to those in the village beyond, and he looked up to see what was happening there. That village, "Baradin", he recalled, was where he first felt welcomed and he remembered as well that it was where Ngaire had first spoken to him about all manner of strange things. It was a place of peace and a place of welcome. But this time, the children were not playing near the lake and the adults were not sitting around the fires. They were running this way and that and screaming to each other. Some shouting out loudly for their children or families, trying to gain some security by being together. As Sam watched, a few of the smaller homes folded in on themselves, smoke and dust rising up as the buildings collapsed. More screams could be heard, but now these were also screams of pain and terror as spars fell and fires started to burn uncontrolled within this small community. Sam noticed a few young ones standing stock still as all around them, chaos started to rain down on them. "Babu," he began, "we need to go and help them." And with determination, Sam started to run towards the village, wondering all the while what on earth he could possibly do to help, but running to do so nonetheless.

"It has come!" was the prophetic statement from Babu, and then, all hell broke loose.

From deep within the bowels of the earth, a wrenching, churning noise began and grew in intensity until, with a large thunderclap, the ground underneath one of the large houses, burst up and out like a paper bag being exploded and a huge rent in the ground opened up, swallowing the house and the people around it as quickly as snuffing out a candle. Sam was finding it difficult to keep his balance as the ground around him increased its shaking and oscillating.

"Do something!" he seemed to hear in his head. "Stop it while you still can!" Again, this instruction pummelled his brain, but he had no idea what he could possibly do in an event of such cataclysmic proportions. "What *can* I do?" he cried. "I can no more stop this than King Canute could stop the waves."

"Sam. If you don't act, those people are going to DIE!" This shot into his mind like a hot brand, burning him.

"Of course they are," he returned. "People die in dreams after all, don't they?" He was getting fed up with the line this probing was going.

Before he could argue any further, a major shock wave blew him off his feet and he hit the floor, hard. Dust and stones splintered into him and cut his hands and face. He pushed himself up and looked again over to Baradin, but what he saw defied all expectations. The ground was now undulating through the village. Force waves under the earth were literally moving through it, cracking houses and buildings like weak, old kindling. A large crack was now rapidly expanding both in width and in length and was moving rapidly towards the lake, disappearing under the waves momentarily until the waters themselves fell into the gaping maw of this terrible onslaught. Sam saw the children and adults overcome by the rents in the earth, disappearing into the blackness, their screams, desperate for a second, until they were cut off as the people were crushed in the tempest under the earth. The boats fared no better. Boats, sails, nets and men were pulled into the gaping hole to be lost forever in the horror beneath them.

The earthquake did not stop! Indeed, Sam noticed that the rip in the fabric of the earth was heading his way. "Bloody hell, it's heading towards us!" he shouted. "Babu. Run!" And with that, Sam turned and started to run away from the impending calamity heading straight towards them. The ground around him was grinding furiously and the noise, if anything, had now reached deafening proportions.

"Sam. Stop! Stoooooooppp!" Clear as crystal within the din of the undulating ground around him, this warning screamed out, but it was too late. He sensed rather than felt his next step landing not on terra firma, but on air and he looked down in horror as the ground beneath him opened up, tipping him headlong into a bubbling, bouncing, terrifying chasm in the landscape. In a blink, Sam disappeared from view, his shock and pure terror blinking out in an instant as his head smacked soundly against the rocks.

David

Sam felt every bounce and jolt as he tumbled down into the dark chasm. He was aware of the jostling and of being pushed from one side to the other, wishing this could all end. "Wake up!" An urgent, distant shout from somewhere. "Wake up, mate!" Again, a strange call to him. He opened his eyes to see a strange man standing over him, shaking him roughly. "Wake up mate," the man said. "You were shouting out in your sleep and screaming for someone called Babu. Who is Babu? Is he a friend of yours?"

Sam's disorientation continued for a moment as he struggled to look around his surroundings to get his bearings. In front of him stood a *normal* looking man and he appeared to be in a *normal* room and even a *normal* bed. There was no earthquake, no pounding noises or rocks cascading around him. No children dying, no people screaming. No Babu, he realised, only this man standing over him trying to wake him up.

Sam pushed himself up, feeling his head throb and sharp knife-like pains stabbing into his brain. "Oh my goodness!" he began, rubbing his temples. " I am fine, thank you. I must have been really tired last night as I dropped off. Bad dream I am afraid. Must have been that dodgy hot dog!" He tried to laugh it off and make light of his predicament, feeling embarrassed that a stranger should find him in this way. "That's OK," said the man. "As manager here, I have to ensure that everyone is fine. We do get some *interesting* characters in here from time to time, you know?" That last said as he looked down at Sam with some questions unanswered in his eyes. "Well," he continued, " I hope you enjoy your day, sir." And with that, he turned around and left, closing the door behind him.

Silence! Utter quiet pervaded the room and for a while, Sam sat where he was, trying to recall what had just happened, and why, for some reason, his head hurt like he had been beaten up. "Maybe I have a cold coming," he said to himself. In the distance, he heard the sound of the waves again, lapping gently against some shore. No boiling, bubbling cauldron of hell this time, just waves as they should behave. Normality appeared to have returned. *Wow*, he thought, *that was so real!*

Sam pulled the covers away from him and slowly got up, walking over to the single small window to see what the day to come looked like. The sun was already shining through to the rear service yard that greeted his view, and, looking up, Sam saw that the sky was clear and blue and "just right" for a walk and a stroll along the beach. *And perhaps a chance for me to work out this headache!* he thought.

Sam got himself ready, moving to the bathroom to brush his teeth and gazing at his face as he did so. "Bloody hell, you look rough!" he said to his reflection. He turned, got his stuff together and left the room, walking down the emergency stairs to the reception desk where yet another young zit-kid-time-waster-no-plans-for-my-future youth sat, behind the counter, bored already even though the day had just begun. Sam checked out and left the hostel wondering what to do next, the dream, as before, shelved in some distant memory bank, seldom opened.

Sam gazed down the Promenade and spied a Maccy D's in the distance, so he hurried down towards it and disappeared inside for a quick breakfast. He eventually worked his way through the small crowd, ordered his food and sat down at a corner table, away from the younger kids who were already poking each other in the ribs as they spied the odd school girl walking past, egging their friends on to chat them up. Sam ignored them. Instead, he pulled out his phone to see if anyone had bothered to contact him recently. The flashing light suggested that someone at least had tried to call. A few text messages beeped up at him. One from someone at school asking him about a school test, which he really had no desire to respond to. Another about a "must see" television programme that he simply *had* to see. That one was sent straight to the delete bin. One spam mail about a hotel bargain (although why on earth he received those sorts of messages was anyone's guess), another offering him a *once in a lifetime, never to be repeated, paint balling venture…* And one from his dad! He almost deleted it before opening the message, but something stopped his hand and instead, he pressed down on the text icon.

Hi Sam, it's dad here. ("Well duh! Who else would be using dad's phone to text?") *Waking up this morning to find, not one, but two sons missing, is more than any parent can bear. I cannot pretend to imagine your sadness at the moment and mum and I are probably lost in ours. David is gone and will not be coming back and our grief knows no way currently of helping us to deal with his loss. But to be so closed so as to chase you away because of it is a step too far, and so I am writing this, just to say Hi. To say, I love you son. Are you there? Are you safe? I am here if you want to talk, Sam. Dad*

The egg burger lay, uneaten, on the table. The coffee was cold. Sam wasn't hungry. Instead, like a vortex, the simple text message from his dad sucked him down into the one place he wasn't ready to visit. He picked up the phone and threw it, with all his strength, down the length of the restaurant. It skittered down the polished floor before coming to rest against a table occupied by a young family. The impact against their table leg causing them to look down at what had caused the noise. They looked shocked when they discovered the phone. A young girl got off of her perch and bent down to scoop it up, looking around to see where it had come from. Her eyes rested on Sam in the corner and she walked over to him slowly, looking back to her parents for reassurance, her arm outstretched and wide blue eyes looking at him. "Does this belong to you?" she began, holding out the phone to Sam. Sam nodded, not wanting to make eye contact with her, afraid she would see his utter loss. "Don't you want it anymore then?" she asked with young innocence.

"Thank you," Sam mumbled, reaching out to take the phone from her. The girl scuttled back to her parents, her face beaming as she felt a sense of accomplishment at doing this small but so important deed.

Sam quickly gathered his things and left. The door swinging slowly shut, the only sign he had ever been there. His mind was beating him mercilessly. Anger and frustration and deep sadness all threatened to combine into a maelstrom of emotion, and he definitely did not want to have his *little break from normality* to be spoiled by conflict and grief. *Why did dad write?* he thought. *They just don't see me. Don't understand me. Don't want me!* He pictured his mother, walking in a shadow world and forgetting that she had more than one son. *No! Let them suffer for a while. See how they like it.* And with that he walked on once again, down to the pebble beach, found a quiet spot, sheltered by the concrete board walk wall, and, sitting down, gazed out over the pebbles into the water, thinking about David.

David. Three years older, always looking out for him. Taking him out into the world and once, even sneaking him into an age restricted action movie that he really wanted to see. David. Sometimes a right bully, but always his brother. They were close. Closer than most siblings, he thought. They shared secrets, frustrations, and even dreams. More than once they had discussed working together in their own business once school was over.

All for nothing! Sam thought. *Bright and healthy one moment, then diagnosed with leukaemia the next and dead six weeks later.* No time to prepare. No time for a final holiday. No time for even a last *goodbye.* Just… gone! And the terrible emptiness that followed. One that never seemed to reach the brim, always wanting more from you till you just had nothing left to give, and still it sucked at you like a leech, affecting every waking moment of your existence in some cruel, cruel joke. Never letting go.

In the quietness of the place Sam found himself that day, as if, somehow, he had stumbled across a holy space, he welled up and cried hard for his brother for the first time he could remember, talking all the while to him as if he stood next to him. Talking to him about his hurt, his loss, his loneliness now that David had gone. Gone, gone, gone! Never to return. Never coming back.

Amongst his tears, Sam managed to say, "You would have loved this weird dream world I visit. We could have had such fun there." The thought of the place, suddenly kicking his emotions into anger. Anger at the pure injustice of it all. "David was healthy, for goodness' sake! No one did a bloody thing." In his eyes, everyone just stood around and waited for David to die, and they did nothing!

Sam sensed another door closing over his eyes as coldness crept, once more, into his thoughts from deep inside.

Wiping away the tears and dirt that streaked his face, he forced himself to focus instead out over the beach towards the waves. He would not allow himself the place to accept that things happened, and David could no more have stopped the course of that disease than he could have stopped the sun rising. Sometimes, shit did happen.

He stared at the waves with their rhythmic cadence, crashing lazily against the shore, and slowly found himself relaxing with the sound of the waves lulling his senses.

The storm begins

The sound of the waves filtered into his mind and, with his eyes closed, he thought about the fact that they always seemed to have a calming effect on him. The rhythmic ebbing and flowing of them as they crashed onto the shore, sucking back after a few seconds, drawing the shore back into itself, cleansing it ready for the next upheaval. It was like life; a bit of turbulence helped clean away the grime and dirt leaving the surroundings clean again to carry on down the path it had been sent.

Today was no different. He heard the waves crashing nearby, almost comforting him. He was sure that he was sensing a faint wetness on his legs from the spray, but of course, that was mere fantasy as the waves were much too far away to reach him here.

There was an even louder crash as a wave broke close to him and the foam and spray ran in a deluge up the shore line and soaked him to the skin. The numbing coldness of the water immediately shook him out of his reverie and he opened his eyes, thinking that he must have dozed off and the tide had come in, which would have been a surprise given the tidal changes here at Sandhaven… But what greeted him was definitely not Sandhaven. Instead, he looked around trying to get his bearings. He was sitting on a rock ledge of sorts, and the waves were crashing against it, way too close for comfort. He found himself in what appeared to be a rocky enclosure of some sort and, through a rent in the wall in front of him, he could see the waves out to sea were much larger than he was used to and the rock pools around him were slick with spray and lichens. He had been lying in one of these and he was already wet from the standing water and spray of the waves. "What on earth?!" he said. "Where am I?"

He was aware of noises above him, high up. Scrabbling noises of something walking amongst rocks, calling... "Sam? Sam! Are you hurt?" seemed to filter into his mind and he sat up to see what or who was calling him. He almost passed out from the pain of a massive headache and, reaching up, he felt a large bump on his forehead and wetness that could only be blood trickling down from it.

Above him, he saw a rock face stretching ever upwards and boulders strewn around like a giant had thrown them out in a fit of rage. Total chaos greeted him as he gazed around him and as he looked up and up, the scene just got worse. Bent trees in unnatural positions, cracked and ripped in various rigid forms, held grimly on to the torn rock face. Far above him, he saw a chink of light, sunlight, filtering down into the green gloom of where he lay.

The scrabbling attracted him again and he focussed on the point of noise. Babu! Babu was there, some twenty metres above him, clinging to the rocky face, his talons extended and his body low to the rocks, trying to work his way down towards Sam, jumping from crevice to outcrop, to rock, getting closer until he jumped down the last few steps and landed next to the pool that Sam still occupied. His eyes scanning around him constantly, looking for danger, and when not, Babu was looking across at Sam with what could only be described as concern etched on his face. "We saw you fall, Sam. We thought you had disappeared for good but we followed. Trying to find you. Down we came, until we saw you far below in a crevice. We have come to help and to get you out of here, quickly!" And with that, Babu reached out with his front taloned leg and gently touched the bump on Sam's forehead. Immediately, the pain disappeared! Gone!

"What? How? I mean… How…" Sam stammered out as he felt a calming healing come over him where before there was just a throbbing pain.

"We can do many things." Babu said. "Bringing healing is one of these. Now, we must get up and leave. The tide will come and this space is getting smaller."

Sam stood up slowly and promptly keeled over as a sharp pain shot up his leg. "I think I may have broken my leg," he cried. Babu stopped and turned back to look at Sam, casting a quick glance down to his leg.

"No. Not broken. It is just twisted," he said with calm certainty. "Come, we must leave this place before the tide closes off our only escape." And with that, Babu sprang nimbly down the slippery rock face and towards the gap Sam had seen earlier, through which now, the waves appeared to be much closer and more dangerous. Sam hobbled slowly down the incline, griping onto the surfaces with both hands as he tried to keep pressure off his injured leg. The cave echoed with their passing and bounced the sound of the crashing waves up into the high chasm above them, reverberating and increasing the sound of what had started as being very calming, now only sinister in its intent.

Eventually they reached the edge of the gap in the rocks. Sam could see the waves dash the sharp edges to either side, white spume and cold blue water flooding and spraying into the space and filling it more with every second. Only a few metres of free air now remained between the top of the gap and the cold water below, and Sam stopped. Babu, with one last glance behind him, jumped through the gap and disappeared to the other side, leaving an empty space that used to be occupied by him. But not for long. His head bobbed through the gap again after a few short seconds. "Come, Sam. Now! There is a ledge this side which will take us safely. But you must leave, NOW!"

Sam crept the last few steps down to the very edge of chaos. The sound of the waves and the crashing, pounding water causing him to take extra care in making sure all fingers were firmly gripping something solid. He did not want to finish up falling into that maelstrom below as he was quite sure that, dream or no, it would not end pleasantly. Grabbing an outcrop of rock just outside the edge of the gap, he pulled himself bodily through the opening until he popped out the other side and at last stood, legs quivering, looking at the sea beyond and, at last, a shingled beach off to his right.

Sam didn't notice at first that the mist had now receded such that he had a better appreciation of where he was. Off in the middle distance and to the right, the shingle beach stretched away to a tree-line which kissed the sea before disappearing behind a rocky outcropping. To the left and immediately beyond the gap he had just exited, Sam was able to gaze up at the large rock face and noticed a waterfall cascading over the lip of the cliff face, high up above them, the water plummeting down before slamming into the rocks at the foreshore.

It took some time before he noticed a familiarness to the cliffs. "I've been here before," he said, looking to Babu. "Up at the top there, is the village of Baradin and that large lake…" His thoughts trailed away as he remembered what had happened when he was last here. "Were there any survivors?" he asked quietly.

Babu remained quiet, looking out towards the shingle, scanning the area as before. Almost as if he wasn't listening. Almost. "Not many," was the simple response in his mind. Babu's shoulder blades were sunken into his flanks, tension evident in the way he stood. There was something there, Sam sensed. Something thought yet hidden from him that Babu was not yet ready to express, but something tangible and relating to Sam in some strange way. Babu cast a quick glance back towards him and moved on, down towards the shingles, for once, his voice still and his back firmly towards Sam.

They walked carefully down across the scattered rocks and boulders, mindful of any of them becoming loose under foot, occasionally having to evade the odd rouge wave as it crashed against the rocks near them. As they walked, Sam's thoughts turned to his predicament. *How did I land up here and where on earth is* here *anyway?*

"This is not *earth* as you know it," came the surprising thought back to him. "You are here because you must be here. You are here because we are here. You are here because you are *The One,* chosen by the Ethereals. And yet, I am at a loss as to why you remain!"

Babu continued stepping over the boulders until he reached the shingle beach beyond, where he sat down and started preening himself, all the while ensuring that eye contact was avoided…

He continued, exhaling loudly. "But we are Babu. We are assigned and joined with you and as such, we walk where we must, without question. Trusting and waiting, always waiting for our destiny to be realised. We yearn for the time that was and the time yet to come, but," and with that, Babu turned to face Sam, as if at last resigned to ask what had been causing his distress. "But we fail to see right now where *The One* ends and *Sam of the Shades* begins! This mystery is beyond us."

Sam, having just evaded one near disaster, was certainly not ready to have this other one hit him so forcefully and he responded in kind. " Babu, I have no idea what you are on about. You surely cannot suggest that the bloody earthquake had anything whatsoever to do with me!" As was rapidly becoming the norm to him in this weird place, he felt that everyone, including Babu now, was somehow expecting him to perform miracles in a place he knew nothing about, had never intended on visiting, and, more importantly, was, after all, just a bloody dream!

"You and we are one," cut across his thoughts.

"So you keep reminding me!"

"Maunga-Atua and you are one also!"

Sam was completely lost in where this *conversation* was going. "Who the bloody hell is Munga toa?" he shouted.

"Not who," Babu replied, "what." And he looked out over the sea as he continued. "This place you see as just a dream world," prompting Sam to look out over the ocean, "is our world. Maunga-Atua, *the mountain of the gods,* it exists as much as you do standing there. And, as Ngaire and Ma-aka and Pania, and Pip and all the others you have been in contact with, from when you arrived, through to when you can remember, and up till now, have all been telling you the same thing. You, Sam, are not here by some random chance. You are not here through some fanciful imagination concocting this place. No. You are here because you were chosen. The only one in all worlds and dimensions, in all times and perceptions, chosen, searched for, found, and brought here, for one purpose and one purpose only. To stop that which will destroy all. Sam, you and this place are as closely linked as you and us are. And one day, we hope and yearn, you will remember again, and Lord Elim will rue the day he ever thought to destroy you and stop the Anahim from pursuing freedom."

Sam looked across at this strange creature in front of him. The same one who had scared the bejesus out of him when he first remembered this weird place. The same who came to his rescue when he was surrounded by those marauders in the tent. The same, he recalled, who somehow, managed to extricate an arrow from his chest and patch him up. *The same*, Sam thought to himself, *who I have treated like absolute dirt for no reason other than he scares me and yet, he remains by my side. Whether by choice or by will, he is here, with me and I have somehow caused him great hurt. Great! Again with the stuff up, Sam.*

Before he could continue further with this self-deprecia-tion, Babu cut across him. "Sam, we are here not by instruc-tion. We are here because, like so many, we see and we believe. We believe in you, Sam, and whilst we are unsure what happened when you tackled The Nameless One, you remain intrinsically you and, for that, we stay by your side. We are unlike all other Padme in that we can exist with-out melding with an individual, but with you, we chose to. Sam, we *chose* to. To be with you, through all weather. We chose you, as the Anahim chose you too."

Sam knew, without doubt, at some deep level, that pure truth, and more, had been spoken. Babu, despite his creepy looks and googly eyes and talons that could rip the face off anyone, belonged to him. *No! Not* to *him*, he corrected him-self, with *him. Willingly. Constantly. To the end, whatever that might mean.*

Sam turned away. It reminded him too much of David and he feared he was not ready or able to open up to anyone or anything again right now. The real fear, he knew, was that if he opened up to another, how would he cope if he had to lose that which was closest to his heart once more. *How can you compare bloody* Babu *with David?* he rebuked himself. But he knew that truth had been uttered and this time, from his heart. For some inexplicable reason, he, Sam, felt a complete and utterly unexpected "Oneness" with this strange creature, and it soothed his heart.

"Why do you keep calling yourself, *We*?" he asked Babu, trying to move away from the mix of emotions coursing through his mind.

"Is an egg one, or three?" Babu challenged. "Is the shell more important than the yolk? Or the yolk more important than the egg white?" Sam wondered where this was going. "All coexist together," Babu continued. "None bigger than the other. All needing each other and yet it is called a singular, an *egg*. In a similar way, and this is difficult to explain easily, *we* are not just *shell* or *yolk*. What you perceive us to be here, this creature walking on the beach, is like the shell. When we communicate with you, we do not need the shell to be able to do so and indeed, being able to talk to you even if we were in the farthest reaches of the mountains of Kairaki, the *sky eater* and you were in the depths of the mighty Moana, the *mother ocean,* this shell would have no part in us being together in mind. This is like the yolk. And then there is the last, the *egg white* if you will. Sam, we don't just communicate in words and thoughts. We don't just physically walk side by side, we also are One. Do you know what I mean? You can already *sense* when I am in danger, in the same way I knew I needed to come to your aid when that coward, Napayshni of the Bjarke, attacked you in Ōmakere. You did not call, but I came. Being *One,* sometimes, even communication is not enough. The *egg white.* We all exist together. A family. Independent and inter dependant at the same time. We. But we are called a singular, Babu."

Sam laughed inwardly at the simplicity and the sheer enormity of what he had just heard. It somehow gelled with him as nothing else in his life had done before. "I think I know what you mean," he said. "I somehow *know* without knowing. And *that,* my dear friend, Babu, is as deep as I am prepared to go right now!" Sam found himself grinning as he looked at Babu who, with one shake of his tail, blinked knowingly and reassuringly at Sam and turned away again to continue their journey.

"What happened?" Sam asked as he limped along the beach, pointing up towards the top of the cliff face. "How did I finish up at the bottom of that hole and what happened to Baradin?" he grimaced as he thought of little Pit and his father, Niko. Were they alright? Safe?

"As you will come to realise," Babu replied, "Maunga-Atua is being hit on a number of levels by The Nameless One. The Nephilim, under Lord Elim, have driven their disease throughout the world to bring destruction against the Ethereals.

"Until recently, this was usually against their people, as you have already witnessed, and before that, when you were powerful, they also attacked the very fabric of this place and the universe around it. You started to stop this advance before you were lost to the mist." Babu looked again at Sam as he said this and Sam had no response to give. How could he when he had no recollection of anything that was supposed to have happened prior to when he was first aware of this place? Dream world though it was. Babu continued.

"It would appear that he has decided to attack the fabric once more, and the earthquake you experienced may well be only the start of his next chapter. You ran off when the first quake hit Baradin and then you disappeared into the large hole that had opened up in front of you. Luckily you didn't see it and so you were relaxed as you fell, but you still hit your head on the way down. We were lucky to find you alive!"

"And what of Pit, and Niko and the people of Baradin?" Sam asked. "Did any of them survive?"

"Of that, I do not know," Babu replied. "Many dead, no doubt. Many more injured. The fishermen all disappeared and they are lost. As for the village, Baradin is a shell. There is great hurt there as in all places where the Nephilim are allowed to direct the Bjarke." Again, Sam sensed that Babu was not saying what he was feeling, but he didn't press him further. He wanted to get up to the village and see if he could help in some way. See if Pit was still alive.

Sam noticed now that the beach line ran back into an inlet, partly protected from the waves by a large sand bank, although this had been destroyed by the recent earthquake. And torn trees and huge boulders now lay haphazardly around, having been hurled from the top of the cliff above to smash into the ground around them. Sam noticed a few boats were in the inlet. Some overturned, others, strewn around the rocks and smashed to smithereens, timbers and spars mixed with torn sails and rigging and stillness greeted them as they approached.

"Be careful," Babu warned. "We do not know what has happened in these parts. We sense much here, none of which is comforting! We are in a bad place."

Passing the first few boats which had been hurled up onto the beach, Sam saw a few fishermen standing around a still form lying on the shingle. They were all swarthy and bearded and were lost in their silence and concentration as they gazed down at the form. As they approached, Sam saw that it was of a man. Face down. Still. Dressed like one of the fishermen. Blood oozed and caked around his head and his neck was bent backwards in an unnatural position, broken beyond repair.

One of the men noticed them drawing near and beckoned to the others, who looked up to see who was approaching. Babu's scales along the ridge of his back suddenly extended and his tongue darted out, tasting the air.

One of the men on seeing Sam shouted out a warning. "Do not come any closer, Death Walker. Go and climb back into whatever hole you came from and leave us here to grieve for our comrade and brother. Come no closer so you do not see what you could have prevented."

Sam heard exactly what the men meant him to!

"I do not understand," he shouted in exasperation. "This has absolutely nothing to do with me."

"This has *everything* to do with you!" shouted one. "You, the so called 'Wielder', wielded nothing to stop this quake. Nothing to stop the loss of life of our brother, Banner lying here."

"And nothing..." shouted another, bending down to pick up a broken spar, "to stop Ōmakere and Baradin from being attacked and our children, mothers, wives, fathers, brothers being slaughtered, all for standing up for YOU! Arana, my father, would still be alive had you done what you said you were here to do." And with that, first one, then a number of the men turned and started running towards Sam, spars, oars now held as clubs, raised in anger. Men in rage ran towards Sam with blood on their minds.

"Run!" screamed Babu and Sam saw that he had already tensed, his talons gripping the beach and his back leg muscles flexing, ready to spring at the first attacker who ventured nearer. But in that brief bubble of the moment when neither fight not flee registered with him, Sam did what most would do in the circumstance thinking their lives were about to come to a sticky end; he cowered down into himself, his arms reaching up to protect his head in defence, and his fingers found each other and interlocked...

A blinding flash of light exploded out and away from the tips of his fingers, hurtling outwards, picking up his would-be attackers and bodily throwing them every which way, their screams of rage and anger quickly overtaken by shock and terror as they briefly flew through the air until they were slammed into the rocks, their bodies impacting with wet, sickening crunches. And then their screaming stopped. Forever!

Sam, his eyes still tightly shut in terror expecting the first blow to land on him for one of the vicious looking oars, wondered what had happened and he slowly opened his eyes to see why the men's cries had all been snuffed out. Around him stood not one of them. Instead he saw their twisted bodies tangled in amongst the rocks in various poses. None of them moving! He slowly got to his feet, gazing all around him in terror and fright. "What the...?" he said, with total confusion. "What just happened? Babu...? Babu?" Sam looked around him now, searching for Babu, the slow fear that he too might have finished in amongst the rocks filtering into his mind. But of Babu, there was no sign.

Sam walked over to the men to see if he could help them. First one, then the next, always looking out for Babu. But the men were far from saving. Sightless eyes and broken limbs were all that remained of the fishermen.

Sam bent over, gripping the nearest rocks, and threw up, his stomach retching at the sight that greeted him. He had to leave this place and seek help so, with eyes scanning everywhere for his Padme, he staggered out from the rocks and towards the distant tree line and hopefully, to help.

The smoking remains of a village greeted him with its stench as he finally emerged from the end of the tree line. Silence hanging over it like a blanket. Despite his emotional overload, he recognised the place immediately. Rudhjanda was a film set after all the explosions had gone off! The mist that was normally present was nowhere to be found. This, he put away for consideration at a later stage but, for now, he just stood and looked out over a world of calamity. Burnt trusses, steaming grasses that had been used for roofing, and twisted posts, stood like jagged sculptures in the landscape. Small tendrils of smoke still meandered amongst all the brokenness, wrapping the components into one scene of terror and despair. "Yes, I recognise this place," he concluded. Distractedly, he rubbed his chest as if to feel for the barb from the arrow which had been fired at him from the bridge he observed across the dry river bed in front of him. A crack brought him back to attention and he quickly ducked, scanning to see if the same marauders as before were still there, but they appeared to have long since left this place. Only the noise of the slow settling of the roofs and walls as they succumbed to gravity and fell to the ground rumbled now and then through what was left of Rudhjanda. Over the whole village, like a sickening flag, the stench of the dead and dying pervaded his senses. He saw the bodies of the villagers, struck down as they worked in peace, now silent, bent and burnt. Arms outstretched in a final plea as if frozen in time. The words of the villagers coming back now to haunt him.

"Sam, help me."

"Sam, if you had been here…"

"Sam."

"Sam."

"Wake up!"

Channel 5 News

"Wake up!"

Sam felt hands on him, shaking him roughly. The jolt made him jump with a start, immediately assuming that the marauders had come back to get him and had sneaked up without him being aware. "Don't kill me!" exploded from his lips in automatic defence.

"What?" came the response. "Mate, I am not going to kill you, just get you to stand up before you get swamped."

Sam opened his eyes in confusion. Where a second ago, smoke and destruction lay before him, now a wide expanse of beach and a tide too close for comfort assaulted his gaze. And a man leaning over him trying to get his attention.

"You need to move away, mate," the man was saying. "Lucky I saw you asleep against the wall. If I hadn't walked along here, the sea would have woken you up very shortly." Sam looked groggily out from his vantage point and saw that indeed, the waves were crashing very close to where he sat so he pushed himself up quickly. His back went into spasm and he realised he must have been sleeping there for some time, for not only had the tide come in, but it was nearly dusk and the sun was low over the horizon.

Sandhaven greeted his weary eyes once more. He looked

across at the man and grunted his thanks, then stumbled up and walked back down the boardwalk towards the town.

His back refused to ease up and he sensed he had pulled something whilst sleeping there. *Boy!* he thought. *I will need to see someone if my dreams continue to be so vivid!* Looking at his watch, he noticed that it was already gone 7pm. The evening crowds were piling into the various seaside restaurants and amusement arcades and a few were enjoying their early evening jogs along the Esplanade. A dog or two running alongside them, barking occasionally at this new piece of entertainment, tails wagging and tongues hanging out as they disappeared off into the sunset. Sam, in a brief second of pure vision, experienced such a sense of peace, that he had to stop to savour it. He realised that here, of all places, no one was expecting anything of him. No one was telling him to do anything or go anywhere or *be* anyone. He was an island in a sea of people, and they just didn't care. He loved the feeling of not having to explain his actions or his dress sense. He could just be himself and the people around him would not bat an eye lid.

With a new found spring in his step, Sam moved off from the boardwalk and walked towards the lights of Sandhaven, the last rays of the sun casting beams onto the fronds of the palm trees over him. In the process, they also washed the terrors of his dream into a mist of obscurity.

He enjoyed the anonymity of being able to walk along the pavement without being stopped and he was able to look around him without fear. A few kiosks were selling donner kebabs or burgers, attracting the odd couple or two, but, for now, Sam was not hungry. He just wanted to wander and not have to think or take any responsibility for a moment.

Sam slowly became aware that his fingers were tingling and that they had been flexing ever since he was woken.

Looking down at them, he was shocked to see that they appeared to be blue and the tips seemed to glow with a deep cobalt intensity. "What on earth?" he began, bringing his hands quickly up towards his eyes to look more closely. Nothing! No blue fingers and no glowing digits, instead, a very real tingling as if they had been cramped and the blood was now slowly bringing life back to his extremities. *Weird?* he thought. He flexed his fingers experimentally and they did indeed feel as if cramp had set in, but slowly the sensation eased and he eventually dropped them to his side, aware that his breathing, for some reason, had increased in tempo. Parts of his dream filtered then into his mind and he looked again at his hands, remembering how he had cowered as the fishermen ran towards him with rage in their eyes. How his arms came up over his head and, "Yes, they did. They interlocked and then..."

Sam slowly, secretively, brought his hands together and, making sure no one was watching, interlocked them again.

Nothing! No bolt of lightning. No death and destruction... *Sam. You are a bloody idiot, aren't you?* he cajoled himself, quickly unlocking his fingers and swinging them instead vigorously from side to side to get some feeling back. He was ashamed that he even thought to believe anything could actually have happened. Annoyed, he decided to head to the nearest chippy and grab a burger, chips and large soda, with loads of tommy sauce.

"What now?" he said to himself. Here he was, in a town of "nowheresville", fed up and bored and wondering what to do with himself. The number 12X bus grumbled softly in front of him, parked by the bus stop, waiting to depart. As if given a sign, Sam decided there and then to jump on board. The bus, he knew, would take him slowly back out of Sandhaven, through the windy lanes snaking between mile after mile of farmland, and back towards

Greyshott and home, there, perhaps, to sneak back into bed and face the music he was sure to have to endure in the morning.

Bus journeys often seem to be great opportunities for the mind to meander in and out of consciousness. Sam found himself thinking about his last few days, how his parents would probably flip at his absence, how he had actually enjoyed being by himself for a while. He also flitted between his reality and the dreams he had been experiencing recently. That worried him slightly underneath the surface, but, as is often the case, the natural foil between a dream world and reality was sufficient for him not to allow panic to enter. After all, seeing all those people killed, hearing the stories of Ngaire and Ma-aka, starting to enjoy the company of Babu, of people he had met, Pania, Pit, all flowed through him, some with a smile, others with a shudder. He found himself missing them, which was weird in itself.

The signpost marking Greyshott 3 miles away flicked another switch in his mind and he recalled the link between the dream world and Alice of all people. *I mean, Alice! Seriously?* he questioned himself, laughing at the unusualness of it all. *About as realistic as mum and dad welcoming me with open arms!* he concluded.

By the time the bus trundled into Greyshott, darkness already covered the area and, looking at his watch, he saw it was 8:30pm. The town was empty of life other than around The Governor's Arms, the local pub, which never seemed to close… He got off outside Timber's, surprised to see the lights still on inside at this hour.

Whether it was random impulse or something else speaking to him, Sam, standing outside looking into the café, suddenly decided to confront Alice about his strange experiences. So he pulled his hoodie tight against his body, rearranged his back pack and slowly pushed open the door.

As Sam was later to rebuke himself, having a plan *before* an action is normally recommended!

He stood now, inside the threshold of the café knowing it was officially closed and not open for service and therefore, as it was not open, anyone could quite rightly question him about what possible reason he could have had for being there. And, to add insult to injury, he then realised that the *reason* he appeared to have entered Timber's was to ask some random woman why she was in his dreams and whether she really was the bravest and fairest of the Anahim, called Aronui?

Brilliant plan, Sam! and he started to turn to head back out onto the street. But it was too late.

"Sam?"

Sam turned back to see Alice standing in the doorway to the kitchen, the light beyond illuminating her head with a halo...

Bloody get a grip! he screamed internally.

"Alice! Um, hi... Are you well?" (*Oh, I am so going to die!*)

Alice stood silently by the opening, studying him for a moment. The irises of her eyes flashing purple briefly before she blinked and offered him a bar stool to sit on. "Sam, the café is shut, my dear," she said gently. "Is everything OK?"

Sam moved to the stool as Alice moved behind the counter to click on the coffee machine. Her movements were unhurried, fluid, as if choreographed prior to his entering the café.

Sam, with no idea how he was going to extricate himself from this particular hole he had made for himself, blurted out the first thing that came to mind. "My parents and I have had a bit of a fall out, that's all."

Silence...

"So I have come out for a walk to get some fresh air."

Alice tinkered with the coffee filter.

She said nothing.

"Do you normally get some fresh air by travelling on a bus from the opposite direction, Sam?" she asked.

(*How on earth had she seen that?*) "Um, I have been out for a while and went to Sandhaven. Just got back!" (*There. That was, at least, honest.*)

"Would you like a drink?"

"That would be nice, if you are having one."

"What?..."

"What, what?..."

"What drink would you like?" A faint smile played on her lips for a moment.

"Coffee please. Milk no sugar."

Sam was fidgeting as if his body was screaming to leg it out of there and never return.

Alice flicked on the television screen, the grainy image slowly gaining focus and the noise level lifting his head to see what was on. Channel 5 news was playing. A weather girl was droning on about a deep weather front coming up from the south, bringing torrential rains and driving winds. A few choice shots of broken trees and posts flapping in the wind were set behind her to add to the effect. Alice turned the sound down and then settled opposite him. He was acutely aware of her eyes studying him and her fingers toying with her neck.

"Were you busy today?" he offered, trying to break the spell she seemed to be putting him in.

Alice ignored him. "Tell me what's going on, Sam," she said instead.

As if a tiny crack had formed, insignificant in itself and yet sufficient enough to break a damn wall, Sam found this simple invitation and her honest face hard to resist and he found himself unable to stop the outpouring of his heart to her despite not really knowing her at all.

Slowly at first but with increasing velocity, Sam lost who he was and just emptied himself of all the hurt, frustration and rage of the last few months at her feet. The loss of David, the feeling of rejection and, somehow, of blame, he sensed from his parents. All the pain flowed out and away from him and was held. Held gently by the person who sat opposite him, listening to *him*, for once.

The coffee cups were left where Alice had placed them. Neither of them touched a drop, too important was this space Sam found himself in. His story ranged far and wide, sometimes making complete sense to him, sometimes sounding, to him, like the ramblings of an utter fool.

The night grew sterner outside as the weather front started to make its presence felt here in the village as the weather girl had predicted. The branches of the nearby tree started to bend and creak, the outer tendrils brushing against the plate glass window of the café, causing Sam to slowly falter and then to stop what he was saying and look up to gauge what affect, if any, his diatribe had had on Alice.

Her eyes were incandescent purple! Flecks of red and violet seemed to move over her eyes like insects chasing each other, and her teeth were gripping her lower lip tightly. But the greatest surprise for Sam was to see this *stranger* opposite him, tears coursing down her smooth cheeks, unashamedly weeping for him. Alice took a deep breath and then sat up and blinked a few times, looking away as she wiped the tears from her face. When she returned her gaze, the vivid eyes had returned to deep blue, all signs of *otherness,* a mere memory.

"Well, Sam," she said eventually after they had both regained some semblance of order, "it would appear that I came just in time after all."

Sam, who, moments before, had unburdened himself and opened up that chest buried so deep inside him, he felt it would never be opened again, was hit by this random statement from Alice. *Is she allowing me to ask that which I am too afraid to utter, even though it is totally preposterous and stupid in the extreme?* he thought.

"Perhaps if I had not opened the café when I did, and instead went elsewhere, you and I would never have met and you would not have been able to unburden yourself so bravely as you have just done. For that, Sam Gilbert, I am incredibly humbled and thankful."

"I dreamt you were an angel!" he said weakly, not daring to look up.

"Did you indeed?" Alice replied. Her face wrinkled up slightly in curiosity. "Well, we can't discuss that now," she continued. "Let me warm the coffee back up and then you need to get yourself back home and be yourself to your parents."

Alice busied herself quickly, rearranging the glass coffee decanter, and then went off to fetch the milk from the fridge. Sam looked back up at the television. A western was now playing and the sounds of the horses thundering down the wide open prairie, and the warming colours that massaged his eyes, slowly all collided into a warm fuzziness and his head folded slowly forward until it nestled into his arms on the counter top and sleep took him far far away, if only for a while.

As such, as before, he failed to see Alice come out from the larder, see him sleeping on the bar stool and then, softly placing the milk on the work surface, come around the counter and stand behind him. She looked carefully behind her, peering out through the window to see if anyone was around, then, looking back at him, she lifted her hand and, outstretched, she held it hovering over Sam's head, her eyes closed and her lips moving quickly in silent incantation.

Pania

Sam snapped awake, feeling a fine spray mist his arms, which he had been previously using as a pillow. Without doubt, a raging torrent seemed to be right next to his ears and he opened his eyes to see a large, wet rock before him where before, the smooth, slick surface of the counter should have been. He sat up and gazed with astonishment at the sight in front of him. A raging river flew past his eyes, the waters spraying and cascading with speed a few paces in front of him. He was in a bed of rocks all lining the banks on one side, the water flowing around and over them and spraying up in the process. The noise was deafening.

"Dreaming again, Sam," he said to himself, once he regained some sense of order. Looking up and around him, he saw that downstream, a short distance away, the river seemed to lunge up into a mighty wall of spray before it disappeared from view, crashing down what was probably a waterfall. Upstream, the river bounced between rocks, broken trees and steep banks on its way to join its brother downstream to leap into the unknown and on past the waterfall.

In front of him, he noticed a number of boulders in amongst the middle of the river. Nets seemed to be stretched between them, all held from disappearing into the maelstrom downstream, by three men, who were staring at him as if he was a demon from the pits of hell!

Sam fixed his eyes on them, shocked at seeing people fishing and, supposedly, in one of the most dangerous places possible. At their feet, an otter and what looked like a snake dived or slithered off the rocks and started to circle the men. A strange looking bird also loosed itself from the area and flapped up into the air, hovering over them in protective fashion. The men, having seen this apparition appear before them as if by magic, cast all experience to the winds and dropped the nets, which, in a few seconds, dislodged themselves and tumbled in a ragged, fish-filled mess off down the river to bubble over the edge of the falls and disappear from view. The men paid no notice that their hard-won catch was now consigned to fate; instead, one of the men drew an evil looking spear from the rocks and crouched down ready to attack if required. The other, after looking at Sam for a few frightened seconds, lifted a horn to his lips and blew a long, loud note.

A deep, powerful noise erupted and Sam was aware enough to realise he had made a call for help from somewhere else. The third man, with bird in tow, had already turned and was now fording his way carefully back across the river to the opposite bank, glancing over his shoulder in terror, fear etched in his face as he fully expected this being, who had appeared magically before them, to grab him and confine him to his worst nightmare.

Sam remained completely still. The look from the one holding the spear made it quite plain that were he to hurl the spear towards Sam, it would not end well for him, and, having already experienced the pain of one shaft, he was not ready to receive yet another and bigger looking one rip through his body.

By now, the third man had reached the shore opposite and had run, screaming, into the tree line beyond, disappearing from view in amongst the branches and the mist, which hung like a wet blanket around them. But not for long, for shortly, a commotion beyond attracted their attention and, like bubbles of molten lava appearing from out of the ooze, a line of men all started to push through the tree line along the length of the river until they stood in a haphazard line from the edge of the waterfall and all along the bank up to the mist bank further upstream, all standing silently, yet with deadly intent, staring at the lone figure who had mysteriously appeared to their friends a few short minutes earlier.

"Bloody hell!" exclaimed Sam, wondering what sort of dream this one was going to turn out to be. It did not appear to be heading in any direction he would care for it to go right now. A mini stand-off had occurred and he was not sure what to do next.

"Saaaaaammmmmm!"

Off on the opposite bank, he was sure he had heard his name called, but that was ridiculous.

"Sam!" Again, his name. He looked along the line of men, wondering where the noise was coming from. His day suddenly improved totally, when, looking at one of the men, he saw the arms waving, and the form jumping to get his attention, of the one person he was genuinely happy to meet in any dream.

"Ma-aka! Ma-aka!" he shouted with joy, for there, was the same person who had spent time opening up to him about their past in the hut of Ngaire, the healer. It was the same. Ma-aka, the leader of the tribe of Watamka. *And could it be*, he thought, *that these are the very rivers where he told me about the loss of his father, Ari?*

From the other side, Ma-aka whistled shrilly into the air, and a large bird flew out from the trees and headed straight for Sam. Ma-aka's Padme, the eagle, flew over Sam, searching around it for any danger and, on satisfying itself, it landed in front of him screeching back to Ma-aka. For a brief second, Sam wanted to reach out and hug it, such was his joy at being *rescued,* but one blink of the eagle's black eyes at Sam was enough to warn him that looking was fine, touching was definitely NOT.

Seeing the eagle sitting there, prompted Sam to think of his own Padme. *Babu!* he remembered with shock. The last time he has seen him was when something had happened to those fishermen and Babu disappeared. He thought he had been killed in whatever had caused the destruction of the men, but… *Perhaps!?* Sam reached up slowly to touch his neck. The comforting feel of the necklace was like balm to his mind. Reaching down, he found the familiar charm he had used to call Babu, and, in a moment, he had lifted it to his lips, and blew.

For a moment, there was no change around him. Sam peered intently all around him. The eagle, he noticed, had lifted its head and was looking with concentration past Sam and into the forest beyond, its crest feathers lifting in anticipation. Then, the slight, distant sound of branches and undergrowth crashing behind him, growing louder.

Sam turned.

Something was heading towards him with speed. He did not want to hope, but, he sensed his smile forming and his eyes glistening against despair. And then, Babu, sleek, incredibly fast, and very alive, burst out from the forest and skidded to a stop right in front of Sam.

"Babu!" Sam cried. "You are safe." And without thinking, he bent down and grabbed Babu around the midriff and picked him up to hug him.

For a while, Sam was lost in the furry scales of Babu, sensing the breath within his body. "I thought you had been killed," Sam eventually said to Babu in his mind.

"Not this time," came the response. "But perhaps next time we meet an enemy, you should control your hands!" And Babu leant away from Sam and peered eye to eye at him, blinking a familiar welcome and humour.

Babu untangled himself from Sam and dropped down to the ground, heading towards the eagle. They touched noses and rubbed their faces together in old greeting. Babu then turned and told Sam that they needed to walk upstream where a bridge stood, so they could cross over the mighty river and at long last, meet up with Ma-aka and his people. "I am sure that *someone* will be very pleased to see you again," said Babu, mysteriously. The eagle jumped up into the air then and headed upstream. Babu turned also and walked on, looking back to prompt Sam to follow. The men on the opposite shore had already dispersed into the forests. All except one! Ma-aka, a grin wider than his face, was climbing and crawling up the shore line, matching Sam's party, no doubt making sure his friend was safe and didn't decide to disappear on them yet again.

After navigating along the river bank, climbing over rocks and broken branches, they spied a rickety wood and rope bridge slung across the raging torrent. It appeared to have been built before civilisation had arrived and Sam was not sure it had any purpose still standing, let alone being capable of carrying anyone. The eagle flew back over the river and finished up floating down to sit on Ma-aka's shoulder who now stood at the opposite side of the bridge. "Come on over, Sam," he cried. "It is quite safe." That didn't encourage Sam one bit, but, he climbed the last few rocks and boulders until he stood on the beginning of the bridge, his hands clinging tightly to the rope hand holds, wet with ancient spray and water.

Babu skipped across without a care, arriving safely on the

other side where he joined Ma-aka, sitting down by his side. Sam was sure he was daring him to *man up!*

"Right then," he said to himself. "In for a penny and all that." And Sam took his first step onto the rotten looking planks, taking him over hell's cauldron, the waters just waiting to get him and throw him over the waterfall with delight!

The bridge creaked and waved like an old banshee but Sam managed to make his way over, not daring to look down at the turbulent waters within arm's length of his shoes. He kept his eyes firmly on the party waiting for him on the opposite shore until finally he reached the other side to a bear-hug welcome from Ma-aka.

The next few minutes were lost in both trying to speak and ask questions and discuss what had happened recently, until Ma-aka lifted his hands to bring some silence to bear. "Sam," he said, "it makes my heart glad to see you again. You seem to have a habit of disappearing. Perhaps this time, for a while at least, you will deign to stay here and be welcomed. This," he said, extending his arm back along a path behind him, "is the village of my tribe. Welcome to Watamka, my home." And with that he turned back, a slight shrug telling his Padme to fly off its perch and scan the area around them, circling and swooping as they made their way through the forested area, mist around them, a clear, arrow-straight path behind them, and on towards his village.

The forest slowly started to thin out and Sam saw the beginnings of what appeared to be a strong, well-defended palisade of stout trunks, all tied together and acting as a protection for what lay beyond. As in the village of Rudhjanda, Watamka had a natural defensive river bed around it, however, here at least, the banks contained a river which flowed past its main gate. A wooden draw bridge had been lowered, affording access over it and, as Sam and Ma-aka slowly approached, some of the village folk started to gather around them, all without exception, looking at Sam in recognition and hope. A few hands reached out towards him as if to touch his clothing. Sam was not used to any form of attention like this, but, he remained respectful of his friend, Ma-aka as leader, and said nothing.

As they approached, the crowds started to hold back, allowing the bridge to be crossed by their leader and Sam first. Sam was impressed at the love these people seemed to have for Ma-aka as his face roamed the crowds around him, animals and birds of all sorts moving among the throng like a choreographed dance.

Sam looked up and across the bridge to see what lay beyond, but his eyes were stopped instantly from progressing by the person who stood, slight and petite, within the archway which announced the boundary of Watamka. A small girl, her hair in pigtails, which were shifting in the breeze, held the hand of a young woman, who was looking down at her charge with a smile, and, with one look up for reassurance, the girl let go of the woman's hand and started to run towards Sam, her arms rising up towards him as she picked up speed to dash towards him.

"Pania!" Sam shouted. And with a leap, he sprinted forward, closing the gap between the two of them in a few wonderful seconds. She leaped up at him and buried her face in his jacket, tears overcoming her in an instant. For Sam, he just twirled around and around, overjoyed that he had found her safe and well.

After a moment of pure bliss for Sam, he lowered her to the ground and looked up to follow Ma-aka's lead. He felt Pania slip her little hand into his, and for once, he did not try to release it, just looked down at her and gave her a deep, welcoming smile. Her grubby face, still lined with tears and messed up hair. For him, a perfect picture. Ma-aka held his arm outstretched towards the archway and said, "After you, Sam. My people are waiting for you." Sam could not have experienced a more welcoming fanfare had they been blowing trumpets from the ramparts! It seemed that everyone had come out that day to see this person who some had already known, others had already seen what he could do, and still others who had been told of his remarkable and magical powers and wanted to see this *man-myth* for themselves. Sam was blissfully unaware of all that the people knew. For now, he felt loved, welcome and alive and he disappeared into Watamka, the crowds following him in, hugging and discussing the phenomena that had entered their village.

Soon, quietness descended around the outside of the palisade wall. The animals of the forest went back to doing what they always did, the river continued to flow past the entranceway, and the gate lifted and was secured, once again, keeping Watamka safe from the dangers around it,

Peace settled over the area, for the moment.

Inside, peace certainly was not evident! A raucous, loud throng of villagers gathered around their leader and his guards, all straining to get a glimpse of Sam. Some of them calling out to him in familiar greeting, but they turned away in confusion when Sam looked at them briefly, continuing his gaze around the crowds, not recognising any of them. Already a few were buzzing, starting to question each other. "Is it really true then?" said one. "Does he really have no memory of this place?" said another. "What is to become of us if he is lost to us?" said a third.

They eventually got to the village square where the crowds moved out into the wider expanse, some climbing up onto higher vantage points, others opening windows and scaling walls to gain a better glimpse of this amazing event, to the consternation of some of the owners of the properties now being used as climbing walls.

Ma-aka and Sam, with Pania holding tightly to him, stopped at the fountain in the middle of the square and, as if by secret communication, the people started to settle down, the noise levels dying down and extending outward in concentric circles until even those furthest away had stopped their discussions to see what happened next.

Ma-aka climbed up onto the surrounding of the fountain and turned to face his people. "You have seen, and some of you have heard," he began, his voice booming into the furthest recesses of the village square. "You have all been party in one respect or another, to the man who stands here before you today," he pointed down to Sam, continuing. "This is Sam. This is 'The One', called from the Shades to rescue Maunga-Atua from 'He who will not be named'. You saw him in the past and beheld his deeds with wonder and amazement." Ma-aka paused, looking at Sam, then continued, with some seriousness. "And some of you were with me when we saw him pass into the Kairaki mountains, there to face Lord Elim, and, like me, you were lost in despair when he did not return. We feared he had been defeated and our hopes for freedom and for peace once more were cruelly dashed." Ma-aka looked down to the ground, trying to find words to explain what was heavy on his heart. "My people, Sam, who you see before you, entered into that den of despair and something happened that lost him to us." The crowds started to buzz again but Ma-aka held his arms out calling for silence. "Something happened whilst there, that caused Sam to lose himself." The crowds started talking again, this time ignoring the call to silence from Ma-aka, who had to increase his volume accordingly. "People! Sam was lost, but he is here again. It is our job to unlock that which has been buried away. He did not die when he met Lord Elim, and we know not what happened, but here he stands. Sam-of-the-Shades no longer, but 'The One'. He has returned and we must have faith that the Ethereals see what we cannot and that this battle has not ended. Sam has returned and we must rejoice, though we see not what can occur to allow him to once more wield the powers he had and may still have. We must have faith and we must have hope, for without either, we are lost. Sam is here, my people. He needs our help and he needs our friendship." Turning now to Sam, he continued. "Sam. I rejoice that you have returned. I believe in you and I believe in that which I cannot see. But overall, you are more than 'The One'. To me, to Pania, to Turi, who is forever lost to me, you have become, and always will be, our friend and our brother." And with that, Ma-aka pulled Sam up to stand alongside him and hugged him tightly, as the throng started to chant and dance around the two men, Pania looking up at them with shyness as the people around her patted her head in acceptance and love.

Sam was as happy as could be expected. Amongst all the throng and dancing, the acceptance and the love, he was grateful that at least this dream world allowed him to forget the loss of David, if only for a brief moment. He saw now how his mind had created this place, to enable him to heal and to provide a platform from which he could hopefully learn to forgive his parents, and David, for leaving him on his own.

The day lost itself in Sam being ushered from one crowd to the next, always with Pania in attendance, and being asked about his journeys so far, which in itself Sam found difficult to describe. He could sense that they wanted to ask him more questions, but, thankfully, before the questioning became too intense, he was grabbed by yet another group to enter into yet more questions. He had little knowledge of this *world* and often, places and towns were thrown into conversation by the crowds, and Sam could only look blankly at the people, hoping the question would move away to something else. Not for the first time, he gazed down at Pania, wishing they could just escape for a moment so they could catch up, and, Sam thought, to allow him to let her know that he was here for her, never to leave again.

As the fires started to light up around the square, a group of older people managed to sideline him off away from the crowds, and, turning their backs to Pania, which infuriated him, they gathered round him in silence for a moment, before one of them, urged by the others, ventured a direct question to him. "Sam," he began, "as the elders of this village, we share with the others, our joy at receiving you again into our home, and we trust you will feel welcome and one of us, for that is what you are," he continued, struggling to voice what he was being made to say by the rest. "However, we would like to know why it is you refuse to use those powers given to you by the Ethereal leaders now that you have returned? We would also like to know what you intend to do to stop the Bjarke rampaging through our sister villages, killing, maiming and destroying the innocent."

For a moment, Sam was stunned into silence, such was the sting in the questions posed to him. That, and the fact that these *strangers* had rudely blocked Pania from integrating, as if they were above inviting her into their fold, caused him to react in a somewhat foolish manner. "Actually," he began, bending down slightly, whilst at the same time, quickly glancing around as if to hide his intentions from others, "the powers have *not* disappeared!" He fixed the old man with a direct look, his face as straight as a poker. They all, without exception, bent in towards Sam to hear what they hoped was a vindication of their *wiseness.* "In fact, I have been trying to hold the power back for as long as possible so that any of the enemy who might have infiltrated themselves into this place…" The elders found themselves looking out and around as if, at any moment, one of the Bjarke chose to reveal themselves and pull out some mighty broadsword. Sam was enjoying this immensely! He continued, "…Might send the wrong message back to Lord Elim saying that my powers had indeed been destroyed. However, I can see that you have kept the faith over all the others and so, if you will permit me, I will show you, here, just a little taste of what is to come when we next meet that all-destroying Lord Elim." And with that, he proceeded to swirl and wave his hands around himself, all the while turning around like a spinning top, his voice starting a low chant and his eyes getting larger and larger as his hands and arms whirled themselves into a frenzy until, with dramatic pause, he shot out his hands towards them and said one word…

"Boo!"

The elders all flinched as they fully expected some bolt of lightning to explode from Sam's fingers. Instead, with arms covering their faces and heads, all they got, was the sound of Sam's high pitched laughter as he walked away, Pania's hand tight in his, his shoulders shaking with uncontrolled laughter and his back firmly to them.

"Now Pania," he said, "how about you and I go and find something to eat in this place and we can spend time together, just the two of us?"

Sam and Pania found a quiet spot at the top of a flight of stairs, in an alcove in the ramparts. *Presumably,* thought Sam, *for someone to stand and fire at a supposed enemy through the slits in the timber wall.* Both Babu and a small ferret clambered up to sit in the slit in the wall, preening themselves as their charges sat down in the dust below them. "Her name is Pugs," said Pania softly, looking at the ferret. "She has been with me now for the three months of my youth. She is very naughty at times!" This said with mock laughter. Sam smiled to see her feeling relaxed with the creature and could well imagine her stamping her little feet in annoyance when Pugs decided she did not want to be dressed in small clothing,or have to endure a bonnet on her head.

For a while, Sam and Pania talked about the excitement of the day, with Sam telling her how scared he was at crossing the rickety bridge and how happy he was when he saw her at the entrance to the village. Pania smiled shyly at this. She, in turn, told him how the news arrived at the village when the young man had come screaming in crying that a demon had appeared to them whilst they fished the mighty Manganui-a-te-Ao. How Ma-aka had assembled the men to follow the youth back to the river to see what had appeared to the frightened men on the river. "But I knew it was you," Pania said with young confidence. "I knew as soon as the man arrived, that you had returned. Ma-aka would not allow me to follow, so I stayed with Marika at the gate, waiting for you to arrive." Pania shuffled up and curled into Sam's side, his arm, naturally coming up to draw her closer to himself.

"Are you..." Pania said with a slight stutter, "are you here to stay now, Sam?" As oftentimes happens, the innocent questions of the youth have the most profound effect. Sam found himself struggling to form an answer that he felt she would be able to grasp, but he knew enough not to lie to the one person here who actually seemed to need him, just as he was.

"Pania," he began. "Do you know those times when you wake from a dream (*how ironic that someone in a dream can have a dream*), and you just can't remember what it was you were dreaming about, even though it seems it had just happened?" Pania nodded her head. "Well, for me, *everything* that occurred here when you first knew me is like that. Try as I might, I cannot remember anything, in fact, I am still getting used to all you people talking to me as if I grew up here." Pania smiled. "You all say that I was chosen and came here with great powers, but, Pania, if that is true, then I am afraid all I *had* is lost and I have no idea how to get it back. I am just like you in that sense. No different to these people here. Just me, Sam. Grateful that at least you want to be with me."

Sam looked up to stare out through the slit and into the misty fields below, which were rapidly being lost in the gathering darkness of night. He continued. "But, this I can promise you, Pania. You and I are closer than brother and sister." Sam had to swallow hard as he heard his own voice talking of things hard for him to recognise. "I had a brother once and I lost him, Pania." Sam knew his voice was choking up a bit, but he continued, Pania looking up at him with concern and love. "I lost him, Pania, to a cruel, evil, horrible thing that took him away from me when we still had everything to discover together. He is gone and I will never see him again." And looking down once more at the quiet form in his lap, he said. "I lost a brother once. I will not lose this, my sister, again." And he leant forward and kissed her softly on her head.

Pania just snuggled in tighter to Sam, the silence of the moment, stronger than any bond. Her final words before sleep overtook her, prophetic in the extreme. "We will just have to go and find your powers then." She yawned as she finished, saying, "If you lost them, we can find them again. Maybe Babu knows where you left them." And she fell asleep.

Pugs moved down off her perch and settled down, sitting in Pania's lap. Babu stayed where he was looking out to the world beyond, scanning, as always, for danger.

"Do you know?" Sam said to Babu.

"Have you forgotten how to breathe?" came the instant, cryptic response. Sam screwed up his eyes in confusion. "You breathe without thinking," Babu continued. "Just because you don't think about it, does not mean it is lost. Your body takes over, leaving your mind to concentrate on other things. Everything you were and everything you are, remains the same, Sam. Even the strength and power you had when you first came to Maunga-Atua. Lord Elim hasn't stolen it. You haven't been stripped of it either. It is a part of you as much as your hair is. What is missing is the means to retrieve it. *That* is the thing we need to find, and we, for once, are at a loss at the moment as to how we do that."

Sam stayed silent for a moment, contemplating. "If this is a dream, perhaps back at home, I need to unlock my acceptance of mum and dad as they are now, which may well then unlock my super powers here. Hah, imagine me, Sam, with a cape, spandex at the ready and the evil lord cowering in fear. Yeah, as IF!" Sam cast the idea aside as easy as a fly. Dreams were dreams and the quicker he moved on, the quicker he could also move on with other dreams.

He settled down, his eyes growing heavy, but not before Babu said one last thing. "What we need to unlock, is your lack of belief that we exist as surely as you do. You see and yet you do not believe, and yet *we* are asked to believe without seeing. We do, Sam. We always did."

Sam heard no more. His eyelids dropped and he fell into a restful sleep.

A low, constant thrumming entered into his consciousness. He thought at first that it was the throbbing of the fridge under the café counter, but he was not yet ready to wake up, instead preferring to relax in early morning drowsiness. Unusually though, it did feel particularly cold, which was strange seeing as he was inside. *Perhaps Alice had turned the heating off,* he thought, moving his head to another position, where it struck a cold, damp wooden post.

"Huh?" he exclaimed, opening his bleary eyes. Rather than the familiar surroundings of the café, he was greeted by the coldness of a timber post, strung to another and another as far as his eyes could see. The thrumming, if anything, was getting louder and he noticed that the dust around him was oscillating slightly at the vibrations being caused. *Where am I?* he thought.

"You are here," came the reply. "You slept, but now you must wake up. Great danger is coming!"

"Babu! What are you doing here?" Sam started to rouse himself from his cramped position.

"I live here!" Babu replied. "Wake up. Danger is at our door!" Babu scampered off to another corner, climbing up the wooden posts to get a better vantage point from which to study what was causing the vibrations from outside.

"You mean I am still here?" Sam said with confusion. "I fell asleep and woke up in the same place?" Now he was confused, and a little scared. For the first time, he had fallen asleep and NOT woken up back in his reality. "Well this is bloody novel!" he exclaimed to himself. He opened his eyes. Pania was still sleeping next to him, her tousled hair and arms folded over her face, showing she was still deep in sleep. Pugs, her ferret, was standing next to Babu, staring off into the mist beyond.

Sam got up and looked back into the village to see ordered chaos already occurring in the dim early morning light. A misty veil swam over the village square and here and there, flickering torches hurried between houses, voices at a low pitch, men and animals all moving around, assembling themselves into groups.

There was a commotion from the bottom of the steps and Ma-aka suddenly appeared, his eyes and face already streaked with dirt, a wicked looking spear held tightly in his hand.

"Sam!" he called. "I have found you. I thought at first you had disappeared again to the world you come from. I am relieved you have stayed. Come." Starting to rouse Pania, who was not ready to wake up, struggling and moaning under her breath to be left alone. "Pania. Wake up. You must leave this place and get to Marika. Quickly now, child. GO!" And with that, he pulled Pania up and ushered her off down the steps, her sleepy face starting to turn to one of fright as she looked back to Sam for reassurance.

"Pania, do what Ma-aka says," Sam said quickly. "We need to see what is going on. Go quickly and I will come and get you as soon as I am able."

Pania disappeared down the stairs, Pugs in close pursuit, and Ma-aka turned to Sam with eyes black as the night.

"Sam," he began, looking first at him and then through the slitted opening in front of them. "Get up quickly. If you have anything to offer us in this time of need, then we have no time for formalities. Use what you have and stand with us. If not, go with Pania and hide with Marika. We will defend this place to our best abilities."

"What are you on about?" replied Sam. "What can I offer and what on earth is going on?"

"Look for yourself." And with that, Ma-aka turned his gaze fully to what was happening outside.

Sam followed his gaze, trying to get the sleep out of his eyes. The thrumming and shaking had, by now, become much clearer, and voices, chanting and jeering were starting to make some sense in amongst the cacophony from without. What he saw, froze the blood in his veins as he recognised that, once again, his dream had taken a turn for the worst.

Outside, the early morning light was being filtered by the misty banks he was becoming accustomed to. Here and there, particularly around the space where the bridge was yesterday, and then disappearing off into the forest beyond, a clearer space was evident and Sam recognised that the mist bank had, as before, not reclaimed the space where he had walked earlier. *Strange!* flashed through his sub-consciousness. The throbbing and noises were coming from the forest beyond, but, now that he was concentrating, he realised that the noise was not coming from just one area, but seemed to encompass the entire stretch of his vision. A rhythmic pounding of what sounded like drums, reverberated through the trees and now, the unmistakeable sound of men's voices could be heard, chanting with a deep, dangerous, cadence. It was a chant that, without doubt, was bringing destruction to the village of Watamka.

"What is happening?" he asked Ma-aka, looking quickly to one side to observe what he was doing. "It would appear that the enemy has crept up to us under cover of night, and intends to attack," Ma-aka responded simply.

Sam gulped down a dryness and looked back into the mist bank.

At first, he saw nothing change. The mist shrouded the trees such that their form appeared only vaguely from the shelter of this veil. Soon, however, he started to see one, then another then another, then scores of flickering torches weave their way in between the trunks of the trees moving towards them. Darkened forms started to materialise at the base of the torches as they moved with singular intent from the shelter of the forest. Slowly, line upon line of forms resembling stick figures in the mist, their silhouettes forming cut-out shapes, stretched away as far as Sam could see. The mist moving around them like water in a river, the torches burning the air around them with wet spittle of flickering flames.

A large, dangerous looking army of men stood now in front of the walls of Watamka and the sounding of the deep battle drums reverberated in loud percussion, waking all around to witness what was to come next.

The Bjarke had finally come to Watamka, and death was on their hearts as surely as night followed day.

Sam sensed the hairs on his arms and neck rise in fear and his breathing rapidly increased. Babu was crouched on top of the palisade fencing, his tongue flicking in and out and the scales on his back, erect and stiff. His body was snaking in sinuous fashion as he attempted to look at the crowd in front of him from multiple viewpoints within his small frame. Ma-aka was crouched next to him, staring through the slit, his spear resting beside him, his arm flexing in readiness for whatever was to come.

With a final flourish, the drum sounds reached a crescendo and then stopped. With it, the voices and chanting of the men. Silence reigned all around, save the flickering, spluttering sound of the multitude of torches. Directly in front of the draw bridge, which was now firmly locked and retracted, a single form stepped out from the line of "stick figures" and made its way slowly forward, the arms held aloft. One holding a flickering torch, the other a mean looking double-headed axe.

"Watamka!" shouted the form, deep in tone and strength. "You see who is here before you. We are not here to talk, we are here to take and to destroy!" The men around raised a loud chant of glee at this, silenced shortly afterwards by the man. One of the villagers stood up from behind the walls of the ramparts and shot an arrow towards him. It flew harmlessly past and the crowd below laughed at the folly. "Word has reached our men that 'The One' cowers in your midst. Whether he is there or not makes no difference to us. Whether you stay protected behind this excuse for a wall like children hiding behind their mother's skirts, or you come and face us like the vermin you are, the outcome remains the same. You will not see another night and this village will follow all the others and be a burning heap before the sun hits the trees. We are the Bjarke and we take no prisoners. I am Otaktay, 'He who kills many', and I am here to feast on your blood. Flee while you can, little children, flee, flee, for here, you will find no mercy, only death. My men are hungry for revenge and the blood of Napayshni cries out to us for release. This day, he will be released. Open up your doors, for today, the Bjarke have come to visit." And with that, the man bent his arms back and uttered the loudest war cry Sam had ever heard. As one, the army before him, ran screaming towards the ramparts, their war cries and ululations rippling through the early mist.

The battle for Watamka had begun in earnest.

The men within the ramparts were not ready to give up without a fight. With a single command from Ma-aka, who stood up and waved his spear once, twice, to the ground, the men who had assembled along the battlement of the palisade walls stood up and, aiming down the sights of the arrows notched into their bows let loose a barrage of black, whistling death.

The satisfying thunk of arrow through flesh and the cries of some of the enemy caused the men to cheer, but only for a moment, as they saw that most of the horde below them, had swiftly lifted up their hide shields over their heads as the arrows came flying, which gave them protection from above.

For their part, the enemy looked well rehearsed to the casual eye. Whilst some of the men shot their own arrows snaking up and over the parapets, causing most to duck for protection, others, under the security of this storm, aimed their own at certain places along the wall, and let their arrows fly. Some were attached to sturdy rope, which, on the arrows embedding themselves into the wood, became links down to the army, allowing them to start to clamber up this quick link to gain access to the top ramparts. Others, were coated in bitumen and burned brightly as they flew towards other sections of the wall, in particular, the sturdy drawbridge and its surroundings. Here, as they sunk into the wood work, the fires and bitumen were flung onto the wood where some fires started to light up the vertical spars.

Loud cries of the men below encouraging others to continue were mingled with those less fortunate, who met their fate early that morning, falling to their faces with angry barbs protruding from their bodies. Still, the numbers of the men below were vast, and as one man fell here, another three came and took his place, all with one common goal; to bring this inconsequential village before them to rack and ruin, and to kill all who stood in their way.

Sam was aware of some of the Padme flying off their perches around the battlements, or flying out from the base of the village to run, full speed into the marauders in front of them. They brought swift justice to many who stood in their way. But some fell, and as they did, those to whom they were bound within the village walls, collapsed where they stood, death overcoming them in macabre fashion. "Be aware!" shouted Ma-aka. "Keep your Padme close for now. It makes no sense seeing them perish and you alongside them at this stage. Hold them." Suddenly, one, then another, then all the remaining Padme who had run into battle turned back to rejoin their kindred people, the men and women recalling their charges with mind melding efficiency. Babu remained close to Sam, concentrating his attention towards the leader of this pack of men, Otaktay. He stood to one side for now, observing his men create the right battle movements. Moving people here, commanding others to assist elsewhere. His main guard keeping a tight cordon around him, protecting their leader from any harm.

A ladder slammed into the wall near to where Sam stood. He was shocked that impending danger suddenly had appeared so tangibly close to him. Ma-aka, with one quick cry, ordered the men to attack the ladders, pushing a few off the walls, the ladders and the men climbing them, slamming into the ground below with sickening thuds. Still more ladders came to join the first, and soon, ladders, fires and ropes were criss-crossed over the structure of the palisades, fires burning fiercely now in many places and the cries of the exuberant were mixed with those of the weak and the dying, on both sides of the wooden barrier.

"Protect the Keep!" screamed Ma-aka to some of the men below. "Strengthen the Gatehouse and reinforce the drawbridge. Quickly men. The Bjarke are gaining."

"Sam," he said, turning to him, "If you can recall anything, do it now. Do it now or we are lost as Otaktay, that worm, predicted." Sam, for all that was exploding around him, felt like he was trying to react whilst stuck in a vat of glue. Every movement seemed to be taken in slow-motion and his arms and legs seemed to be moving in extreme sluggish fashion. He was at a complete loss as to what he was expected to do and he started to panic, as he had done at the bridge to Rudhjanda, fearing for that thin sounding "thunk" and yet another barb pushing out of his chest as he fell to the ground.

Sam made his way, with Ma-aka and Babu, down towards the village square. Ma-aka disappeared to a fire that was now raging out of control in one of the store houses within the walls of the palisade. Sam felt he had no choice other than to run towards the drawbridge, there to offer whatever help he could bring to the men who were sweating and swearing as they simultaneously tried to shoot at the enemy whilst dodging a few arrows that flew by and trying to extinguish the flames that were licking around the spars of the drawbridge with fierce determination.

"Babu," he summoned within himself, "if those men even appear to be gaining the upper hand, you go and do what you do best. You go and kill them and send every last one of them to hell for me!"

Babu, without a second glance, shot off towards the walls, sneaking through one of the arrow loops, his tail the last thing Sam saw, before he disappeared from view, his fate now in the lap of the gods, wherever they were camped out right now!

All around, Sam heard the cries of the men as they called and sent instructions to each other. The air was filled with the cawing and screeching of various birds of prey as they sought to bring assistance from the air, advising and moving their human partners to areas of weakness. He had no time now to be afraid. Instead, with grim determination, he stood side to side with the men and women of Watamka and waited for the drawbridge to collapse.

It was only a matter of time before the creaking in the wood became a constant din and finally, with a mighty crack, the central spar gave way and the rest of the drawbridge folded in on itself slowly, like a pack of cards. As soon as the opening had been forged, a brace of arrows flew into the opening, pinning a number of the villagers where they stood. Their shocked cries at being hit, quickly cut off as more black barbs followed the first wave, flying and sticking into the unfortunate men like pins in a cushion.

Those to either side, ducked behind the side walls of the gatehouse and peered out from time to time, sending their own arrows out through the opening, hoping to hit anything coming their way. Above them, other men were busy aiming through the arrow loops at the approaching horde sending arrow after arrow into the throng.

More than once, Sam heard one or the other scream at him to do something, anything, but Sam stayed mute, not able to summon any of the supposed powers he was supposed to have in this world. Even interlocking his fingers as he had done before, offered no spark of lightning. He felt useless in himself and instead, looked around to find a bow with which he could at least try to fend for himself and perhaps knock out a few of the Bjarke before they got too close.

Outside, the cheer at seeing the drawbridge crumble, echoed around the army and a new spearhead-formed echelon of men gathered together and started running in earnest towards the breach in the wall, their war cries loud in their chests and their axes and swords whirling over their heads as they advanced. As the men started to collect together into a large swarm, bloodied, dirty, crazy with blood lust, the constriction also created a concentrated zone into which the village men all started to aim and fire. For a while, it appeared as if the tide was being stemmed as man after man fell out of the swarm, pierced through with the shafts of quivering death, sent their way by the brave villagers. It was only a matter of time before sheer numbers started to outweigh the remaining arrow shafts available to the men around the opening, and the Spearhead moved ever closer to the river's edge and the now gaping entranceway.

Babu shot off, leaping and clearing the river in one bound, his eyes fixed on the leader's position now set behind the wedge of marauders stampeding towards the opening. His aim went straight through the tip of the *spear* and, as at Ōmakere, the furry of his passing terrified the men, who faltered as this blur shot into and through them like a red hot knife. Men fell where they stood and Babu disappeared into the throng, ripping, slashing and maiming as many as entered his field of vision, his principle aim, to get to the main group and kill Otaktay.

Suddenly, from behind them, Sam heard the cry of despair and fear as the marauders breached yet another area to the rear. Looking back, Sam saw the first of the men cresting the top of the palisade and gaining a strategic foothold on the battlements. Their arms swinging their axes and swords in a blur and their heavily muscular bodies, slick with sweat and blood.

Ahead, the main thrust of men swarmed over and past the disturbance, which was Babu. Sheer numbers overwhelmed the position even though more and more of the Padme darted off to enter the fray with Babu. They left their comrades to die or fight. For them, the prize lay ahead of them and they were eager to get their hands on it.

The remaining villagers started to retreat back towards the heart of their square as more and more Bjarke poured into the various breaches in the palisade walls and the villagers were slaughtered where they stood. He heard the keen wailing of women and children as they abandoned hope and gave in to fear, waiting for the end to take them. Of Ma-aka and Pania, there was no sign. All he did know was that Pania was last seen heading towards the Keep to one side of the square to stay with Marika. He hoped she was safe.

"Sam!" A cry from one of the women, pinned to the ground by an evil looking shaft, "Where are you?" her eyes quickly losing their sight as her life escaped, spilling out onto the hard floor around her. Sam had no answer for her, only fear and confusion and a desire to get "the hell out of Dodge" and wake up in some nice bed somewhere, away from all this chaos. Babu had disappeared into the enemy and who knew if he was still alive? Sam had tried to communicate with him, but only silence greeted his calling. He feared the worst and started to lose faith in his surroundings and the abilities of this place to stay the welcoming safe place it had been when he first arrived. Men and women around him tried in vain to stop the marauders advancing, but soon, the remaining villagers were forced to stop. Their tiredness and demands to drop their weapons, forcing first one, then others to give up, dejection and fear etched across their faces as they started to look around them at the carnage that had been their village a few short hours ago, now already a burning hulk of destruction and sadness.

Ahead of him, Sam noticed a disturbance in the group of men. They were all breathing heavily and many were bare-chested, blood and dirt mingling freely on their bodies. The group of men slowly parted, allowing an avenue to be formed, through which the author of this carnage slowly approached. Otaktay! Huge, evil looking, tattooed everywhere and with a thick ponytail draped behind him, Otaktay walked slowly up towards the remaining inhabitants, his eyes scanning the crowd for potential danger.

Otaktay stopped at the edge of his group of men, staring into the crowd in front of him, looking, searching… finding.

His gaze fell on Sam and seemed to stay there for an eternity. He moved his arm up towards his mouth, rubbing his chin in thought before he moved away from the crowd and towards Sam.

"So you are *The One*?" he questioned, his axe held loosely between his two hands. "You are the one who was supposed to have defeated the Bjarke only to be lost to Lord Elim?" He started to circle Sam, as if inspecting a sickly insect. "You are the one," he continued, "who took the life of Napayshni and all his men!" The crowd of angry marauders started to growl, some lifting their swords in expectation of exacting revenge. Otaktay stopped their movement with a wave of his hand. "How is it possible, little man, that you, who stand here before me, was able to demolish over 20 hardened Bjarke and yet here you are, without so much as a weapon or ability to strike?" He continued his circling. "And, are you the one who controls that demon who decimated some of my men?"

Sam dared not breathe.

"Alas, little thing, your *Padme* was last seen running for the hills in terror. I am afraid it is the last you will see of him." Otaktay seemed to enjoy goading Sam and seeing how it pleased his men. They jeered and spat at Sam, their evil eyes dissecting him as on a microscope.

"Have you no tongue?" Otaktay asked. "Are you unable to speak, or are you, after all, nothing more than a wet pup, not worthy of any title other than 'The *Useless* One'?"

Sam saw that Otaktay was gearing up to humiliate him, but in front of this huge being, Sam had little to say, let alone challenge him on, so he remained quiet, his eyes downcast and his body sagging into itself in despair at the apparent loss of Babu. He continued to call him, but still, Babu remained silent. A sure sign if ever there was one, that Babu was indeed dead.

Otaktay stopped his pacing and stood in front of Sam, measuring him up. Deciding what to do next. He opened his mouth to pronounce his decision, only for him to be interrupted from the most obscure of places.

"Sam!" A cry from within the shelter of some rubble next to the keep. Sam recognised the voice in an instant, and wished he had never met her. Pania, seeing her closest friend being interrogated and hurt, decided to spring to his aid in the bravest way possible for a young girl just over her ninth birthday. She sprang out from her hiding place and started to run towards him, oblivious to all around her. The Bjarke looked down in surprise as this young thing hurtled past them towards the man standing in the centre. Sam cowered into himself as he heard her voice, wishing she had kept quiet, and therefore, safe, now, exposed, left to the whim of these people who *took no prisoners.*

"Leave him alone!" she screamed, her hair flowing out behind her and her dirty knees pounding her legs into the ground. "Leave him alone." The Bjarke stood aside as she past, leaving this whirlwind to be dealt with by their leader. Otaktay, on seeing this new event unfold before him, and sensing the close connection between Sam and Pania, saw his next decision alter into a glorious composition of pure revenge.

"Helushka, grab that whelp!" Otaktay ordered to one of his generals as Pania moved closer towards the group. With one fluid movement, the man addressed as "Helushka" leaned out and swept Pania off her feet as if she was made of feathers. He held her in his iron grip as she fought to be released. He paid her hitting and protestation no mind, looking instead with deep glee at his leader, awaiting further instruction for the tasty morsel now fighting to be released from his steel grip.

"I said to you people before our attack, that revenge would be sought for the loss of Napayshni." Otaktay looked over the crowd as he spoke, slowly bringing his gaze back to Sam, where he continued. "I longed to taste the blood of the one who had taken Napayshni's life and those of his fallen braves. But for him," looking firmly at Sam with steel, dark, dead eyes, "his fate is to be decided by those greater and more worthy than this rag-tag group of warriors, I have the privilege of calling *Comrades.* We take him to Lord Elim, there to see his life leached out of him by the ancient ways of the soul reaver. There to meet his end."

Sam shuddered as he began to see what Otaktay was leading up to and he hated him more for it. "Don't you dare!" he started to say under his breath, gazing sternly at his enemy standing mockingly before him. "Don't you bloody dare."

"Kohana, Achak, grab him. He will want to remember this for as long as he still holds breath." Two pairs of hands grabbed Sam, forcing him bodily to the ground. He could no more fight these men off than he could have flown through the skies.

Otaktay looked out at the people around him and raised his voice in final pronouncement. "I am Otaktay, leader of the Bjarke and clan tribe leader of the people of the mighty Nephilim. We exact revenge on our comrade, Napayshni here today, and leave this place as a sign to the other tribes of your people yet to be visited and defeated. Let this defeat flow down through the ages to your children and your children's children. Let it remind them that you are but nothing. A speck of dirt to be trodden underfoot. The Bjarke come and go as they please and none will stand in our way."

"Helushka, come. We take but one today." He looked at his general, who grabbed Pania and threw her over his shoulder, and together, Otaktay and Helushka turned around and started to walk back out of the wreck that was Watamka. But not before Sam heard his last instruction to those left behind. "Keep that one alive," pointing to Sam held in the vice-like grip of Kohana and Achak, "the rest are the spoils of battle. Do with them as you will!" And together, they walked away from Sam, Pania screaming back at him in terror. Screaming for Sam to save her as the rest of the Bjarke, with wild, ecstatic glee, shouted out a prolonged battle cry and launched themselves into the terrified villages, swords and axes scything through what remained of the frightened innocents.

Seeing Pania being taken away from him brought an anger up to the surface that he had not experienced in many months. Here was someone he had grown to love despite his fears of letting her down, and she was being taken from him. Just like David was taken from him a few short months previously.

"Noooooooo!" he screamed. "Drop her now before all hell is let loose on you!" Sam struggled to get out from the grasp of his captors. Pania was slowly being taken further away amidst the carnage around him, her cries of terror echoing through him and grabbing his heart like never before. He could not lose another one so close to him. Not this time.

Heat consumed him from within and his body burst into a white hot brilliant volcano of fire. Both Kohana and Achak recoiled immediately, their hands and arms destroyed beyond repair. Their screams were the last thing they heard before they sunk to the ground, dead before they knew it. The others around Sam, on seeing what had happened, sprang back in sudden shock as this person, who a few short seconds ago was a weak, insignificant youth, was suddenly glowing in front of them. White hot fire pouring out from every pore of his body.

Sam had had enough!

"I am coming for you, Otaktay," he cried. "Stop while you can for here there is no mer…" The rest was lost as one of the Bjarke, in sheer terror, swung his spear shaft at the head of Sam, hitting him soundly on the skull. Sam's world exploded in stars, pain, and bright light and he remembered no more.

The Awakening

"Sam. Sam! Wake up. You have been having a nightmare." An insistent, urgent voice moved into his head. Sam groaned, sending feelers out into his immediate surroundings, trying to regain focus. His head pounded in pain and he opened his eyes.

In front of him, stretched the long cold surface of bright, striped linoleum. A number of bar stools were placed next to a counter above him. Two stools were on the floor, one under a table. "Argh my head," he groaned. "Where am I?" His head throbbed in agony and he stretched up to rub his temples gingerly as he sat himself up off the floor.

"You had a nightmare, Sam. You had a nightmare, and then you threw yourself off the chair and whacked your head on the footrest of that stool there," said Alice, pointing to the stool now lying under the table.

Sam rocked slowly back and forth, trying to nurse his head and to ease the pain. Without thinking he said, "I need to get back. Pania has been taken." The response he got back took a little while to register. "Pania is still alive, Sam. Pugs watches over her. We have to get you up and ready, ready to face the world."

"My head bloody hurts!" His mind had been tracking what had transpired since he came to, and suddenly, as a penny dropped, it stopped him saying anything else. He focussed his eyes, staring straight at Alice.

Alice's eyes were an iridescent purple! Flecks of red and blue were moving within the depths of them and she made no attempt to blink the colour away. Not this time. Her face was definitely glowing and Sam knew enough to register that no light shone behind her to illuminate her this way.

For a second, Sam just sat and stared, and then his world blew up inside him.

"You are *kidding* me!" Sam started to struggle to get his feet under him, to get away from acknowledging what his brain absolutely *refused* to believe, let alone accept. "You are bloody *kidding* me! Uhh uhh! No way, Jose. This is not real! You are for sure not real. What the bloody hell is going on? Where am I?"

Sam found himself glancing all around him for a quick exit, at the same time, staring with horror at this apparition in front of him, who, only yesterday, was serving him with a "Coke and a bloody *normal* smile!!," now sitting there as plain as, eyes bright purple and her face bloody glowing!

"Sam, stop! Please! You must stop, and listen. You *know* who I am!" Sam was too panicked right now to listen to anything. This was way the hell out of his comfort zone. Distant dream planets, strange folk, people dying for no apparent reason; *that* was all well and good. Having the dream now start to infiltrate his real world, *his* bloody world, that was definitely not cool! This simply did not happen, couldn't happen! Wasn't bloody able to happen, damn it! His rambling thoughts flew every which way assaulting him with merciless efficiency, the pain in his head now a distant memory, the impossibility of what he was seeing before him, very much taking front and centre stage.

"Look to your self, Sam,"Alice said, with calmness flowing through her words. "Ask yourself how it is possible that

I know about Pania, about Babu, Ma-aka and Ngaire. I was the one who sent Babu to be with you in the first place, whilst I came here to get you. If all this is true, then you know that the thoughts you have had about me are true also."

The scariest of movie scenarios was forcing its way into his world and he was not ready for any of it. Standing up he ran straight towards the café door, grabbing the handle as he approached. It was locked!

"Let me out!" he screamed in terror, looking back at Alice, who now stood by the edge of the counter, as he furiously tried to rip the door off its hinges. Alice blinked once. "It is open, Sam," she said, and the door flew open in his grasp, catapulting him out onto the street and into a crowd of people out on a typical Saturday morning shopping spree.

"Careful young man!" one of them exclaimed in haughty tones. Sam didn't care, he just needed to get away from here, from her, as quickly as possible. Run away and hide in the darkest cave if one revealed itself to him. Just get away and not think about what had just happened. What couldn't have happened, though try as he might, the events of the last few minutes refused to dissipate and instead, they stood to attention right in front of him, refusing to budge.

It's not possible, it's not possible, it's not possible thundered in his mind with every step he took, matching his running with regular cadence. His route seemed to take him naturally up and away from the heart of Greyshott, up the windy roads towards Blacknest Hill which overlooked the town. "It's just not possible!" he uttered again, to no one in particular. But it was possible. It had occurred and, try as he might, he could not deny it. "This can't be true," he tried to argue with himself as he reached the summit of the hill, rapidly running out of steam and slowing down at last.

"It can't be true!" he screamed aloud out into space, the

breeze snatching his words away and flinging them off into the air for a moment, leaving him, finally, out of breath and alone.

With body bent from the exertion and arms pressing onto his thighs for support, Sam gazed down onto the town nestling in the trees below him. He could see the chimney pots and roofs of the various buildings in the centre. The cars, busses and people going about their normal activities for a Saturday. Further afield, the shops and office buildings started to give way for the residential apartment blocks and single houses of the outskirts of Greyshott, and, if he looked closely enough, he could spy his own road peeling off from the High Street and taking his eye to his own home, now camouflaged in with the other houses.

Peace seemed to be the natural bed partner with the area, much like it must do, he surmised, with most towns and villages that weekend. Here there were no marauders intent on maiming and killing, no Lord Elim waiting to send the fear of God into the inhabitants, no strange creatures who could communicate with you over time and space.

Looking down towards the town church, he saw the area in which Timber's Tea House should be sitting and he stopped to consider further.

Of course, we are not allowed to get away scot-free! he said to himself. *Oh no, Sam Gilbert. In this world, we have to live with gods who casually reveal themselves to you with purple bloody eyes and faces that glow of their own accord, all the time whilst serving us traditional breakfasts and cups of tea!* The events of the last hour replayed themselves in his head, but now, with distance between him and *her,* he was able to reassess what had happened.

Well, he said to himself, finding a large boulder to sit on as he gazed down over his town, *If she really was all powerful and was out to get me, regardless of whether I was standing right in front of her, or hiding up here like a coward, she could, I suppose, quite easily magic herself from there to here and do whatever she wanted to me! But she hasn't. She is still down there, and I am safe up here,* he continued this line of argument and deliberation in his mind. *How she knew about Ngaire and Babu and Ma-aka...* He stopped as another name entered his thought patterns. ... *And Pania.* He hoped she was alright. Hoped that the next time he dreamt, she would be there, safe and sound and playing with Pugs without a care in the world. But somehow, he knew he was kidding himself. *Anyway,* he continued, *I don't know what the problem is. Who has ever heard of dreams being reality? Maybe I said something in my sleep whilst I slept at Timber's and Alice heard me say their names and used them against me in jest when I woke...* He allowed that particular nugget to rotate a few times.

No! That is equally stupid, Sam!

All this time, his eyes had stayed on the area from where he had recently fled. He knew precisely what he was going to do but, for the time being, he refused to give that thought any room for manoeuvre. He could not deny, no matter how he tried, that something weird had just happened. Indeed, he would not have been more surprised if someone in the Saturday crowd had literally grown a third leg right in front of him.

Regardless of how I argue it away, Alice somehow knows about the dreams I have been having. This, he thought, was as good a place as any to start an argument whose outcome he already knew the answer to. *She knows what has been happening, somehow, and yet, for that to be true, then the dreams must be real, which obviously they cannot be and therefore...* He was working his argument into knots so he stopped and tried again. *Her eyes were definitely purple!* He knew that that had not been imagined. He reached up to tug absent-mindedly at the charm necklace, which was no longer there. *Ah! And I am not convinced about her story that she gave her necklace to* a friend. *Hah, likely one, that. So she gives me a necklace which only appears when I am dreaming, has purple eyes and is one of the Anahim of Maunga-Atua. No, correction. She is THE leader of the Anahim! Equally preposterous.*

Whichever way he tried to rationalise and cut up this particular cake, Sam kept on coming against a blank wall, forcing a re-think on his logic. He tried again.

OK. I have been having a series of dreams, all seemingly related, which, when you come to think about it, is not normal. I wake up today to see a purple eyed demon woman staring at me seemingly knowing what has been happening. I have been told about this woman in my dreams by Ngaire. Alice knows about Ngaire because I know as sure as hell that I didn't tell her anything about the place or the people. I have been told that Alice is the leader of the Anahim although she lost her powers to come here, and yet, when I saw her this morning, she definitely was not *being* normal*! She had a necklace similar to the one I wear in the dream world and it has mysteriously disappeared from around her neck. Bloody hell, Sam, if you continue down this route, there is only one solution that is possible, and that, me old mate, is absolutely the most* stupidest *theory in all this relative world!* He threw his hands up in exasperation. "Aargh!" he screamed out to the surroundings. *But what choice is left to me? Unless I have been dreaming that I have been dreaming and what I saw this morning was still part of a dream, which would really set me off, then I must accept that somehow, somewhere, Maunga-Atua exists, Alice exists, and I am supposed to be this ONE, ready to save the day and rescue the princess, wherever she may be hiding!* he thought in conclusion. He looked down again into the town. Still safe. No angels or demons flitting around causing havoc. No whirlwind of power coming in from the east. Just a quiet town, as it always had been, and probably always would be.

He paused.

You have to get back down there, Sam, and have it out with her once and for all or you are on the fast route to the loony bin.

Sam gritted his teeth against his lower lip a few times, scratching his head absent-mindedly as he plucked up courage to go back down and confront the only person who could possibly explain everything, much though he was not looking forward to the outcome.

With a final exhaled breath, he stood up, dusted himself off and turned back, walking over the grassy surroundings, back onto the windy head road and down into Greyshott, to have it out once and for all with the leader of the Angels of another dimension.

"You are a bloody idiot, Sam!" The last thing hovering in the air where he had stood, before it too was taken away by the breeze to disappear into the air, dancing away to join with all the other statements, promises and devotions that had been made over the centuries from this self same spot.

His journey back down into the village was filled with second thoughts and scenarios proposed placing him anywhere else but where he was about to go. The skies didn't cloud over bringing with them the certainty of heavy rain. In fact, as days went, this one was just fine.

Sam eventually reached the High Street and turned up towards the church and the *den of adders* which, until recently, was a very nice café serving the best English Breakfast going. As he approached, he saw that, as usual, a few punters were already sitting down inside enjoying their early morning brew and fantastic fried egg sandwiches. Outside, people passed by as if nothing was different. *How wrong they are!* Sam thought.

He found himself standing at the threshold, his feet refusing to take him any further. The decision was made for him as the door opened, spilling two people out onto the street. Inside, he saw Alice standing in the centre of the space, tables all around her. She was looking straight at Sam, ignoring everyone else around her. Thankfully, her eyes had returned to their normal blue hue and her face had stopped glowing. She had that look on her face as if to say, "And?" Sam stepped up into the threshold and entered Timber's Tea House.

"Mary?" Alice called back into the kitchen. "Take over here for a while will you? That's a dear." Mary bustled out from the kitchen, smoothing down her apron and casting a suspicious eye at Sam, wondering what business he had here with Alice at this busy time of the morning.

"It's not as if I don't have anything else to do back there," she protested as she huffed and puffed past Alice to take an order from one of the window tables.

With a final look back at Sam, Alice turned and disappeared into the gloom of the kitchen. Sam followed, feeling like the proverbial lamb to the slaughter.

Sam realised in all the time he had been coming to Timber's, he had never seen the back of house areas. The kitchen was spotlessly clean. Stainless steel counter tops, shiny utensils and numerous pots and pans were all on display. A kitchen showing someone had pride in what they did. Off to one side, attending to a few pans sizzling away, the cook was busily preparing food. The heady smell of eggs, bacon and sausage wafted over to him. Breakfast was already in full swing.

Beyond the spotless kitchen, a corridor led off. A small office to one side and a store room to the other, and beyond that still, a rear door, which was open.

Sam walked down towards the open doorway, causing

"cook" to cast a few surprised gazes in his direction before she turned back to concentrate on making sure the bacon was done just right and the eggs didn't burn. Outside, there was a small car park, the rear of a number of shops, all jostling for height, shape and size, and a single ship's container, door open, Alice disappearing into its interior.

Now why on earth does she need a container? echoed through his mind, as he approached the open doors and plucked up the courage to enter a place which only had one exit! With one last look back, hoping that at least someone had seen him step into the container, he pulled himself into the cavern and disappeared from public view.

Inside, there were two rows of shelves on either side of the long walls, stacked high and holding all manner of articles, most foreign to Sam. A workbench was positioned at the end of the container and Alice was standing over it, her back to him. Head down, her shoulders hunched and her fingers gripping the edge tightly, she waited for him to draw nearer.

The container door closed softly with a silent clink behind him and the interior lit up with the soft glow of a "somewhere else" light. All sounds from outside had ceased, as if they were in a sound-proofed room.

"My name is Aronui," Alice began softly. "I am what is called an Anahim in my reality. Most of what Ngaire told you is true, to a fashion. If you will, I will try to explain that which is missing from the telling but suffice it to start by me saying that you and I have known each other for many years. Longer than you realise. When you first entered Maunga-Atua, you entered with courage, wisdom and a power we had *never* seen." Alice paused for a moment, thinking back to that time, and then she continued. "When you returned, the Sam I know had been lost in the shadows and a shell remained. My world stopped that day, Sam, and every attempt from that day till now, has been on trying to unravel what happened when you challenged Lord Elim in the depths of the Kairaki mountains. My despair cannot be imagined. It's not every day that an Anahim, a creator of worlds, is brought low!" She said the last in attempted weak humour. Sam could have heard the pin drop and its noise echo through the chamber. He said nothing.

"Ngaire was correct about why we, why I, came here. I came to search, and find." Alice turned to face Sam now, continuing. "The Anahim and the Nephilim were locked in a *no-win* situation. We know each other's ways much too completely for any one side to triumph and whilst the Ethereals are more powerful, the Nephilim have greater numbers. The only solution was to seek the one who held the source of the awakening of our existence." Alice spoke softly and slowly, always scanning Sam for some reassurance that he was listening and understanding what she was saying. She continued.

"When we had created all that you have experienced in your dream, we knew that a time would come, when that order would be challenged. We knew that the source of creation, the essence of all that is, would be sought, attacked and possibly destroyed. We could not allow this, so one volunteered to take our purest essence into themselves, becoming one with it, and left our world, in every sense of the word. That Anahim was Hahona, *The Healer*. He merged with the oneness and moved himself out of our existence, reforming himself anew here in this world reality that you live in. Where else could we hide what is pure? The Nephilim do not have our powers, so we knew they could not follow in the same way as we were able to. We therefore also knew that being here, should our world order be threatened, the purest essence that creates all things would still exist and would be able to be rekindled should we all face defeat. Hahona came here, Sam. Many eons ago. He came here and he merged with one person. They were unaware of the merging and indeed, that was the intention. They were to go on with their lives as if nothing had changed, and, in effect, this remained. The life force was past down from generation to generation." She paused again, waiting for Sam to make a connection. "It now resides in you. Is now you, Sam! And, crazy as it might seem, inside you, you hold all the power and creative ability to make worlds, form time and mould life itself. I can therefore well understand that you are having a problem accepting what is happening to you at the moment!"

Alice stopped talking, allowing the silence to work its healing on Sam. For Sam, that would still be a long way in coming.

He heard all that she had said, but the concept explained, was so far from his reality, that it almost felt like he was watching a film from the safety of his own armchair, or indeed, like having a dream, knowing one would be waking up at any moment and would leave whatever transpired in the dream world, safely locked away.

Alice continued. "When I arrived, Sam, I was able to communicate with you, not just on a 'human' level, but I was also able to tap into our own energy that resided within you such that you felt at one with me and you understood and accepted this series of events for what it was. Not as a pure human being, but as a *bigger* entity. You were able to understand and therefore, you were able to be trained in how to wield what lay dormant inside you and, most importantly, how to keep that which is within you, locked away from this reality. Should it have been released here, we hate to think what the consequences would have been."

In some strange way, Sam sensed that what Alice was

saying, was true (to her) and, incredible though that was, Sam felt relaxed that whatever had been going on, was under some sort of control, control that he maintained. However, bits of conversation that he remembered Ngaire telling him, rose to the surface and he interrupted Alice to challenge this incredible message.

"Ngaire told me that when you arrived here, you lost all your powers. If this is true, how then do you know what has been happening to me in Maunga-Atua with such clarity?" Sam did not, for one minute, believe that his dream world was anything other than a dream. He accepted, however, that some weird stuff had been going on recently, sufficient enough for him to question his interpretation of events, and indeed, in this instance, to question the proprietress of Timber's Tea House, who looked and acted no differently than any other human he had interacted with, other than her eyes were known to change colour and she apparently was able to glow at will.

"Did you ever question Babu when he said he could communicate with you regardless as to how far away you were from each other?" Alice replied. "You knew that what he said was true, even though you had never experienced this before or had any reason to believe that a creature, as you thought he was at first, was able to communicate with you through thought!"

She has a point there, Sam pondered. And then, without thought, "Is he alright?" Sam suddenly yearned to see Babu again and to see that he was alive. "Is he still alive?"

"Babu is not like the other Padme we created,"Alice replied. "Babu exists and is not that easy to destroy. Like you, he too is *different*. Yes, Sam, he is alive."

Alice allowed Sam to absorb this good news, then she continued.

"We, the Anahim, created each and every Padme. Do

you not think that we are able to communicate with them also, regardless of where we are... or when... or whether we are in another time, place and dimension? Shell, Egg, Yolk, Sam. Remember? One and the same. Time, space, infinity... to us, there is no difference! We know and see everything! At the same time. Because, where we exist, time does not. It is a created thing just as much as the Padme are."

Sam was battling to come to terms with this incredible explanation of everything in a whistle-stop tour of quantum dynamics, faith and other things for which he had no words by which to describe. It was if he was looking at a picture but his eyes were out of focus. Try as he might, he could not see the picture clearly.

"Hang on, Alice. You were supposed to have lost your powers when you came here. How then can you communicate with Babu if those powers are no longer there?" Sam thought that question was going to cause her problems.

It did not!

"My powers are not lost, Sam. They are merely laid down. If you will, they are not allowed to exist in their true form here because, if they did, this place as you know it would be utterly destroyed, but aspects of our being remain. Communication being one of them."

"Did you create us?" Sam thought he would close that particular anomaly down seeing as they were talking about *out of this world* things presently.

"There is no easy answer to that, Sam," Alice said. "We did and we didn't. If I can explain briefly: Do not see this earth as confined to a sphere flying through space around a star which is one of billions of stars flying in a galaxy which is one of billions of galaxies in the universe. When you were in Maunga-Atua, was there anything about it that made you feel it was not real? Were you able to touch the trees, feel the water on your face, talk to the people there? And yet, even though you could experience all these things as much as you experienced the waves crashing down at Sandhaven yesterday, you believe *now* that it is not real because you do not experience it in the here and now. But, do you experience the furthest galaxy in this system? Have you ever seen the Magellanic Clouds? You have not, and yet you know they exist. Why? Because someone has told you they exist and you believe them. You have experienced something in another world, and seen and touched it first hand, and yet you refuse to accept what your eyes and heart are telling you. What makes more sense, Sam?"

Before Sam could assimilate all this, Alice concluded. "The concept of 'all-ness' is difficult to grasp for one who has never experienced it. But you have, Sam. You have experienced and lived in both the here and the there. That which is within you, whether you accept it or not, continues to function, to operate and, thankfully, appears to still be able to work. What we have to do, is switch on the part of you that was switched off when Lord Elim confronted you."

There is that name again, thought Sam. *Why is it that everyone keeps on telling me about Lord Elim and yet I have no recollection of him, no recollection of travelling to some mountain area, no recollection of having any battles with anyone prior to a few days ago?*

"Sam, when you were discovered, lying in a heap at the foot of Mount Ohanzee after you went into the mountains of Kairaki to do battle with Lord Elim, Babu summoned the Anahim. A mighty army of the greatest of us came to protect you and no one dared enter our protective cordon around you. You were brought safely back to health and then you re-appeared here, in this world domain. I have tended to you ever since and have been waiting. Waiting till you were ready to return. Waiting until today. I have something for you."

With that, Alice turned back to the worktable and opened a silver chest in front of her, lifting its lid up and back. She delved into the depths of the chest and brought out a small object. Closing the lid, she turned back to Sam and slowly offered out her hand, open for him to see.

A small, tightly tied satin cloth was lying in her outstretched hand, holding an object in its care. Alice proffered it to Sam, who, with trepidation, reached out and took it gently from her. He untied the string and slowly unrolled the material until the object within lay open for him to see.

"When you left to bring order back to our world," Alice started, "You took with you the Staff of the Ethereals through which your powers were to be focussed and expressed. When you returned, all that remained of the staff was that."

Inside, glowing softly in the light of the container, was what appeared to be a silver haft. Brilliantly engraved with motifs and emblems, and embossed with gems, the handle willed Sam to touch it. He picked it up slowly. It fitted his grasp as if it was always intended to reside there. At one end, an opening existed which appeared to have once held another piece. The timber staff itself was missing. The haft felt worn and smooth in his hands, as if waiting to be wielded. It was a thing of beauty and Sam was entranced.

"We do not know what became of the staff," Alice said, cutting into his thoughts. "But we know it still exists and that somehow, the reconnection of it to the handle will somehow reunite your mind with what happened, and perchance, reignite that which remains to be concluded; the end of Lord Elim and the realignment of order within Maunga-Atua and our worlds. Sam, you need to find the staff again. Find the staff, destroy Lord Elim, rescue Pania and rebuild that which is dying. We need you to be Sam.

The One. The Chosen. The Wielder of All Power. And we need you now!"

Sam could sense the strength of feeling emanating from Alice. It was as if the world as he knew it, for a moment, had disappeared and everything that existed and always had done, was refined to this one moment where two people stood facing each other and everything else disappeared. Sam was not able to fully digest what had been thrown at him, but he knew, in the back of his mind, that he would.

Soon.

The Turangai revolt

"We cannot just stand here and do *nothing*!"

"We must take stock of all that is…"

"Enough about waiting! If we wait, we die, and I am tired of dying!"

"Be still! No one can make any decision if we are all talking at the same time. Ngaire, say something."

The mists moved silently through the forest, its tendrils, like feelers, moving over the moss, searching for prey. It covered everything without exception and flattened the colours into a dull, generic grey, too tired to push brightness into the offering.

Within the forested area, in a clearing long since swept clear of covering trees, a shape shifted in and out of focus as the mists moved past and over it. The shape was large and cumbersome and seemed to have grown out from the undergrowth, its walls forming the same dull green as the surrounding woodland and the roof glistening with moss and droplets of water, trapped from rejoining the mist banks beyond.

A large tent, tied down with guy-ropes and seemingly erected a great many years ago, lay nestled within the clearing. Almost nondescript in itself, other than at one end, where a gaudy set of low-glowing lamps illuminated a flap in the fabric of the walls, through which, from time to time, groups of people could be observed entering or leaving it. Around the outside, like sentinels, the various Padme sat in a concentric circle. All facing outward. As more people entered the tent, their Padme peeled off and joined their comrades. A secure force, protecting those within from anything and anybody foolish enough to try to attack on this most darkest of evenings.

The tent was being used as a nexus point for a gathering; A very large and important gathering, and it was from within the dull walls, that the sound of many dissenting voices could be heard, rising and falling in volume like the tide of the ocean.

"Ngaire, you must accept that the situation cannot be allowed to continue?" said one elderly man, his beard flowing over his hands and twisting in and out of a gnarled stick he used as a cane.

"Ngaire is not the only one who sees what others cannot," said another. A younger man who had arrived late, his burlap cloak still covering his head such that his features were in shadow underneath his hood. "We do not have to follow her counsel just because she hears the heart beat of some of the Anahim."

"Be silent, Kahurangi. If you have nothing positive to contribute, then stay hidden under that blanket you call a cloak and listen to what the wise have to say instead!"

Tai, one of the elders of the Turangai folk who had all assembled in the tent that night, glared at Kahurangi, daring him to speak further. His staff, already gripped tightly in his hands, was poised to strike out at this young upstart of a man who generally seemed prone to speak rather than to listen. Turning back, he addressed Ngaire.

"Ngaire. No one knows more of the world order and

of the events of the last few years than you. Your counsel and wisdom is regarded and recognised amongst all the Turangai, and, most importantly, amongst these your fellow elders." Tai gestured around the gathering, pointing to a few key members as he spoke. "We listen to what you say, but we cannot wait. Hard though it is, we need to act and act decisively if we are to *ever* get The One to accept who he is and, more importantly, what it is he needs to do."

Tai looked down at Ngaire, who, until that moment, had remained quiet, her pipe fixed to her mouth as usual and the thin stream of smoke flowing up and into the eaves of the tent to join the smoke of others, who had similarly brought their pipes and weeds to assist them as they debated what was to be done with Sam, The One.

Ngaire, with a final, deep puff of her pipe, looked up at Tai through wrinkled eyes and said, "And what is it *exactly*, you feel we should do, Tai, to get Sam to accept his destiny?" Ngaire had been sitting in the same spot now for a few hours and her bones and backside were starting to throb. *These people prattle on like old women!* she thought, not for the first time. Ngaire was rapidly losing patience with her kinsmen as they debated and shouted and cajoled, but just didn't *listen*.

"Are we to call the Anahim one more time?" she continued. "Call them and insist that they sort Sam out once and for all? Would you, Tai, Anaru, Ariki?" Pointing to the three main culprits who were advocating decisive action. "Would *you* like to summon them here, to this place and *demand* that they do something?" The men stayed silent, not knowing how to answer a question that they were too afraid to consider themselves. "Where is your faith, that what was started by them, will be finished by them also? When all appears to be lost, the only thing that remains is faith, otherwise we are no different to the Nephilim and their brood, the Bjarke. They have abandoned faith and their fall is complete. Do you want to be like them?"

The tent fell silent for a while after this as the crowd heard the pronouncement from Ngaire. But only for a moment. And then, everyone clamoured to be heard.

"Ngaire speaks the truth."

"If we wait and do nothing, we are surely doomed. Look at the towns of Rudhjanda, of Baradin, of..."

"We need to assemble the Anahim and get them to act."

"Ariki, you speak without thinking, as you always have done. Who is it that ran, when the rest of us..."

"You are all old men who babble like a brook but your words lead nowhere..."

"There is another way!"

With perfect timing, this sentence was uttered in the pause between arguments, causing the crowd to focus in on it in an instant, looking back to see who had uttered this proclamation. From the back of the crowd, the elders parted slowly making room for one, lone, seated individual who, to this moment, had remained silent. Listening, thinking, and now imparting.

"Tensa. You are one of the oldest among us," said Kuhurangi. "What could you possibly know of another..."

"Silence, whelp!" came the iron response as Tensa looked up at him from the bench on which he sat. "You wear fine clothes, young Kuhurangi, yet underneath it all, you are skinny, lacking substance, and your words, likewise." Tensa, sat huddled up inside an old, threadbare blanket, his feet brought up onto the bench so that he was sitting cross-legged on it. If anything, he looked even older than most and his weather lined face resembled parchment, which had seen many seasons come and go. His beard was full, yet wirey and his nose was creased and incredibly large. However, within the tapestry of his face, his green eyes blazed with intensity and were most definitely not the eyes of a doddering old man, resigned to rock backwards and forwards on his chair until Father Time called for him.

"Like Ngaire," he began, "I have seen this world grow, flourish and rejoice with life. There were times when we could walk among the Anahim and communicate with them, be one with them. Most of you are too young to remember, but I do. I remember the mighty waters of Moana, the mother ocean, when she was clear and bright and her waves washed the shores of all Maunga-Atua with peace. I remember the snows of the Sky Eater, the lofty peaks of the Kairaki range when all was as it should be." His audience listened with intense concentration now that Tensa had their attention.

"But do you not remember as well, the days of the ancient time? When the power of the Anahim flowed through us, their people. We lived and moved with their ways, with their powers, with their magic. And it was the way of the Turangai because it was the way of the Anahim and the Ethereals, who are to be honoured."

Tensa stopped for a moment as he gathered the blanket around himself where it had slipped away from his ancient shoulders.

"Some of you," he continued, "will also remember our forefathers telling us how the Anahim spoke of many other things then. Of lofty places one could only dream of. Of times even further back in the eons of the birthing of Maunga-Atua and of places locked away beyond our times, this place or this reality."

Tensa gathered his thoughts. The next part was critical for his ideas to have any chance of holding sway in this group of peers. Some were nodding their heads in acknowledgment. Some, but not all.

"Do you therefore also not remember that mention was

made of the ability of the Anahim to *world swap*?" Some of the crowd started to utter incantations of protection around themselves, such was the sense of fear suddenly palpable in the gathering. Tensa needed to strike, and strike quickly.

"They spoke of the ability to move between worlds, and times and dimensions," Tensa said, raising his voice slightly to regain the control. "This, some of you must accept, is what we have been told. But, we have also been told that this world swap was NOT just a privilege of the Anahim, but was also possible for their people, the Turangai, under extreme situations and with very, very careful control." Tensa had to shout now to be heard as the elders all threatened to revolt and lose any chance of seeing where Tensa was going with this.

"If this is true," he shouted, "and Aronui moved dimensions not a few years back, why is it therefore not possible still, for the people of the Turangai to do likewise? If the chosen one will not accept who he is, then we must go to him and convince him. Nothing has changed since the days of old other than the Nephilim spit in our faces and we stand there and ask them to spit harder!"

"You are mad, Tensa," shouted one with disgust

"How can he speak of these things as if they are merely the small talk of the children and gossip mongers in the villages?" asked another.

"Tensa, you go too far. This is utter fantasy. How can you sit there and spout such things especially now when we need clear direction?" said a third, turning away from him in frustration, ready to ignore any further comments arising from that corner. The crowd started to move into puffed-up anarchy.

"Actually," said Ngaire, after the crowd had spewed out yet more shouts and comments to the four corners, "Tensa speaks truer words than all of us put together."

At first, the crowd hadn't registered what she had said and the import of it. But slowly, like a gentle ripple, her words filtered out, stopping the various discussions in their tracks, flowing out towards the periphery of the elders gathered.

"Tensa speaks the truth," she repeated. "Tensa speaks with wisdom that should shame all of us." She looked around as she said this, looking with daggers in her eyes at some gathered around. "Aronui did indeed make that journey and we all know that she went of her own accord and is lost to this place, for ever. BUT, it is true that should we feel there is no other way and we accept that Sam *must* be convinced that he needs to remember again and so unleash all that is still inside him, then we have no choice. We must depart from this world and risk losing ourselves in order to regain it once more. Our talking must end and we must journey to the citadel of Maqata, there to find Fastana, the last of the monks of Anahim and seek his blessing to unlock that which has been hidden from us now, for eons."

The silence was palpable as the gathering choked down on what had just been suggested. It was pure senselessness, surely? And then, like a dam bursting, everyone started to clamour and shout and try their hardest to be heard, to try to argue any other option other than one which, so far as they were concerned, had been locked away for ever, and rightly so. Outside, the calm of the forested clearing remained. The various animals and forms of the Padme remained seated in a concentric circle around the tent, looking outwards, protecting, scanning, waiting. Ignoring the noises emanating from within. For them, they sensed what was being discussed within and already knew the outcome. Without a word, first one, then the rest stood from their protective cordon and started to move to the front of the tent, to wait.

Inside, chaos reigned. Men and women shouted and stamped around, arms cartwheeling in agitation with some, their cloaks and long sleeves flowing up into the air like a strange dance. But it was not choreographed. This was control banished to sit outside until they were all good and ready to allow it back in.

Within this upheaval, Ngaire sat quietly, bringing her pipe up to relight it. Allowing the dry tinder within to light up slowly, the smoke starting to filter into her mouth. Through the smoke, her eyes moved to fix on Tensa. His eyes were already focussed on her. Together, they turned their gaze to look over to one of the younger leaders in the crowd. Hauku normally kept quiet in these gatherings, but both Ngaire and Tensa knew that when Hauku listened, she really *listened.* Her youth belied her wisdom and she was destined to go far as an elder amongst her people.

They were both looking to her, their eyes communicating what did not need to be uttered. Hauku, looking at both of them in turn, brought her hands together and lifted them to her mouth, the fingers pressing together, forming a spire. She looked down once as if to seek acknowledgement, then she looked at Ngaire and Tensa and nodded her head imperceptibly.

In amongst the throng, the three of them slowly stood up and started to make their way to the entrance of the tent, where, without a word, they disappeared outside to commence the journey, with or without their comrades. Their parting at first, went unnoticed, but, as one support can weaken a structure, when three principle pillars are removed, it did not take too long for first one, then all to register that there was an imbalance within their gathering.

"Ngaire is gone!" said Uriah.

"So is Tensa," said another.

"And where is Hauku?" said a third.

A quick look around confirmed that they had indeed left, and, as often happens with a leaderless group, regardless as to whether they might feel they can carry on without them or not, a stream of people slowly started to exit the tent to find and follow the intrepid three.

The tent returned to being a dull green-grey structure within the clearing. The lights still glowing at an entrance of a space now devoid of life, save for the wildlife around it, who nibbled on the grasses as they had done since time began. The mist sending strands of dew to caress everything until the place disappeared once more into memory.

As this unlikely group of travellers moved, their passing, from the air, resembled a long line of rag-tag, shuffling blankets all hobbling and wobbling forward. It did not look at all like any army that might cause concern to an enemy. The Padme flitted around their charges like mosquitoes, but generally, they all moved forward in singular fashion, all moving slowly, inexorably on towards the foothills of a mountain range they wished they never had to visit again. Ahead of them, leagues away, sat the cold, impenetrable rock of the mountains of Kairaki and the lair of that worm, Lord Elim, his household of the Bjarke and the resting place of the Nephilim, the sworn enemy of the Anahim, and all the Turangai.

The travellers moved off to the west, away from the head mountains of Kairaki. Instead, they made their way to where mountain met ocean. As they travelled, they attracted other curious groups of people, wondering what auspicious occasion was happening to attract such a troop of esteemed leaders and elders so that, when they eventually started to climb the first of the foothills kissing the ocean, the group of some 30 elders had now expanded to over 200 as they all walked silently onward towards the destiny of their world and their existence.

This group of nomads grew and flexed as they travelled

onward. Padme could be seen flying or running off into the undergrowth, to relay their charge's orders to the villages still remaining on the western shores. Slowly others came to join the group, summoned by those already travelling. At the head, Ngaire, Tensa and Hauku continued with grim determination, from time to time, stopping to get their bearings but always onward to a place they had heard about, but till now, never visited. The citadel holding the last of the monks of Anahim was ahead of them, and more climbing would be required before they stood finally at the gates, hoping someone was there to let them in.

The band had grown to close to five hundred people by the time they approached the steppes leading them upwards at last to the final track and the gates of the citadel of Maqata. The remaining peoples of many villages and towns were, by now, represented here. Solidarity was being shown where it was at all possible. Dotted thorough the crowd were one or two from Baradin, Tangaroa, Anduin, Ruhdjanda, even Watamka, which had similarly been dessimated. News moved up along the lines to land at the ears of the leading group of three, and it was both balm and acid to them when reports eventually reached them of survivors, of loved ones, still alive but in hiding in the forests and caves around the areas.

From Baradin, news that Pit and Niko and a number of the others had managed to escape and were alive.

From Tangaroa, five still alive.

From Anduin, thirty.

Ruhdjanda, ten.

Of Watamka, that mighty town numbering in the hundreds, only forty survivors so far.

But, for Ngaire, both elation and despair as she heard that Ma-aka, though badly injured, was alive. Pania however, her favourite and cherished sister/daughter, and for Sam, his closest link to this place, kidnapped and taken away by the Bjarke. If anything, this news spurred her on. Spurred her to climb, determined to get to Maqata, smash open the doors, climb into hell itself if necessary. Do anything possible to get Sam by the scruff of his neck, and bring him screaming and shouting, for all she cared right now, back into Maunga-Atua to finally finish what he had started and to finally meet and destroy Lord Elim and all his brood of scum, and even all the Nephilim at the same time.

With teeth gritted and steel in her eyes, Ngaire stood at the first stone step leading up into the darkness above and into the depths of the mountain pass, leading to Maqata. She turned to see the crowd spreading out below and around her. It made no difference whether she saw a thousand or just one. For her, she would battle "the Nameless One" himself right now, just to get one opportunity to summon the only one who could possibly bring an end to all the misery coursing through her beautiful land.

Ngaire turned back to look ahead, and with one thought shot to her falcon Seria, she gripped the first rocky outcropping and started her climb up into the darkness and the citadel of Maqata.

Up and up the crowd of stragglers moved, winding their way through the cuts and gashes of the rocky peninsula which merged the beginnings of the mountain range of Kairaki with the Oceans of Moana. Climbing slowly yet steadily onwards. All the while, their protective flank of Padme flew, climbed or scuttled around them, wary of any danger, ready to attack should anything come towards them uninvited.

The waves below them crashed against the foot of the steppes and seagulls flew off from their perches to soar on the air currents around them as they climbed higher. Otherwise, the gathering climbed step after step, ever upwards until at last, Ngaire reached the narrow straight that announced the path that led to the gates of the citadel. Slowly, the rest of the group arrived at the landing, their bodies pressing into all the nooks and crannies to accommodate the people who had come to offer support or, for others, to seek comfort in these dark days among their own kind.

Ngaire looked over to Tensa and Hauka, who, like her, were breathing heavily from the exertion and, with renewed vigour, she gathered up her shawl around her, tucking the odd strand of her long hair back into a hide hair band, and moved down the track to find the gate and seek entry into a place she had only ever heard about, never believing she would ever need to visit this austere place of mystery and silence.

The stony path wounds its way between rocky outcroppings and, as they progressed, the sheer rock faces of the mountain slowly rose above them until they were walking along a canyon, overshadowed by the vertical sentinels of a menacing, cold and silent mountain. Occasionally, a few rocks lost their grip with the vertical surface and bounced down the face, slamming into the floor of the canyon and spewing pieces of stone over the surface, such that their passage slowly became more of an obstacle course than a smooth path.

With a final bend in the canyon route, Ngaire was presented with a view that simply took her breath away. Ahead and to either side of the canyon, the steep rock faces peeled away from each other such that a framed view out to the northern expanse of the Moana Ocean was created. Ngaire noticed that the mist banks lay below them out towards the ocean such that she was able to gaze out for miles over the expanse in front of her. Green fertile fields, huge forested areas and the ocean, all merged into a tapestry laid down over the earth to fold itself into the striking yet severe faces of the main body of the Kairaki range which disappeared off into the distance until it too was lost within the mist fields that still lay like a cloth over everything. Placed within this framed view as if sculpted there on purpose, sitting clear of the vertical rock faces, sat a structure of pure beauty and simplicity, yet exuding strength from its solidity.

Maqata had been carved out from the living rock centuries ago. The enclosing walls were smooth and polished by the winds that whipped through the gaps to either side. Beyond the main walls, the crowd could see some of the roofs of the complex within, poking up over the top. If Ngaire had expected a massive castle, she would have been disappointed. The citadel was fairly small as citadels go. Small, but exuding strength borne out of the starkness of its form and the impenetrable nature of its purpose.

A few small windows could be seen dotted around the external walls, darkness within them like sightless eyes staring out over the crowd. Ahead of them, a stone archway at the end of the path cleaved through the solid rock. Within the archway, an ancient timber door could be seen, closed and uninviting. And lying down at the foot of the door, as if it had been waiting for them, sat the largest lion Ngaire had ever had the misfortune of seeing.

It was watching them.

The gathered people all took a collective breath when they saw this mighty beast ahead, obviously guarding the fortress from people just like them. A few on the sides started to edge slowly backwards but a slight twist of the lion's neck in their direction, and the eyes casting an all-seeing watchful glance at the movement, stopped any further shuffling from within the ranks.

"What now?" asked Hauka, as the three of them considered

their next move. "If we turn and run, that beast will have us in a moment, and if we stay..." The rest remained unspoken.

"Perhaps it is a test?" Tensa suggested, looking carefully at the animal, now licking its right forepaw.

"You want to be the first one to see if you pass?" retorted Hauka.

A stalemate almost existed between man and beast. To move forward would surely enrage the creature ahead of them and undoubtedly cause a horrible sticky end to befall whomever decided to make the first move. To go backwards, would have a similar outcome, if slightly delayed. By a second or two!

Ngaire stayed silent through this discourse of her colleagues, her mind sifting through permutation after permutation. Her eyes scanning every opening and shadow of the silent citadel to see if there was any sign of life whatsoever.

Suddenly, Hauka and Tensa heard Ngaire huff to herself in acceptance of what could not be changed, and looked on in horror as she slowly put one foot in front of her, followed by the next. "What are you doing?" they both cried under their breath, fearful that any loud noise would provoke the beast. "Shht!" came the quick response as Ngaire moved away from the crowd, her hand pushed out behind her, fingers pointed up. The universal symbol for "STAY THERE!"

Ngaire, at this moment, did not feel even a little bit brave. Indeed, every pore of her body was screaming for her to turn around and hobble the hell out of the way of this creature, who now had his eyes fixed balefully on her slight form. Tongue licking slowly against massive canines. As she slowly approached, she still cast glances up into the openings over the animal, but, as before, only silence and emptiness greeted her. She thought, not for the first time, that somehow, she should have come up with a better solution than to march a troop of innocent civilians off over dangerous enemy ground and up to a citadel she had never been to before in the vain hope that some partly mythical monk might still be alive AND living here AND able to assist them with opening whatever portal there might be to enable them to get to Sam in his world.

"Bloody idiot!" she said to herself, remembering the expletive Sam had sometimes used in her company. She laughed inwardly as she felt a humourous adage flash through her mind, of a wild woman laughing like crazy as a lion came and ripped her to shreds.

She was now within a few metres of the creature. Close up, he was, if anything, even more huge and dangerous looking than from the relative safety of the gathering behind her, who, until this moment, had stood stock still for fear of upsetting "IT". She took one last look back at her companions, which was a mistake!

With head turned back to her people, she sensed and felt the ginormous beast rouse itself and could almost believe that its breath was now within a hand's width of her face. The end, she hoped, would be mercifully quick and painless. She slowly, *very* slowly, turned her head back to look on her fate.

The lion had now decided to sit up from his prone position and his head was now some two metres higher then Ngaire's tiny head. His paws alone were the size of her torso and his claws raked into the dusty, rocky path as if flexing and stretching out any kinks remaining in his body prior to dinner. Its eyes were fixed on Ngaire. Its breath brushed her hair slightly and she felt the sheer power of this magnificent yet terrifying beast vibrating through the ground around her feet.

She stopped and bowed her head, arms clasped together in front of her. Awaiting whatever fate had decided to pitch to her, here on a rocky path in front of a silent citadel housing a supposed monk who might be able to aid them in their most direst of needs, right next to the most fearful creature she had ever beheld.

The door creaked open. Its swing causing a loud, screeching wail to echo through the canyon, up to the throng gathered at the bend. To Ngaire, the sound was as if the lion had decided to roar before springing on her and she naturally cowered into herself and screamed.

Nothing!

No feeling of huge teeth sinking into her neck. No sense of a paw lifting to swat her to the ground. Nothing! A few seconds past with Ngaire frozen in a cower, waiting for the end to come, before she opened her eyes under the cover of her arms and squinted out at the lion, who by rights, should have been polishing off her bones right now, looking for the next tasty morsel. Instead, the lion was not where it had been a few second before. It was now walking majestically back through the now open doorway, its tail swishing slowly from side to side. Every now and again, it turned its head to look back at Ngaire, then continued on its walk through the archway and into the citadel itself where it stopped, turned around to face her and then sat back down on its haunches, apparently waiting for her.

Ngaire, with another look back at her friends, shrugged her shoulders at them and proceeded to follow the lion, passing through the archway and the timber door, and entered into the citadel to find out whether Fastana was still alive or whether dusty bones would be the only thing left to mark his existence.

From within, the sense of proportion was completely out of this world. Walls were leaning in every which way, appearing as if at any moment they would succumb to gravity and collapse under their own weight. The buildings dotted around the enclosure were a mixture of heights and sizes. They all seemed to have been designed by a toy maker intent on creating strange and bizarre buildings to suit his or her particular quirkiness. The craziness of the buildings were heightened by their proximity and comparison to the surrounding citadel walls. These, from the inside, were of similar style to the external appearance. Smooth, polished stone walls disappeared up to the battlements above. A few old staircases notched into the walls could be seen spaced out around the circumference, leading one up to a thinly cut walkway overlooking the expanse beyond. Ngaire hesitated to have a guess as to how many people this place would have once held. But now, judging by the silence that greeted her, the inhabitants who must have once graced this place, were long since gone and forgotten.

And yet. Her trained eye picked up that although the buildings were all dark and empty, and there were no lamps lit, still, the forecourt in which she stood, had been recently brushed clean, the fodder rack to one side was stocked with grass, and there was no sign of dirt or abandonment anywhere.

Curious, she turned back to look at the lion who, until that moment, had been sitting there looking at her. Again, as if by command, it had turned and now it faced one building, bigger than the rest. It was looking intently at a staged area half way up the building, where the upper levels were stepped back, leaving a flattened viewing gallery. Its eyes and focus was now no longer on her, but on what was happening above and beyond it.

Ngaire turned to follow its gaze.

At first, there was nothing untoward in that direction and Ngaire wondered what had caught the lion's attention. She was just about to look elsewhere when, out of the corner of her eye, she noticed a slight movement up above the balcony area of the building towards which the lion now stared. A figure, difficult to pick out in the closing gloom of the early evening, shuffled slowly forward until it stood directly behind the balcony line. A pair of gnarled, ancient hands reached out from beneath a darkened robe, one hand moved out to grip the handrail, the other lifted up out of the robe, revealing a staff, incredibly bent and twisted. The figure raised the staff up into the air, the ends horizontal to the ground and, with an incredibly low and deep, almost guttural tone, proceeded to chant.

The words and cadence were alien to anything Ngaire had ever heard. If this was a language, it was one long since lost to the Turangai. The chanting increased in depth and slowly, the ends of the staff held aloft started to glow, getting brighter and brighter until with a final flourish of the wrists, flames streaked out from the tips, hitting the various buildings dotted around her, lighting up the lamps and prepared timber pyres, until the whole area around her was lit with a warm and comforting glow, fires licking out from underneath bone dry tinder and the place transforming into a place she felt safe in, despite the fact that Ngaire thought she had just witnessed magic. And magic used as if this was an everyday occurrence here.

"Ngaire." Thrummed through the air to cause her to look back at the figure. "Ngaire, come up here. We have been waiting since the stars darkened to see you. You, and your kin who wait outside. You have come looking for Fastana, the last monk of the Anahim. You have found him and despite his appearances, he still lives." And with that, Fastana turned back and walked away from sight. Ngaire, looking back, was surprised to see that the gathering had sneaked forward and had been peering in through the archway, and, on seeing the pyrotechnics, were all ready to hot foot it out of this place and back to their relatively safe houses in comparison.

Tensa and Hauka rejoined Ngaire and there was some relief and hugging that took place at seeing the other still alive and in one piece. The crowd moved naturally out into the quadrangle, exploring this weird looking place, their Padme flying or flitting to various cracks and crevasses to wait for further instructions and, for some, to preen feathers and sharpen claws. It was not too long before some had found food ready for cooking in one of the buildings and the heady smell of meat cooking over an open fire started to waft over the group, bringing a sense of relief to the party that the first chapter of this ordeal was now at an end, particularly now that the lion beast had disappeared up the stairs to go and sit somewhere else, away from the tiny people who had stood before it earlier.

Ngaire, Tensa and Hauka, with a last look of pride back at the group of rag-tag people who had chosen to follow them to a place never seen before, turned as one and headed off towards the stairs, taking them up to the balcony and at long last, to meet with the one who, they prayed, would be able to assist them, where no other could. Sam was needed, and time was disappearing fast.

To enter is to perish!

They arrived on the balcony to see Fastana disappear into a dark archway ahead of them, buried into the side of what could only be described as the great house. The roof was split into a number of lofty turrets and steep sloping tiled areas. Holes were dotted around in places, showing that some disrepair had occurred. At the foot of the arched doorway through which Fastana had left, a few stone-carved steps were visible, badly weather-beaten. The view, however, from this vantage point, was even more impressive than what they had experienced previously. Off to the east, the two moons of Adelphi were already rising. Bright red and virulent green, they shone in unison as they travelled through space. They were particularly bright that evening and their reflection was intensified both off the veil of mist lying below them and through the reflection off the distant ocean waves, barely visible from here. But the stars! Bright, vibrant, almost within arm's reach, they peppered the darkness like so many millions of night bugs, all clamouring for attention.

Ngaire's Padme, Seria, screeched from the top of the tallest turret above her. All was safe from her vantage point. With one last longing glance towards the distant ocean sparkle of the night's reflections, they turned once more and climbed the few short steps, following Fastana into the gloomy darkness.

Inside, rather than expecting to enter into a grand hall, the archway led them into a darkened passageway, a few torches held in stands fixed along the wall giving some illumination. Of Fastana, there was no sign. They halted at the threshold, wondering what to do next.

"Hurry up!" they heard from within the gloom ahead. "Keep up and don't forget to keep to the right."

Ngaire looked with a questioning face at Tensa, who, on shrugging his shoulders, exclaimed, "Keep to the right it is then." And he proceeded to move down the passageway.

They soon came to a fork in the corridor, the *obvious* route seeming to continue on as if nothing was different. An even darker and smaller corridor branched off to the right. They turned right, weaving their way between some tree roots sticking out from the foot of the surrounding walls. They sensed that this path was slowly descending but other than that, all other sensory perceptions were lost on them. Again, they came to a branch in the path, and again, the fork to the right appeared even smaller than the one they were in and more unstable. With looks all around, the three dived right, hoping that this little game would come to an end soon so that they could discuss their concerns with Fastana once and for all.

This time, the path spiralled down and down and even the roots from the trees above them, were now only visible in the roof area. They were deep underground, or so they thought.

Ahead, Tensa stopped, his hand raised. "Do you hear that?"

At first, both Ngaire and Hauka could only hear the sound of their own laboured breathing, and yet.

A distant thrumming could be heard, echoing up

towards them. A strange noise. Almost as if the very rock they were buried under, was breathing. They continued on slower now.

As the spiralled path slowly flattened, they could hear for the first time that the sound was not of a mountain breathing, but the pounding and sighing of waves crashing onto rocks. They came at last to an area which ran straight and true to a natural barrier. Ahead, the pathway disappeared amongst a number of large and very wet boulders. Beyond that, they saw that it was indeed waves from the ocean that were now crashing into the rock pool, now receding, sighing as they departed. The pathway had opened out into a well lit cavern, the roof high up above their heads. The waves of the ocean crashing through a gap in the rockface ahead of them, allowing the water in. The rock pool was huge! Easily thirty metres across, this natural bath was obviously a rock pool at the foot of the mountain they had just climbed. They had, effectively, walked straight through the naked rock and exited on the other side, at water level. With unspoken commands, Ngaire, Tensa and Hauka sent their Padme off to inspect the environment and they all shot off in various directions, scouting for any danger.

The cavern was well lit with a number of lamps and candles. To one side and sitting down amongst the wet rocks, the self same lion was present, its tongue flicking out every now and again, as if testing the air for another meal. Ahead, and sitting at the very mouth of the opening out into the ocean, his face turned towards them, sat Fastana, the last known monk of the Anahim. He was studying them curiously.

The three didn't know how to start the conversation and they all looked at each other with embarrassment, none of them having considered just how to broach the subject. Their decision as to who was to talk first was made for them.

"Have you noticed how very misty this place has become?" Fastana mused.

An obvious question and one not really considered by the others as being anything else other than within the realms of ordinariness.

"Did you notice when it arrived?"

This question caused the three to turn to one another, trying to come up with a feasible response.

"I think it happened a few weeks ago," said Hauka, tentatively.

"Twelve days," Fastana replied. "How many days has it been since Sam disappeared to face Lord Elim?"

This, the trio needed no time to reply to. "Twelve!" they all exclaimed collectively, the penny thrown into their midst, certainly dropping if not fully dropped.

"When The One disappeared," began Fastana, "it was marked by this entire system being encased in mist. The mist will stay as long as Sam does not disturb it, but his passing has been noted and the mists receive and part for him. He still is whole, but his mind is not."

The trio were at a loss as to where this conversation was going, as they had intended to go down another line of questioning. This had them stumbling to express their important reason for the visit. Again, they needn't have worried, Fastana seemed to know and sense everything.

"You have come seeking to enquire whether I know if a way exists to bring you to him," Fastana began, shocking the trio into amazement.

"How did he know that this was the sole reason for travelling here?" they said to themselves.

Fastana continued in a sort of sing-song way, his body slowly rocking sideways, his eyes disappeared up into their sockets, sightless whiteness the only thing emanating from his eyes. "Anahim have travelled there. Nephilim also." This was a shock; Ngaire had never dreamed that they had travelled between realities also. Fastana continued. "And every time they chose to enter, none of them returned! To enter is to perish. The accursed Nephilim, as is their nature, tricked the *holders* into allowing their passing into the other sphere and many there were who infiltrated that place before the Ethereals changed things. The source of this power to enable world swapping, was broken in pieces and infused into the monks such that no one individual could ever harness the power to allow travel between worlds. Since that day, no more Nephilim or Anahim have made the journey, until the day when Aronui sacrificed herself to summon he who alone was capable of ending the scourge here."

Fastana looked quickly at his Padme and a silent command shot between the two of them. The mighty lion immediately stood up and, without a second glance, ran off down the corridor they had come from, disappearing from view.

"When Aronui was here, she gathered me to one side and said, 'ensure the band is not broken and hold fast until the Silver Fern is come, then gather again and do what must be done'. And then she stepped into the light and was no more." Fastana looked up at Ngaire and nodded to her. "You have come, Ngaire, 'Silver Fern', and so I follow my duty and will summon the monks' apprentices once more. Perhaps we can yet, convince The One. Now rest, it will take some time for the gathering to awaken."

With that, Fastana beckoned to a small alcove off to one side, set up above the rock pool. Within, there were a number of couches and welcoming lamps, and fruit and water for the hungry travellers. The three fell down onto the couches and tried to talk about what had just transpired, but the strains of the day and the exertions paid their toll. Within a few minutes, their voices trailed away as sleep overtook them. Once again, the only sound remaining was that of the waves crashing below them in safety. Seria, Pila, the snake Padme of Tensa and Mazina, the half-jackal, half-owl of Hauka settled down around their charges, facing outwards in a semi-circle.

Fastana took one last look out to sea then turned and disappeared into a rock niche hidden from view, to summon his gathering.

The first dappled rays of a morning sun filtered down through a gap above their heads, allowing a little natural light to enter their chamber. A few gulls called out their early morning greeting to their mates as they hovered in the warm currents coming off the face of the mountain walls outside. Three bundles roused themselves slowly from amongst the stark furniture on the platform and looked out with groggy eyes. Below them, already assembled, stood twenty of the fittest travellers who had journeyed with them, along with their Padme and the lion, who had summoned them all when sent off by his charge.

The trio looked down with some confusion, wondering what their people were doing down there but their curiosity was soon eased when Fasatana re-emerged from the niche he had entered the night before.

"Ah, you are all here," he said. "Get up, Ngaire. The gathering awaits you." The twenty, made up of men and women, looked up at their leaders, wondering what was happening. Their Padme, similarly, were flying around buzzing with unanswered questions. The lion remained impassive, as if bored with these procedures.

As soon as the trio were ready, Fastana turned and headed off back through the rock niche, not looking back to see if anyone was following. The assembled group set off behind their leaders, already having explained that they had been summoned by their respective Padme to follow the lion, whose name, apparently, was *The Summoner*, hinting perhaps at his overall responsibility.

The niche opened up into a tight, twisting, damp path, only wide enough for one person at a time. Faint light bounced off the slick walls and floors sufficient enough to give some sense of direction, but, as the trio were rapidly discovering, designed in the same way as the route down to the rock pool. One to ensure that anyone unwelcome to enter would find it very hard to return, or to attack that which they could not see. The group continued their winding path, always following the echo of the footsteps of Fastana ahead of them until at last they arrived at yet another large cavern, almost perfectly circular in form, the walls polished to a smoothness that caused many to gasp at the sheer workmanship. There was only one entrance into the room; the one they had entered. Apart from Fastana and the twenty-three, there was no one else!

"Where are your people?" Hauka queried. She, like the rest of them, was starting to feel that they might have been brought into a trap. With the only escape back the way they had come, and a lion blocking their way, their sense of security started to dissipate in the damp air around them.

Fastana waited silently in the centre of the room, his hand resting softly on his staff. Waiting for the crowd to stop so they could pay attention to what he had to say. "When it was decided by the Ethereals to cease any further opportunities for either themselves or the Nephilim to world swap, a great many debates were held over many years as they discussed how to protect both the other worlds and this part of their being. Too much damage had been caused by the Nephilim in other places and the Ethereals were determined to bring this to an end."

On hearing that the Nephilim had apparently also

travelled over the dimensions previously, a loud clamour rose from within the group. This was news indeed, and not what they wanted to hear.

Fastana had to stamp his staff onto the smooth surface to regain their concentration. "The Nephilim have never since regained entrance," he said. "The last to enter, and fall, was summoned there before any of you were old enough to feed yourselves!" he continued, now that he had their attention once more. "The Ethereals gathered all the Anahim leaders together and they in turn summoned every monk in civilisation to ask them to help as they had never done so before.

"Many weeks passed before everyone was assembled, and this place still echoes with the sounds of their gathering, the camaraderie and the one time when men and the mighty Anahim were collected in one place." Fastana looked around him at the walls as he spoke, trying to recall that day so very long ago, when he stood here as a young acolyte, awestruck at being in the presence of these otherworldly beings who had created him, and being able to communicate with them as easily as walking. Those days were long past and now, he was the last. After him, he was at a loss as to what would become of his central position amongst all the monks.

"We monks numbered over five thousand on that day," he began again. "There were so many that a number had to stay outside of the citadel walls to sleep, but we were all here, with the Anahim." He bowed his head before he continued softly, "It was an honour to be numbered with them and to be found of some worth for them to trust us, trust me."

At last he was ready to tell them what had transpired that day. What a master stroke had occurred and how brilliant and outrageous the plan was.

"The Anahim were directed to take their powers enabling them to world swap and, in effect, breathe it out into every monk assembled there. A piece of this power was thus fused with those assembled there. When they departed back to their own lands and countries, it ensured that no individual could combine all the people together again and so to coalesce the power to form and destroy and create worlds and places again. For this power is pure and boundless, not held to any time, place or dimension. The final piece to this unusual disassembly was to send the strongest shard to another dimension, away even from the monks. It is that piece that has been passed down from generation to generation and now resides in Sam. And so, I can well understand why you want to get him to wake up from his *dream* and do that which is natural to him; allow that which is within to shine, and to destroy that which destroys, and thus bring healing."

Ngaire and the rest had never properly realised why it was that Sam was so important to their very existence before. For some, they believed that he was simply a mighty sage in his reality. None actually knew just what he held inside him. They were even more determined now to find him, convince him one way or another, and bring him back to settle the score finally.

But how?

Ngaire offered up that question. "Fastana. If this power was shattered and placed inside your fellow monks all those years ago, and you are now the last of them, how then are you able to assist us? You are the last of the monks of the Anahim. Are we to seek an alternative path to our plight?" She started to feel the weight of despondency as she heard her mind relay out the seeming impossibility of what it was they were trying to achieve, when, theoretically, their only chance lay in a collection of people who were mostly all dead!

Ngaire was certain that underneath Fastana's demeanour, a smile was lurking. He knew something, of that she was sure.

"I did not say that the power was destroyed," he began. "Neither did I say that the monks were dead, although a great many have indeed moved on from this plain and now walk with the Anahim in freedom and peace. Do you not see? Do you, Ngaire, a healer of the people, not see inside you to the answer that lies at your door?"

Fastana was playing with her, she was sure. She was also getting a little angry that he was seeming to make sport of her in front of her people. "*What does he know of the outside...?*"

"When Hahona, the mightiest of the Anahim left this place to fuse the central shard with one from another time and dimension, he did so generations ago." He stopped to see if they were seeing where he was going with this. The returned stares were still blank, so he continued.

"Sam did not exist then."

Still nothing.

"The shard of power fused with the very being of the first Wielder. And it has been passed down ever since then, from generation to generation until today, where it resides in Sam. Still the same as it was. Still as powerful. Still as pure. It exists today even though the original recipient has long since returned to the dust whence he came."

Tensa called out in uncontrolled excitement, he had it! "So what you are saying, is that whilst the monks also received it, whether they still live or are dead, it also has been passed down from generation to generation until this day. Still as powerful..."

"Still as pure," Fastana continued for him. "Yes. Still exists in all those it has been passed down to."

Hauka, on hearing this, could not contain her youthful curiosity. "But Fastana. You are *monks*! Surely you..." She started to realise the sticky position she was getting herself in to and she faltered.

"We don't!" Fastana said with some mirth. "Not in the way you would normally be required to act to maintain a new generation!"

Hauka had to turn away for fear that her red face would be a beacon to all around her.

"People have one way," he said. "Fish another. Stars have a very different way of bringing new life into existence. We monks are no different. What we are, what we have learned over the millennia, we pass on to acolytes through spirit and through mind, just like I was taught when I was an acolyte all those years ago, sitting in front of the Anahim in wonder and awe."

There were a number of collective gasps from the assembled people. This was indeed an experience they would never forget. Some already had visions of them passing this down to their children and their children's children, gathered around a camp fire at night, as the stars gleamed above them.

"But," Tensa began, "you have brought us here." He pointed to the room, empty of all others save themselves and Fastana. They saw that there was no other way in or out and the place had no hidden walls or elements to hide any other people who, apparently were now dotted all over this world. He was at a loss.

"Yes, I have brought you here," Fastana agreed, looking with pride at the singularly empty, circular room within which the gathering stood. "I have brought you here to reveal that which you seek. For here, you will see just what has been hidden from the world for generations."

At that, Fastana raised his staff above his head, and with a loud, guttural cry, slammed it down onto the floor in front of him. At first, nothing happened. The noise of the staff striking the floor bounced off the smooth surrounding walls and slowly filtered off into the ether. But then, like a leak had occurred under a floor, thin strands of blue started to flick out from under his staff within the rock floor itself. The strands moved in a dance around this central spine and then started to grow and stretch out, feeling for more space, more depth. As the strands of light grew away from Fastana, the people around started to move away from them, fearful that something would happen to them if they were touched by this underground light show.

More and more flashes of electric light shot out from where the source was and sprang out like arrows, heading straight for the walls where they bounced up the surfaces, looking like veins in a body. Living veins that were moving and dancing and flashing slowly become entangled and thicker and more visible, until all the walls and floor were moving as one vibrant and dazzling display of lighting-like flashes of the deepest, brightest blue.

And then the dancing stopped. Instead, the walls were now bathed with a uniform blue skein just beyond reach within the rock face itself. A few of the braver people ventured to touch the surfaces, but all they felt was the same cool face of the rock, but this time, there was a slight, almost imperceptible vibration from within the bed rock of this chamber's walls.

"To venture into Sam's dimension," Fastana said softly, "is to venture into a place from which there is no return. The Summoner," pointing to his Padme, "went back to your people while you slept and gathered those you see before you here. Each one was chosen for a reason. They were chosen because over all the others gathered here, they were willing to go where no one from this reality has ever travelled since the inception of time itself. They were willing to go, knowing that there was to be no return. No guarantee of even finding Sam, but willing to go nonetheless. And go, as a sacrifice if needs be, such that Maunga-Atua could survive. This is no easy burden to carry, Ngaire. No one has ever travelled in this way before and we are unsure what may become of them when they do. Apart from through their Padme who will remain here, we will have no way of knowing whether they will have success or not or whether they will be able to find Sam or not."

Ngaire, Tensa and Hauka looked with shock at the crowd around them. None of them appeared to be afraid. They stood tall and proud, each and every one, looking forward and towards the trio. Their Padme sitting now in front of them, waiting. The import of what they had just heard was almost too much for them to bear. "You cannot!" cried Ngaire. "This is simply madness." She looked around the group of people, searching for at least one of them who would agree with her, stop the rest in going to a place of no return with no guarantee of success. All she received were twenty pairs of eyes looking calmly at her, resolved to carry out what they had determined earlier. Theirs was the responsibility for finding Sam in his world, and so, hopefully, to convince him that Maunga-Atua needed every ounce of his being to believe it existed.

"Ngaire," said one of them softly. "You have led us these many years. You have nurtured us and healed us and cared for us like a mother cares for her young. Now it is our turn, as adults, to care for you, and, in turn, care for our beloved world and people. What we do is a small thing in comparison to being able to bring Sam to his senses. We must go, if only for him to see, believe and so, to act."

Fastana interrupted them. "Ngaire. If you want to get his attention, short of summoning the Anahim themselves again, this is the only way by which you can enter his world. These, your people, are willing to do this, for you."

Ngaire was too stunned and saddened to say much else. Inside, she knew that Fastana spoke the truth, but she,

Tensa and Hauka were unwilling, now that they were actually at the *crossroads*, to actually commit to that which they had started the journey for.

"How?" she asked simply.

At this, Fastana gripped the staff tightly to his chest and uttered one word.

"Watch."

Fastana closed his eyes and, once again, started a low, deep, thrumming chant that reverberated through the gathered people's bones. They could all sense that some deep untapped magic was occurring in their very midst. Ancient strengths, emanating from the rocks themselves, older than time, older than existence, flowed through Fastana and out, under his feet and into the walled surfaces around them. His chanting captured the hearts and minds of those around them and they stared at him as his voice became deeper and stronger and "older", reaching back into the roots of the ancient mountain, calling to the very essence of nature itself.

Slowly, the people were aware of distant responses to the chanting. The noise at first seemed to be coming from the rock face itself in a few locations, growing in intensity. As they looked, in three equidistantly spaced areas around the perimeter, the blue hued walls appeared to lose their solidity and instead, forms could vaguely be seen within the depth of the rock wall. Forms which slowly became more solid as if a focus button was being turned, until, behind the three locations, the people were amazed to see three identical scenes.

Within the solid rock face, these three areas had become as one looking through glass. Beyond, and with their backs to this new *window*, sat three people, their robes covering their bodies and heads.

These were three of the new monks of the Anahim. All

alive, all safe within their own demises, all communicating with each other in a language deep with agelessness. Beyond each of them stood a solitary candle in a silver stand, flickering brightly. Beyond that, and similar to the room in which the crowd stood, the walls of the chambers of these three monks were also completely reflective such that the gathering could effectively look through their *windows*, beyond the seated monks, over the candle and then see their own reflections in the walls within the monks' chambers.

All three monks were chanting in time and cadence with Fastana. Suddenly, it appeared as if the flames from the candles were starting to bend towards the walls they faced. They bent and started to grow in length away from the wick of the candles. Grow until they touched the reflective walled surface within the individual monks chambers. Then, incredibly, the flames continued growing through the walls, appearing instead in the chamber that Ngaire and her people occupied. Three strands of flame punctured out in three different places from out of the *solid* rock and started to stretch towards the centre of the chamber, heading for Fastana.

Those nearest to these beams of flame stood back from them in fear, not understanding what was happening. Slowly, the flames continued to extend, all three growing longer and longer as they grew into the chamber. Getting closer and closer to each other, and to Fastana who still stood in the centre of the space, staff in hand, eyes closed and chanting as before.

And then, the flames merged! Fastana became a torch of brightest intensity within the centre of the space. The chamber lit with the reflective glow that had become Fastana, who now appeared to be burning up and yet, looking closely, still standing, his cloak unburnt, his skin not burning off him. Those around him moved away in terror. None of them had witnessed such *magiks* before, and the mood of the crowd started to change to one of wanting to flee. But only for a moment.

From within the torch that was Fastana came his reassuring voice. "Now you can perhaps understand how this priceless treasure has been protected and nurtured over the generations. Each monk is located in citadels like this all over Maunga-Atua. All can be summoned, just like we can summon our Padme regardless of distance. Should any one monk be forced to lose connection, as you see here, another is ready, in a different location, to take their place. And so, whilst I stand, this link to other places, this World Swap, is possible through me. For I am the last of the monks of the Anahim. The last of the original bearers of the flame. The last who is able to wield the flame, allowing passage beyond the here. Fear not. Draw closer and see that I do not burn."

Some of the crowd did indeed move forward, reaching out to touch Fastana tentatively, then retract their hands quickly with surprise. Their hands not singed, their clothing still the same as before. Others in turn, gathered around these braver individuals, looking at the clothing and hands with astonishment, then turning and approaching Fastana to see and experience for themselves. Even Ngaire and Tensa, the oldest of the group, found themselves hobbling forward to see for themselves.

Fastana then announced the time of departure. "Five of you have already been chosen," he proclaimed. "Have faith and approach. Walk towards me as if I were a door, for indeed, that is what I am. A door to another place. Have faith and walk. We will not see you again but your Padme will be able to communicate to us and you, in turn, will be able to communicate with them. Go with blessing. Go with faith. Find Sam and show him that his world is infinitely bigger than anything he can ever recall."

Within the crowd, there was a slight movement as five individuals turned to their comrades, hugging them tightly, then bending down to hold and caress their Padme. Communication not just through thought, but through their bodies and actions. Years of living together, now quickly coming to an end as they prepared to enter into an unknown place and time, prepared only to do all in their power to bring Sam to his senses one last time.

The five finally approached Ngaire, Tensa and Hauka. There were no words that could bring justice to the feelings coursing through everybody. Tears were free to flow as the group of five stood ready to depart. All three gathered the five to themselves and the eight held each other tightly for a moment, before the five extracted themselves from their leaders, turned, and walked towards Fastana with grim determination.

There were no words, no loud noises, no crashes of thunder as they approached him. One minute they were there, the next, they had simply disappeared.

Paris, around 10am

The Boulevard Périphérique (E15) is the busiest road in Paris. The motorway surrounding the city is some thirty-five kilometres long and takes up to twenty-five percent of all Paris traffic on its wide, at times, up to eight lane black top route. Despite the sheer numbers that it carries, there are no hard shoulders generally which means that accidents can cause considerable disruption, as emergency vehicles have no open route to get to an emergency situation easily.

The E15 crosses the famous river Seine in two places, one at Porte de Saint-Cloud, the other at Porte de Bercy. And it is here, that the motorway not only crosses the Seine, but also two of the busiest rail network lines from Paris, feeding most of the south of France.

Pierre de Fontaine and his family, wife, Chantel and two daughters, Monique and Isobel, were travelling counter-clockwise on the outer ring approaching Porte de Bercy in their new Citroen. After a busy few days in the office, Pierre was more than ready to take the family for a well-earned break to Euro Disney. They had left early from their home in the 14th arrondissement, hoping to beat the traffic, but it appeared that a great many people had a similar idea. Joining the E15 at Porte d'Italie, they already saw that today would be a slow one. Ahead, a wide line of vehicles were coming and going along the eight lane stretch, leading to the Porte de Bercy and the north.

Monique was bored and they had only just left.

"Do we have to go to Euro Disney?" she asked for the tenth time. "It's so lame! Jean-Claude and Martine said they could look after me whilst you are gone. It's for kids like Isobel." Monique was a fifteen year old, "yearning-for-freedom" girl. She looked across at her ten year old sister, angry at her for no reason other than she must be to blame for this *mini break.*

"Monique, dear," said her mother, "this is something we all discussed last month. We are going and that's that. We shall soon be turning off the Périph to head away from Paris. If you are so bored, why don't you film the journey with your phone and post it on Facebook for all your friends to see?"

Monique just raised her eyes to the heavens. *Like that would really happen!* she thought to herself. But she got her phone out nonetheless, and started to bury herself in messaging her friends, complaining at the injustice of being an eldest child.

On the opposite, inner ring side, travelling clockwise, north of the Porte de Bercy crossing, Luigi Andretti was battling tiredness in his articulated lorry. Behind him, case loads of tomatoes were stacked in their refrigerated compartments in his container all heading slowly south and down towards Lyon. He should have pulled off at one of the many "Aires de service" rest stations dotted around the E15 by now, but he wanted to leave this Paris collar before the traffic coming into Paris centre added to the congestion, snarling up the road yet further and adding at least another hour to this tedious journey. From his elevated vantage point, he could see the tracks ahead of him and off to his right heading up to the Gare de Lyon, one of the busiest rail stations in Paris. Off to his left, the tracks snaked under the overpass and disappeared off down towards where he was heading, Lyon, about 460 kilometres to the south. Being a seasoned trucker Luigi was doing most things automatically, not really noticing the road movements and their ebb and flow. Nothing ever happened to Luigi when he was driving. He was, after all, an accomplished Italian driver and knew this route like the back of his hand.

He looked down towards the old radio in his cab and started to search for a decent channel playing Italian music.

The 'de Fontaine' family came at last to the turn off on the Porte de Bercy and dropped down onto the A4 heading east away from the daily grind of the Périph and towards their destination. The route ahead cleared and Pierre started to relax into the remaining thirty minutes of the journey.

It was a bright hazy day for this time of year, for once. Cirrus clouds were painted in the azure blue sky, as if blown by a street artist. A few contrails could be seen winging their way high above the crowded streets of Paris. Visibility was good. Traffic was flowing, which for this hour, was a blessing at least.

A huge, reverberating thunder clap exploded around the Porte de Bercy and surrounded the area with unimaginable light and noise. Instinctively, many drivers in their cars, fearing that a terrorist event was occurring, cowered down in fright or swung their steering wheels to one side in defensive reactions. Cars rear-ended other cars, spewing metal carnage around and over the bridge in short order. This only added to the natural course of action that was to follow on that fateful day.

Luigi was still concentrating on the radio when the light ahead shot into his cab, blinding him momentarily.

He looked up in shock to see what was happening, all senses rapidly trying to catch up with events. His last few moments of life were to look on in terror as a lone man suddenly seemed to appear from out of nowhere, standing in the middle of the motorway some ten metres away and directly in front of him.

There was nowhere for Luigi to go.

Luigi felt rather than saw his heavily laden truck crash into the individual and bounce sickeningly over him. His world went into overdrive as he slammed on the brakes, whilst at the same time, yanking the steering wheel off to the right.

Momentum took over.

With the cab now heading straight for the barriers to the side and the rest of the lorry under heavy braking, the rear started to lose traction and skid sideways into the traffic adjacent to it. Luigi only registered one thing. The cab, pushing easily with its own heavy weight, crashed through the side protective barriers as if it was made of paper. The tomato-laden container tipped off its bearings and slammed into the nearby cars, motorcyclists and trucks, spilling its load in its fall. The rest of the articulated lorry disappeared over the edge and for a few seconds, Luigi saw the rapidly approaching tracks of the main rail network approaching him, before the cab slammed into the ground at speed, crushing him instantly.

The 10:30 TGV train from Gare de Lyon heading to Marseille had already reached 120 kph by the time it reached the Porte de Bercy and impacted on the wreckage. The train driver and co-pilot were killed instantly and, without a brakesman, the remaining 15 carriages concertinaed into one another, slewing off the rails and spilling one of the busiest business commuter trains over a 200m area. The full tanks of diesel were ignited by the sparks from the sharp edges of broken carriages and the live electricity coursing through the tracks. A fireball erupted and enveloped carriages 1-4 in a flash fire before billowing up and over the bridge, crammed with commuters in their vehicles.

On the western side of the Porte de Bercy, on the outer ring, another family were travelling off on their holidays, caravan in tow. For them, a holiday to look forward to rapidly turned into their worst nightmare as they saw the lightning flash across the skies before impacting on the bridge, and looked on in horror as cars, trucks and smaller objects all seemed to disappear in an explosive fireball. Hilda de Bryn, the driver, screamed out to her husband who was dozing in the passenger seat, but for them, it too was to late.

The windshield of their car erupted inwards and a human form travelling at a collective speed of 85kph smashed headlong into the screaming face of Hilda. Driverless, the car and caravan hurtled into the side barrier, taking out yet more cars before it mounted the central reservation and crashed head first into the on-coming traffic.

Chaos quickly escalated as panic, bad driving and a lack of knowledge all combined to create an expanding, tangled mess of broken cars, vehicles and bodies. More explosions occurred as another truck on the inner ring bounced off the top of the destroyed caravan and flew over the crash barriers immediately after the Seine, this time plummeting onto the tracks leading from Gare d'Austerlitz.

Within a few minutes, the busiest road in Paris and two of the busiest rail systems were brought to a stand still. Not one call had been made to emergency services, so sudden was the catastrophe.

To the north of the bridge, two objects were seen impacting into the river itself.

Miriam, one of the five chosen to enter through the maelstrom first, was completely unprepared for what happened to her on walking *into* Fastana. She gritted her teeth expecting some pain to occur, but all that happened was that the light became incredibly bright, and then suddenly she was smashing into a big river. She was pushed deep under water and she almost gasped out in shock, but her sixth sense kicked in and she clawed her way to the surface and peered out at a world gone mad, and one most definitely not Maunga-Atua. Treading water, she looked on with horror as a huge, obviously man-made structure behind her seemed to explode with fire. Strange objects were falling off its sides, some in flames. She looked on in horror as the unmistakeable shapes of people could also be seen jumping off the structure, some in flames, others screaming in terror, to land with dull splashes into the river she was in, there to disappear from view.

With her sensory perceptions in tatters, she had enough sense to swim to the western bank, which was closest to her, and claw herself out of the smelly, dirty river before it swept her away into the flaming holocaust ahead. A number of people were looking down at her, grief stricken or in blind panic. They were shouting at each other and at her in a strange language she had never heard before. Some held small objects to their ears and seemed to be screaming into them.

Her feelings of being in an uncontrolled situation rapidly escalated into those of pure terror as one of the passers-by reached down to try to grab her hand and pull her out of the river. As she watched, his hand made contact with hers and, as if being rubbed out, first his fingers, then his hand, then his arm started to disintegrate. The man's pain receptors had no time to register what was going on, but his mind enabled him to witness his own horror unfolding before him. As he watched, his entire body started to melt and he fell down to the cobbled floor trying to scream from a mouth which no longer had form.

The sight of seeing someone disappear like this was too much for one gendarme, who had been happily strolling along the banks of the Seine. On seeing what had transpired, and observing the lady now climbing out of the water apparently unfazed as to what had happened, he pulled out his gun concealed in the safety holster and shot the woman in the head. He briefly saw her lifeless body topple back into the dark waters and the surrounding chaos that had exploded onto his senses before he reached up to point the gun at himself, and pull the trigger.

Pierre could not believe what he was witnessing in his rear-view mirror as the bridge behind them disappeared in a chaotic explosion. His mind went into overload and his scream broke everyone's sense of calm, bringing them all to look at Pierre to see what was going on. Chantel screamed out another warning. "Pierre, watch out!" And pointing forward, she could not believe what greeted her eyes. A second ago she was day-dreaming, looking out through the windscreen, longing for at least a few days' break from the daily chores of life. The next thing, a man wearing the strangest outfit she had ever seen suddenly appeared in front of them from a bolt of lightning. Her mind tried to register that although what she had seen could not possibly have happened, nevertheless, there he stood and unless they stopped and stopped *immediately,* he would hit their car. Pierre slammed on the brakes and managed to stop within 2m of the man's legs.

Monique, who had been deep in text conversation with her friend, looked up to see what was happening. Like her mother, she saw the man appear before them as if by magic and heard the cry of terror from her mother and her father, even though he was looking behind him. She brought her phone up, opened the camera app and quickly pressed the video button, live streaming the ghastly image to her social network page.

"Stay in the car!" her father ordered, as he unbuckled his seat belt and climbed out of the car. "Pierre. Be careful, please," cried Chantel. It was the last thing she ever said to her husband of eighteen years.

For Monique and Isobel, what happened next haunted them for the rest of their lives. Pierre approached the apparition before him, calmly asking him if he was OK. The man looked blankly back at him, speaking in a strange form of English. "Sorry," Pierre replied in his best pigeon-English, "I am not good at speaking English." He offered his hand out to the man who was gazing at him as if he came from the planet "Gog". The man reached out his hand, and Pierre's world ended!

Like the person who had tried to assist Miriam, Pierre could not believe what was happening to him as first his fingers seemed to melt before his terror-stricken eyes, and then his arm and torso quickly disintegrated. His brain was still registering this horror and not being able to assimilate that Pierre was indeed dying right in front of himself as he collapsed to the floor and melted into the asphalt road without a sound being uttered.

The stranger, with one look behind him, ran off in terror, the very ground around him seeming to burn up in protest at his passing. He clambered up the steep embankment and disappeared from view.

Monique had unknowingly captured the entire event on her live-streamed video phone. Within thirty minutes, her video had gone viral!

Within ten minutes, snippets of information started to filter through to Radio France, CNN International and France 24. Their helicopters quickly took to the skies thereafter, shooting off towards Porte de Bercy to capture what was undoubtedly sounding more like a terrorist attack with every passing second.

The police constable on duty that day at the Préfecture de Police in the 13th arrondissement, the closest precinct to the incident, was looking forward to going home at the end of a very stressful shift. He heard the dull explosion and wondered vaguely what had caused it. It did not sound like any explosion he had ever come across. More, if anything, like the noise a plane would make as it went through the sound barrier. Something had happened, of that he was sure. Little did he know that his day was about to get a whole lot worse! As soon as news started to filter into his office that calamity was occurring in his patch, he ordered his captain to switch their monitoring system on that focussed on the bridge that appeared to be in question. The office staff all looked on in horror as they saw a terror situation unlike anything ever witnessed by them before.

His training immediately kicked in.

"Francois, get SAMU on the line. NOW!" he screamed.

SAMU 75 is the regional medical emergency response centre based in the centre of Paris. It is the first port of call for all communications in an emergency situation. The day team within SAMU 75 were quick to link into the monitor system for the area. The views that crashed across their senses numbed them into a state of shock. This could not be happening! This did not happen in Paris!

Now that the system was coming on stream, more and more contacts were made to relay information and seek urgent attention. The APHP Crisis cell was the next to be connected. The *Assistance Publique – Hôpitaux de Paris* together with the *Pitié-Salpêtrière* Hospital we immediately mobilised, the latter one of five civilian level-one trauma centres in the APHP group. The former, after brief discussions, ordered the triggering of the French *White Plan*, which effectively mobilised all hospitals, recalled staff and released all beds to cope with a possible large influx of severely injured people.

The President was notified, twenty five minutes after the first explosion occurred. Paris was brought to a standstill within thirty five minutes of the President being notified. By that time three television helicopters were fighting with the emergency service helicopters for space hovering over the disaster that was unfolding below them. No one had ever seen such a terrible event. The fires were raging on both sides of the Périph and on the main Gare de Lyon line. Rescue vehicles, including fire trucks took over forty five minutes before they were able to offer viable support to the dying and injured. By that time, traffic was stationary for fifteen kilometres in both direction, almost, for the first time, bringing the entire thirty five kilometre circuit of the Périph to a complete log-jammed standstill.

The world woke up at various places to the unfolding events happening in Paris. Confusion reigned as news readers tried to offer some explanation as to what had occurred. Stories ranging from an all-out terrorist attack with poison gas, through to a diesel explosion on one of the TGVs, causing massive disruption flowed through the ether, attracting billions to switch on to see the unfolding events with a collective sense of disbelief. Chaos had come to France. Chaos with a vengeance!

England, 11am. Morning news.

Sam's thoughts were rudely interrupted by a loud banging on the container door from outside. Someone was trying to get their attention and their shouting left little to the imagination that something terrible had happened.

Alice quickly waved her hand over the air in front of her and the glow faded to be taken over by the single light of the lamp on her ramshackle desk. The silver handle, similarly, was quickly covered and put away again into the box from whence it had been taken.

"Alice. Alice, are you in there?" An insistent cry came from a lady's voice outside of the container. She sounded very afraid and panic stricken. Without waiting for an answer, the lady hurled open the door and stuck her head inside.

"Alice, you have to come and see this. Something terrible has happened!" And with that, she disappeared, the noise of her feet quickly disappearing as she ran back to the café, all the while, her voice crying out to anyone who cared to listen, "Oh my goodness. Oh my goodness! The poor people."

With one look at Sam, Alice stood up and followed quickly after the lady, saying only, "That was Mary. Something has upset her, that's for sure. And you can be assured, that nothing fazes her, ever!" Sam and Alice ran back into the café, moving quickly through the kitchen area, which was deserted. A few eggs were still frying on the flat iron but no-one was supervising them and the slow smell of burnt egg white was already reaching their nostrils. The kitchen was deserted and voices of shock and horror could be heard growing from within the café itself. Sam was at a loss as to what was happening, but already he sensed that it was not good.

In the café itself, it was as if the room had been turned into an area for sculptures. The people were either sitting or standing, all looking at the television monitor on one side of the wall. Mary was leaning back against the counter gripping the edge tightly with one hand, the other scrunching up her apron into a tight wad in her fingers... No-one was moving as they tried to take in what was being relayed to them from the screen.

Sam and Alice quickly turned to look at what had caused all the fear palpable in the room and what greeted them, was nothing short of calamity on a major scale.

The BBC had stopped all other programmes for a major bulletin alert. From within the screen, a catastrophic view of a world in disaster was being shown. The camera was obviously in a helicopter, hovering over a sea of broken cars, smashed trucks and smoke billowing from multiple places. Glimpses of flashing blue and red could be seen everywhere as rescue and emergency vehicles tried to move through the turmoil. The anchor lady in the helicopter was shouting as loudly as she could over the din of the rotors, her voice shaking with the shock of what she was seeing, whilst at the same time, trying vainly to convey to the audience what, in her opinion, was happening.

Sam and Alice stared with shock as the carnage slowly unfolded when the camera panned back from the close up of a burning truck, to show the wider extent of the disaster. They now saw the bridge, a river below, smoke and flames somehow burning on the water, and wreckage and mangled burning vehicles stretching off into the distance.

"A bomb or something has gone off in Paris, Alice," Mary cried, tears streaming down her face as she alternately glanced between Alice and the screen. "Something terrible has happened and they are saying that many people are dead!" The rest of her sentence trailed into silence as the graphic views being displayed took all sense of speech away from her. Elsewhere, people from the street outside, had now entered the café to see what was going on, gasps and cries of horror flowing freely from many.

The announcer came back into shot.

"Information is still sketchy at this moment, George," she said, "but we are hearing and can confirm, that shortly after 10am this morning, French time, what appears to have been a major explosion occurred here on the E15, about 6 miles south-east of the centre of Paris. Rescue vehicles and the fire-service are still battling to come to the scene. Cars and vehicles have been thrown around as if a major bomb went off, and I can report as well, that a commuter train leaving the centre's main southern station, Gare de Lyon, was also involved in this terrible incident. We can see carriages scattered over the ground and smoke and flames spewing from at least three, no four of them. There are also many bodies. People who, today, woke up to a normal existence, only for their lives to be cruelly ripped away by the disaster unfolding below us."

"Jennifer," the station newsreader cut in. "At this time, is there any announcement from the government as to whether this was a terrorist incident or not?"

"We have not heard any official announcement from the government at this time, George, but we have heard unconfirmed rumours that the explosion seemed to start from a large articulated vehicle which was travelling south. We can, of course, not confirm at this time whether this is indeed correct, or whether the vehicle in question was indeed part of the disaster here, or indeed if it had any part to play in any terrorist attempt to disrupt Paris. What we can say, however, is that if any attempt was made, today, whoever is responsible for this has been successful. Jennifer Wright, BBC news."

The camera image dimmed from one view, opening instead on another, focussed on the balcony of the president's residence in Paris. The doors to the balcony were shut but the camera zoomed in to get a glimpse of any activity from within. Fuzzy, grainy images of people walking past the windows, their heads ducking from view, the only sign that some activity was brewing within the power house of French democracy.

Sam looked around at the people around him. All were in a state of shock. Some were crying, others held each other for some form of comfort. No one was unmoved. He turned his gaze towards Alice to see her reaction, shrugging his shoulders at her as if to say, "What on earth…?"

Strangely, Alice did not appear to be following the story, instead, her gaze seemed to be looking towards the corners of the screen, as if searching for something that was not obvious. Unconsciously, she moved closer towards the screen until she was close enough to touch it. Her fingers slowly moved up towards the flickering images and hovered over them. Then something caught her eye and her fingers quickly traced a line from the centre of the screen, where the centre span of the burning bridge was visible, and moved down to a small area to the bottom right. One car could be seen faintly on the edge of a road travelling away from the bridge. It, like many others around it, appeared to be abandoned but this was not what was catching her attention.

There! Moving away from this lone abandoned car, a rough line could be seen snaking off in another direction away from the bridge. Sam wondered why on earth this line, which appeared to be a path, was causing so much interest to Alice. And without thinking, he too moved closer to the screen until he stood next to her, gazing at the same tiny piece of the screen. "What is it, Alice?" he asked with some curiosity. "What is it you see?"

Alice said nothing. Her gaze firmly fixed now on the line, her eyes moving up the screen until the line disappeared from view. Strangely, it appeared to have smoke coming from it, which in itself was yet another strange anomaly added to the whole events being relayed in front of them.

With a start, Alice snatched her fingers away from the screen, moved back quickly and looked up to the heavens, her head lost in some thought pattern for a moment until she turned to look at Sam. What she said took a moment to sink into Sam's head.

"They have come!" she said, looking between Sam and the screen. "They have come and they have come for one purpose and one purpose only. To find you. To find you and take you back."

Sam was at a complete loss as to what she meant by "they had come". What on earth did "they have come" have anything to do with a Paris disaster which would surely become yet larger as the day wore on?

"How could I have been so blind?" she said to herself. "Somehow they have found a portal and have made the leap. Oh the stupid, stupid people! Why would they do that? What possible merit could it serve? How is it possible that they could even make the connection? I must research and research quickly." With that, and with Sam completely at a loss as to what on earth Alice had just muttered to herself, she turned to him and, with her eyes yet again blazing a strong violet hue, said, "Sam, we need to leave and we need to leave now! They have come and in so doing, have unlocked catastrophe on this place of a magnitude that will make this Paris event look like a Sunday tea party!"

With that, she grabbed Sam by the arm and almost yanked him off towards the kitchens, crashing through chairs and tables as if they were of no consequence whatsoever.

"What's going on?" Sam shouted, trying to stop Alice dragging him off towards the kitchens. Alice had him in a very strong grip for a woman, he thought, and he sensed that it was a grip that he would not be able to wriggle out of anytime soon.

Alice said nothing until she had entered the empty kitchen and slammed Sam up against the wall to the office. "Listen Sam, now is not the time to pretend. Now is the time to act! Right now I do not care if you think that what you are seeing on the screen is the result of terrorists or a horrible accident, or even fluffy bunnies acting in self-defence. What I *can* tell you is that what you are seeing is the result of someone or something physically entering this realm from another reality, whose sole interest is to seek you and get you to return to Maunga-Atua either to fight or to perish."

Sam could not comprehend all that Alice was trying to tell him. It was not a few minutes ago that she was trying to tell him that he was a supposed saviour or another world and he had a *magic staff* as a toy and was able to defeat all and sundry with it. Now she was simply telling him that, according to her, the people from the other reality, which, when he thought about it, was still too weird and wacky to take seriously, were now intent on saying "Stuff all this waiting around, we are going to go and force him to sort himself out!"

"Bollocks to that!" he exclaimed, the expletive shooting out from his mouth before he knew what he was saying. "What did I do to deserve this? It's not my bloody fault that there was an explosion in Paris, and it's not my bloody fault that all that you say is occurring in your la-la land is also as a result of me not being special enough for you right now!" Sam, his senses yet again assaulted from all sides, reverted to his normal position of striking out at whoever else appeared to be wanting to attack him. He was now more than ready to tell Alice, his parents and the rest of the people of Maunga-bleeding-Atua to take a running jump and leave him alone.

"Do you know why I was more interested in a thin line on the screen rather than the terrors that we were all seeing?" Alice cut into his red mist.

"Because you are all bloody heart and want to save the wildlife!" he retorted, eyes blazing with fierce anger, brought up from the depths of his soul.

"Because," she continued firmly, "what I was looking for was not what was happening, but what had *happened!* That abandoned car and the line weaving off away from it in the opposite direction to the disaster was not some random event, Sam. What it was was probably an event I have been dreading since I came here and one which now appears to have been realised."

Sam, despite his anger bubbling away inside him, listened.

"The Anahim are able to switch themselves, their powers, off if they so choose. They are, after all, the leaders of the Ethereals, able to create *and* destroy worlds. People, on the other hand, are not! What you are seeing on the screen is what happens when foolish people decide to take matters into their own hand and force destiny. Things get broken! That line you saw was proof of this."

Sam was still at a loss and Alice could see this in his face. She continued.

"Sam, no one has ever made a jump from one reality to another other than you. No one. And why? Because if that were possible, it would be like trying to link a black hole here with a normal galaxy. The galaxy would not last long, which is why these things are not supposed to happen. But, for some reason, people have found the way to make the jump and have appeared here. The two worlds cannot exist together, that is why they are separated. Normality in one place is death in the other! What you are seeing in that, what is to you an insignificant little fuzzy line on the screen, is a track of someone or something who has made the link and even now, might be alive and their very existence in this world is starting to unlock the building blocks of what makes this place Earth. We have to stop this and we have to stop this right now!"

There are many times in a person's life when no matter how strong the proof exists that a situation is either true or false, they still choose to believe another fabricated answer. This can be for many reasons. Upbringing, a lack of belief in one's self or of one's place in the order in the world, or, as in the case of Sam that morning, one of bloody-mindedness. Sam had been assaulted, it seemed, for a number of days, where it appeared that everyone was expecting him to conform or be something he was not. Now, it appeared to him that, even Alice had a similar view of what she thought he should be, and this was finally causing him to block every external influence in his world and to tell everyone to take a hike and mind their own damned business. Even in his dreams he appeared unable to escape this cruel injustice that he certainly had not asked for, neither was he wanting. Losing David was enough hurt and responsibility for one life time, thank you very much.

In psychiatric terms, Sam was having a bit of a meltdown right there in the empty kitchen and he did not mind one bit who got to see it. A deeply buried sense of respect for the person in front of him stopped him from telling her where, in his opinion, she could place her ideas.

"Alice, for at least a week, I have been assaulted from every angle. My parents reject me as a result of me losing my brother. A dream world that I know I have never experienced before is now invading my night times and is telling me I am the only hope to save the day there. The people that I remember in that world just stand there and die because they believe I am supposed to be somebody. My friends here all think I should be certified and they laugh behind my back, and then you of all people land a line seeming to say that somehow, because I do nothing, even bombings in foreign countries are apparently my fault also! Man, I am sorry, but from my perspective, that's a pretty shitty message to try to come to terms with.

"I wish everyone in Paris a safe and happy life, but for now, I am 'hasta luego'. I need to get out of here, away from everyone and, for once, get some 'me' perspective back in my life, otherwise I am afraid I will do something stupid and someone will find me in a ditch somewhere with toads and wet lichen growing over my cold body!"

With that, Sam turned and walked quickly out of the kitchen, past the customers still gazing at the unfolding news report, and left Timber's. His head and eyes downcast, not wanting to make eye contact with anyone, just wanting to have this whole experience passed onto someone else who at least would not stuff it up as he appeared to have done and, in his opinion, achieved so magnificently.

As so many times before, lost in his anguish as he was, he failed to see Alice follow behind him to the entrance door of Timber's. There, she stopped, extended her hand upwards and outward in the direction of Sam's disappearing form and, with her eyes for once unhidden from the world, now a vivid purple and green, she uttered one short call, the words full of feeling and emotion, yet the language coming from another world: "Shecha, meod otah. M'nassa té. É racha ma, Sam. M'lay o té tamid." (Shecha, eternal. Keep him safe. The chosen one, Sam. Now and forever.)

“The Padme have fallen!”

Fastana continued to blaze with white hot light as first one, then the other four were subsumed by the incredible energy emanating from him as they approached. And then, they were simply no longer there. Even Ngaire, who thought that in her long life she had probably witnessed enough to never be shocked again, was stunned into silence. The crowd all took an involuntary step away from Fastana, who was slowly reaching his arms up and over himself, the staff delicately lifting off the floor and the tendrils of energy appearing to be sucked back into the wall surfaces until the light was gone, the walls returned to hard, shiny rock, and Fastana stood once more amongst them, tired, dishevelled and, for a few seconds, unsure as to where he was.

“Now, we wait,” he intoned, looking around at the crowd assembled there. Everyone’s feelings and emotions were heightened due to what they had just witnessed. None of them had ever seen or experienced anything like what had just occurred in their presence and, for some, this man in front of them started to hold them in some fear despite them being chosen by The Summoner in the first place for their courage.

Tensa was about to ask Fastana what they needed to wait for, when, to one side of the room, one of the Padme suddenly emitted a high, terrible scream of pure fear. Those nearest to it sprang back, wondering what was causing this commotion.

"It's Pila; Tane's Padme," said one of them. Pila was writhing in agony on the floor, its legs cartwheeling in fury and its body arched back. Every sinew straining against an unseen force. With one violent lurch, Pila uttered a final cough and then all sight left him and his body became still.

"Tane has died," said Fastana simply.

Before the crowd could come to terms with this loss, another commotion occurred at the back. "Pashar is spewing out water!" Came from the crowd. "Pashar? That's Pelot's Padme," said another. Pashar, with one final heave, coughed up way too much water, dying whilst still trying to breathe.

"Pelot has drowned," from Fastana.

Simultaneously, both Padmes of Miriam and Jot'tha erupted and fell without a sound being uttered.

"What is happening?" This from Hauka.

"If you go," Fastana replied in hushed tones, "there is no return. Remember?" Fastana was turning to leave the chamber when another cried out. "Fastana. There were five who left. Five. Only four appear to have perished."

The crowd realised what was being suggested and they all started to look around to see who also had left with the party. "It's Jolenthe," shouted out one of them. "Look. His Padme is still here." The crowd focussed their attention on one of the smallest Padme in the room. A delicate mix of mouse and weasel was still sitting where his Jolenthe had left him. He was quiet, concentrating. His gaze, far far away.

With one quick look, Fastana turned to his Padme, The Summoner and sent out his communication. Within seconds, the lion in turn had moved over to the small creature, bent down to him and touched his nose with his mighty snout, looking deep into his eyes.

Then he looked up towards Fastana.

"Jolenthe lives and is unharmed," reported Fastana. The collective sigh of relief from the crowd was palpable in the air. "The deaths of the others was no more unusual than they all seem to have appeared in Sam's world at a place where thousands of strange carriages moved with incredible speed in confusion. The sudden appearance of our people amongst all this chaos caused collisions to occur." The saddening news was somehow lessened by the realisation that apparently, bad luck had played its hand and four unfortunate souls had paid the ultimate price.

"However," Fastana continued. "There is something else." Fastana was now scratching his wirey beard. Perplexed. Unsure of what he was getting from the lion. "Jolenthe is experiencing a strange energy as he moves. If I can see what he is seeing, it appears that his presence there is having a physical effect on his surroundings." The crowd were hushed as the particles of information filtered out of Fastana. "There is great sadness in him, but I do not know why. Death, somehow, has been imposed on someone by Jolenthe and his mind is too numb to understand why. This area is dark to me. He moves north and is seeking a way to track Sam." Fastana stopped for a second, listening to what the lion was relaying via the mouse/weasel. "The ground vibrates as he moves and behind him, he sees a trail of burning grass. He is at a loss as to why this is, but he is safe."

The crowd gathered around Fastana, Ngaire and Tensa. Hauka was tending to the small Padme of Jolenthe and her concentration for the moment rested solely on him. "From what we can understand," Tensa said, "it appears to have been an unfortunate series of events that occurred. Five have left, only one remains," he paused for a second before uttering what he knew had to be said. "One is not enough!"

The crowd looked perplexed for a moment until the truth of what he said landed on their collective minds.

"One is not enough," some of them echoed. The unsaid response to this was in everyone's thoughts. A brief period past before one called out from the back.

"I will go." A tall man pushed slowly through the crowds until he stood in front of Ngaire. He gazed down at her, somehow seeking her blessing.

"I will go also," said another. Then one, then more called out until the remaining fifteen had formed a protective ring around their elders. Once again, their demeanour and stance showed that their courage and determination to save Maunga-Atua held more sway than any self-preservation.

Hauka, from the side, cried out, "Why do the children stand and do the work of the elders?" She had observed the dialogue from her place with the lonely Padme and her love for her people moved her to tears. "I will go," she said, her frail voice breaking with emotion.

Tensa stopped her. "Hauka. If you go, who will remain to teach the young? You are needed here as never before. To go is to throw your wisdom and importance into the fathomless depths of our mother ocean." He moved over to her and drew her into his embrace, his hand resting on her head in silent blessing. "Fastana," he said. "Open the gateway one more time. Perhaps our sheer numbers will prevail."

Fastana took one look at Ngaire, willing her to countermand what Tensa had just uttered, but her face was a closed to him and he saw no sign of uncertainty in it. Only deep sadness.

"I will summon other acolytes," he proclaimed. "Perhaps their combined linkages will help to get our people closer to Sam." Fastana had never seen such determination and braveness from anyone. Any sense of worthiness he might have felt, was blown away by the actions of the people who stood around him.

Once again, he moved into the centre of the space, gathered his thoughts around him like a cloak, and slammed his staff down onto the floor, as if he was trying to shatter the place into a million pieces.

As before, areas around the solid rock face became permeable and other monks appeared in similar stances to those earlier. The tendrils of light grew out of the rocks, moved towards the centre and, once more coalesced around Fastana who disappeared into a hole of intense white light.

And then, without further discussion, first one, then another, then the remaining men and women walked into the vortex of light, and disappeared.

The silence was deafening. Ngaire, Tensa, Hauka, the lion, Fastana and sixteen Padme remained in the vast cavern.

They all waited, hoping for the best, expecting the worst.

Meltdown

As the remaining fifteen passed into the maelstrom of light, nothing could prepare them for what they were about to experience. Two perished immediately as they landed in a lava flow from the volcano, Kilauea, on the island of Hawaii.

Two arrived at the edge of the city of Yinchuan in Ningxia, a central province of China. It was late afternoon and the sun was already low in the western skies. Ahead of them, they saw a few lights dotted around a city, vast beyond their comprehension. With some trepidation, they gathered together and headed off towards the lights. The grasses below them were dying and grey as they passed.

Three crashed through a light weight roof of an industrial building in downtown Los Angeles, landing heavily on some cardboard packing cases ready for assembly by the morning staff workers. It was 1am in the morning. Nothing moved. As they gathered themselves up from the debris, at first they were not aware that the surrounding walls of tin seemed to be buckling backwards away from them. The low screech of bending steel slowly rising in volume.

A further two splashed into the shallow waters of the Louisiana Bayou near Port Sulphur and within striking distance of New Orleans, startling a number of alligators and a flock of herons. The shallow waters around them immediately started to bubble angrily around them, steam spiralling up and away in the wind, in the direction of that famous city.

One landed on the la Croisette in Cannes. It was a bright morning and the street was already packed with morning joggers and tourists admiring the scenery. A number of people saw a brilliant flash of light on the grass verge and a young man appear out from the glare, momentarily stunned and looking around in some confusion. Strangely, most of the crowd started to clap, believing this was a special effects preview advertising a new film. The film festival was just around the corner and here, in Cannes, where almost anything was possible, seeing a bright pyrotechnic of light appear was not that out of the ordinary. This relaxed excitement at seeing this person emerge, was soon to end very abruptly!

A further two appeared suddenly in a blaze of light in the main car park of Real Madrid football club in Spain. A unique derby between Real Madrid and Atletico Madrid that day was ensuring the car park was packed. The event did not go unnoticed and shortly after their appearance, Madrid was never the same again.

The final three appeared safely in a green, lush field surrounded by lambs, startled into a mini stampede. The field was a verdant green. The skies were clear, the weather fine for this time of year. Gathering their bearings and glad to find that they were not alone, they quickly assembled and looked around. Below them and off to one side, one of them noticed a road snaking past a border fence, a sign wedged crookedly against the incline giving directions for towns nearby.

On it, it said, “Milton Haven – 10 miles. Newton Stanley – 4 miles. Greyshott – ½ mile.” They started to walk in the direction of the town closest to them, little knowing that that one small decision, like the smallest roll of a tiny pebble, was the start of a landslide affecting both realms for ever more.

Behind them, five sheep lay still on the ground. Later, the farmer was to stand over them wondering what had happened to his keep. Five of his hardy sheep, eyes sightless, skin ripped apart as if a wild pack of animals had invaded the field and killed with wanton abandonment.

The jigsaw is complete.

Sam was already making his way out of the town centre. Hands in pockets and head still down, eyes staring into space through the tarmac. Thoughts and emotions were tripping off his mind like droplets of a waterfall on the rocks below. Over all the cadence, his one main thought was *why?* Why was this happening to him? Was it not enough that he had to try and deal with the wound of losing his brother? Everybody else could take a running jump right now so far as he was concerned, but David. Well, that was final, wasn't it? There was no coming back from that journey. He wondered whether that wrench would ever ease.

Ahead, he slowly became aware of a disturbance. Loud noises and screams were coming from in front of him. Curious, he looked up to see a group of people standing around what appeared to be a lone individual. They seemed to at once both be trying to attack the man and recoil from him. He was about to change direction, assuming that some kids street fight was ongoing when something about the scene stopped him.

The man caught in the middle was doing his best to defend himself. He was no child. His hands were raised above his head in a defensive stance and he was bending his head down under his shoulders. He was not attacking.

For their part, the people surrounding him were of all ages. Some men, a few older women and two dogs were all skipping around the central character but almost as if they dare not touch him. Almost as if a fanciful play was being performed. The looks of the would-be attackers, however, were not those of a friendly banter. The looks were those of terror and fear.

As Sam looked on, one man, braver than the rest, cried out in anger and body checked the lone individual, bringing him bodily to the ground. Attacker and attacked fell hard onto the floor, legs and arms flailing as they landed.

Sam drew nearer, then wished he hadn't.

As he stared at the commotion ahead, the man who had slammed the lone man to the ground started to get up. In fact, he *tried* to get up! With eyes looking down in terror, he saw his own body literally disintegrate in front if him. The parts touching the man seemed to dissolve into nothingness and he slowly collapsed into the chest of the fallen man until his head softly folded onto and then into the man's chest. And then he simply was no longer there!

Just like that, and without any stage props, Sam had literally witnessed an impossibility. The attacker was *gone*! He was there, victorious for one moment, and the next, he was no longer there.

"What the…?!" managed to escape from him before the lone man pushed himself up from the ground, unconsciously dusting the residue off of his strange looking clothes. Clothes that, for some strange reason, Sam recognised.

Then, as if the scene ahead had been a focussed shot in a film and now the viewer was invited to see the context, Sam became aware of the bigger picture unfolding ahead of him. Three still forms, all with parts of their bodies missing, lay on the floor in a haphazard manner further back from where this man now stood. It appeared as if they formed a sinuous path leading off behind the man.

He noticed a dog, still alive and trying to pull itself to its owner, now very dead, on two legs. It had not noticed yet that its hind legs were twisted and broken as if a lump hammer had smashed into its poor body. Its look was of confusion and terror but it was determined to reach its master and offer protection. It reached the torn man and licked his still face for any sign of movement, then, exhausted it laid its chin on the owners face and slowly closed its eyes.

The man, who was now standing, was also apparently unaware that his presence seemed to be having an effect on the ground and surroundings near him. Sam noticed that the Tarmac around him, and indeed the route he appeared to have made in getting here, was twisted and torn into so much rubble. Impossible as it seemed, this man's passing was as if a bulldozer had ripped up the street surface to enable some road works to take place. Even as he stood, the ground was peeling back from him like a living animal recoiling from danger.

The crowd, by now, on seeing too much terror for one day, were beside themselves and they all started fleeing every which way to get away from this nightmare that had landed shockingly on their doorstep. This was not happening. Could not happen. "This is England, for Heaven's sake!"

And then the lone man turned and spotted Sam!

Sam, in some sixth sense sort of way, saw the next few seconds almost as a déjà vu movie. Once before, in a dream, he recalled someone coming out of the mist and seeing him. And rather than run away, he had run *towards* him, calling his name.

"...Sam? Sam. Is that you?" came cascading into his mind. The man was walking, no, *running* towards him now. Oblivious to what had just happened. This apparition.

This fiend from hell was making his way straight to Sam, and this time, Sam knew he would not be waking up! As he approached, he was also shouting out to someone else, somewhere. "T'rui! Gasha! Come quickly. I have found him. I have found the one. I have found Sam!"

His face was a massive grin, which, under the circumstances, to Sam was just so unbelievable as to defy description. Here was this crazy person, who apparently had just been responsible for the deaths of four people, at least, and a dog, now running towards him with a huge bloody smile on his face.

"No way, man!" Sam exclaimed. "No bloody way!" And he too started to back-pedal away from this maniac hurtling towards him. But it was too late.

With one more step, the man had reached Sam and bear-hugged him as if they were long lost friends. Sam recoiled, fearing that he too was going to disappear in some sticky mess. Too afraid to react, to scared to think, he shut his eyes tightly and waited for an end he had not expected. His last thoughts were, *David, I hope you are bloody there, mate!*

Nothing happened! Sam's eyes were screwed tightly shut and yet he still felt the tightened grip of this crazy person encircling him and he still felt all his senses were working as normal. Slowly, he opened one eye and looked at the man who still held him, wondering how on earth he was still able to stand.

The man's face came into focus. He appeared to be around mid-30s and a rough beard graced his lined features. His eyes were fixed on Sam, waiting for him at least to respond in some fashion.

And then, almost imperceptibly, the man's face changed. The original look of pure joy slowly evaporated as he started to feel things happening to him that were most definitely out of the ordinary.

He looked down at his body, his look of joy evaporating quickly as he saw with horror what was happening to him. As Sam and man held each other, the man's grip started to weaken and his fingers lost their connection with each other. He staggered suddenly as one leg gave way underneath him, then the other. As Sam looked on in pure terror, the man in front of him started to disintegrate. Parts of him fell to the floor and his face started to sag in on itself. Sam could see so many emotions flying furiously through the man's eyes as he came to the sudden realisation that, for him, all was not well.

And then, as if a dim light came on, illuminating his last vestiges of reason and wisdom, he looked one more up at Sam and garbled, "Sam, chosen one. It would appear that even here in your reality, the people of Maunga-Atua die!" And with that, the sight left his eyes and he collapsed in a heap before Sam.

Sam screamed like never before. He screamed the scream of someone with nowhere else to go. He screamed with pure unadulterated loss at all that had tried to flood him with guilt, depression and self-loathing. *How could I have witnessed an impossibility?* he thought, amidst the chaos in his mind.

A reassuring hand came and rested on his shoulder and he turned back to see who it was. "Alice?" he cried out in loss. "What are you doing here?" Tears streamed down his face as the events of his last weeks came crashing into his world, shattering so many walls he had built, he was afraid they would never be able to be built back up again.

Alice looked at him briefly once more, her eyes blazing their iridescent purple. Compassion and love poured out of her. Then her eyes slipped off his and gazed off into the distance, looking at something. Sam turned to see two other figures approach him. Slowly, carefully. Fearful.

T'rui and Gasha had come running as soon as they had heard their colleague cry out. For them, they had been equally shocked at what happened to this world as they interacted with it. Destruction and what seemed like disease did not occur like this in Maunga-Atua. Here, however, their very passing seemed to affect the very fabric of this place, causing destruction the longer they stayed there.

They came running round a street corner just in time to see their closest friend, Akana, fold into himself, gripping the person who stood in front of them, until he disappeared into a mess on the floor. The remaining man appeared to be unharmed. Their confusion turned to some joy as they too recognised who stood before them and they started to walk towards him, not quite sure what had befallen their comrade, but determined to get Sam to respond.

Their approach was halted as their eyes fell on the one who stood behind Sam. T'rui cried out. "Aronui! Aronui, we are unworthy." They both stopped instantly as they saw this creature, who myth had painted and their emotions had adorned with too many baubles. Here she now stood. Looking at them. Eyes ablaze and hair electrically charged and weaving in the still atmosphere. They had seen an Anahim! They had witnessed what no one should witness and they had found Sam. What a tale this would be in the telling, once they returned.

"Go!" Alice said quietly to Sam, pulling him behind her. "Go and be what you were meant to be and save that which must be saved. Even now, your world is being destroyed and you have no choice but to act, and act now."

Without further words, she shoved Sam backwards and took his place, looking at the two who stood before her, daring them to approach further.

Sam ran! He ran back into and through the town,

oblivious as to who might be watching him. He ran, almost sub-consciously up the winding road that took him to Blacknest Hill until, exhausted and panting for breath, he reached the very top and stopped.

Silence.

Quiet.

Peace.

Like a soothing balm, the space caressed him with its atmosphere. It gave him an immediate sensation that all his troubles and woes really counted for nothing when you saw the bigger picture. And here it was in front of him. Clouds moving lazily in the afternoon sky. Fields waving slowly in the breeze. The town below seemingly unaffected by what had just transpired.

The bigger picture, he thought.

No longer was there any doubt as to the existence of Maunga-Atua. The man dissolving in front of him put paid to that! In fact, he thought, he somehow *knew* that Maunga-Atua was real. He just did not want to believe it. He reminded himself, "Sam, you didn't want to believe that David had died and yet you know he did. It doesn't really matter whether you chose to believe it or not, it still happened."

His thoughts moved onto the other "happenings" that occurred around him, and a moment of pure Eureka-ness burst on in his world. It didn't matter whether he believed anything or not. It was still going to happen. With or without him.

He reached a decision. It was easy now that he had got some perspective.

Sam's eyes fell on the beacon of rocks, built decades ago by the cartographers of the county at the time. It stood dead centre of a clearing, indicating the highest point on the hill. It stood as a sentinal for whomever wished to visit here. It had a purpose regardless as to who knew it. Only it, this mound of crudely constructed rocks, could be the sentinal for this place. And whether you liked it or not, it simply *was.* And it did its job perfectly.

Somehow, standing here, this crude rocky totem seemed an appropriate place for Sam.

Looking around to make sure that none disturbed him, he moved to the beacon and sat down in the lee of it, looking out for a moment towards the fields in the distance, the clouds, the birds. He had no answers, but, like water in a raging torrent, he was willing to be carried now and trust the moulders to mould him for this much much bigger picture.

Sam looked out into his world and slowly fell asleep.

The end of book one.

About the Author

Julian Cheek is an Architect by profession and lives with his partner in Hampshire, UK.

His childhood years were spent in Southern Africa where his parents worked when he was just a young boy. Growing up in a land rich in character and beauty, his free time was often spent playing in the fields and streams around his neighbourhood.

Being a typical innocent young boy, Julian had friends from many cultures, creeds and colour. The fact that people were different was no more or less important than whether it rained or not. The main point was that people were people and friends were made regardless of status or caste. It is this important element that the author wishes to highlight in his stories, some based on actual events. That a friend is a friend! No matter what he or she believes in, stands for or looks like. A friend is someone who is there for you through thick and thin, and obviously, someone who you feel totally at ease with.

It is this ethos that he carries with him in his family and professional life as well. Everyone is equal and everyone has a contribution to make to this place we live in.